CG 8/24

COWLEY LIBRARY
TEMPLE ROAD
COWLEY
OXFORD OX4 2EZ
TEL: 777404

To renew this book, phone 0845 1202811 or visit
our website at www.libcat.oxfordshire.gov.uk
(for both options you will need your library PIN
number available from your library),
or contact any Oxfordshire library

**OXFORDSHIRE
COUNTY COUNCIL**

L017-64 (01/13)

All rights reserved
Copyright © Christine Trueman, 2020

The right of Christine Trueman to be identified as the author of this
work has been asserted in accordance with Section 78
of the Copyright, Designs and Patents Act 1988

The book cover is copyright to Christine Trueman

This book is published by
Grosvenor House Publishing Ltd
Link House
140 The Broadway, Tolworth, Surrey, KT6 7HT.
www.grosvenorhousepublishing.co.uk

This book is sold subject to the conditions that it shall not, by way of
trade or otherwise, be lent, resold, hired out or otherwise circulated
without the author's or publisher's prior consent in any form of binding or
cover other than that in which it is published and
without a similar condition including this condition being imposed
on the subsequent purchaser.

This book is a work of fiction. Any resemblance to
people or events, past or present, is purely coincidental.

A CIP record for this book
is available from the British Library

ISBN 978-1-83975-089-2

Chapter 1

Wreck

The two divers, one larger man, one slight figure beside him, sat adrift in the small boat, floating some distance from the shore on the smooth, infinite expanse of Atlantic Ocean.

Behind them, the sun was a mere pinprick of golden light that cast a broad path across the purple and steel hues of pockmarked water. Above them, a yellow haze burned the stratus clouds, which drifted, feather like, above. They might have been the only two people on the island.

There were few sounds, this time of the morning – not even the gentle rush of waves on the distant shore and the dark, volcanic rocks, nor the cries of hungry, waking seabirds either.

The lead diver put up a thumb as a signal, nodding to his companion, before falling backwards with ease despite his bulky frame, breaking the skin of the water, then sinking down before the other had time to join him.

With his companion now with him, the waters closed over them and they were part of the ocean.

Before long, as they breathed steadily, hearing their own breathing alone mingled with the rush of water in their ears, the thin, light-filled, greenish space between them and the surface, where the shadow of their boat's hull bobbed, was left at a distance and the ocean world grew darker. The second diver followed the first in a close trail through shoals of parrotfish which glinted like quicksilver, both divers descending with ease, confident in a familiar environment.

When the bottlenose dolphin approached them, swimming alongside the larger diver, she appeared to smile and follow their progress, until she was joined by another and a third curious dolphin.

This group of humans and dolphins entered the murkier depths of the wine dark sea, companionable and easy, until the rusted red wreck of a sunken hull showed itself to them, the mast reaching almost to the surface. The dolphins then swam before them in near darkness until the lead diver turned on the torch braced upon his head, to illuminate the wreckage.

The wreck was large, its hull red and orange like the diseased shell of a lobster, but it was impressive in its bulk. Not the oldest wreck near the island, for it had sunk in a fire in 1920, but one of the most interesting. The dolphins were used to it and soon they swam away in search of breakfast tuna.

The two divers approached the wreck, slowing down to tread water before reaching the large slabs of corrugated iron. Their faces were hidden for a moment in a cloud of butterfly fish that left the sunken vessel as they were disturbed.

The lead diver jabbed a finger towards the interior of the crusty hull, intending that the figure behind him should follow him closely.

As he stood in the door's frame, the hand, ghostly in the milkier water, brought out a Jon line, threading it through the nearest rail in a practised knot and with surprising speed, hooking it to the mesh protecting the lead diver's tank as his back was turned. He turned at the light touch and his eyes widened in surprise, his slow movements turning to startled panic, right hand reaching out as though to clutch at the smaller figure. His eyes goggled behind the mask as the fishing knife pierced his regulator hose, and in a swift blizzard of bubbles he struggled to follow the rapid, mermaid-like ascent of the flippers beyond him, now above him, but he was tethered tight and his eyes swelled as though they might burst from their sockets.

For a few seconds he twisted and thrashed in a futile effort to get free of the hook and, in panic, pulled the demand valve from his mouth, then closed his mouth until it was forced open by the instinct to breathe. But the increased heart rate and the shock had already killed him. His head twisted from side to side. One convulsive jerk of the shoulders, but the tight clasp still held him back. The steady suffocation came from inside out, as his blood filled with dissolved nitrogen, water pressure pushing and pounding on his heart and lungs. The bends caused one body blow of excruciating pain which stretched and stiffened him like a man on the rack, and he passed out for eternity.

His erstwhile companion had long gone, but two of the elder dolphins swam back in compassionate concern. One of them nudged the floating man, gently pushing at his body as if to revive him. But he was tethered to the ocean now and there was nothing to be done. The dolphins swiftly retreated to the surface in one streamlined movement, murder a disparity to them, their gentle bodies moving in unison towards the light on the water.

Chapter 2
Diary One

I recall a family party. It's 1980 something; we are in a large hall and we are dancing to Sister Sledge, at least the women are, arm and arm in a wide arc, whilst the menfolk stand back nervously as though they might be asked to join in.

"We are family... I got all my sisters with me!" We're singing loudly, sometimes discordantly, shouting those words that we know whilst leaping about in playful abandon. My two sisters are there, my sister-in-law and my 'new' sister, or rather my cousin's wife, Camilla. She has creamy, olive-brown skin; she is thin-limbed and undeniably very beautiful. She knows how to wear a sparkly frock and has the cheekbones and figure of a young Diana Ross.

"Where did your mum say your family comes from?" I shout at Camilla across the noisy speakers which are bouncing up and down like Disney cartoon characters.

"Saint Helena!" Camilla mouths, silenced by the din and waving her elegant arms in the air. I remember wondering why she wasn't inelegantly sweating like the rest of us.

"Oh yes... Where is that, exactly?" Where in the world is St Helena?

I didn't wanted to appear ignorant in front of Justine, Camilla's mother, and in my mind's eye I am picturing an island in the Caribbean. But no. Camilla collapses as the music draws to a close, staggering towards me on high heels.

"It's in the South Atlantic. A five-day boat journey from Cape Town. There's no airport, you see. It's so remote that it costs a fortune to travel there, so I've never been myself, though we're planning to, someday soon. It's a British island; we are British," she says with a good-humoured smile, as though I might take issue with it, or maybe people have taken issue with it in the past. As though they had to fight for the right, I remember thinking. Perhaps they had.

"I'm rather better at history," I say, excusing myself. "Isn't that where the British exiled the emperor Napoleon?"

Camilla nods, clapping her hands above her head in joyful abandon to another burst of music, shimmying across the dance floor once again. In an instant, I want to be Camilla.

The conversation is forgotten until very recently, dusty in my brain's private filing cabinet, except that I discover that there are so many people who originate from St Helena now living in Swindon that the town has been nicknamed 'Swindolena'.

Across the years I meet with Camilla often, but our conversations revolve around our husbands, our children and our work. Camilla's life is here. The island is forgotten – by me, at least.

It isn't until twenty years later that Mark, my husband, tells me, whilst on a journey to visit friends, that a younger lawyer who once worked for him has recommended him for work on the island of St Helena.

"Really...? That's where Camilla's family comes from," I remind him.

"Is it?" His memory is worse than mine. "Of course, I'd forgotten."

I am upset for Camilla and her family, that we should have paid such little attention.

"I'm absolutely sure it is," I say, realising that he has not included me in the possible plans for working abroad. "So, are you intending to go without me, or what?" There is an unmistakable huffiness in my voice. It didn't use to be like that between us, but of late Mark appears more cheerful than he ever was and is cheerfully disregarding me on a daily basis.

I guess that the last decade has been busy, to put it mildly.

I gave up teaching to look after our daughter's children. I often look a bit of a wreck nowadays as a consequence – nothing like the younger woman at that party dancing to Sister Sledge all those years ago.

I feel as though I have been busy supporting our family whilst Mark has been developing his career; this includes Mark attending a lot of social legal events, like conferences and dinners, that kind of thing, whilst I remain at home as the plumber and garbage man and general head of the family mafia.

I rarely go with him to these events now – frequently wonder who he takes instead of me. Of course, the earring, caught in his shirt, didn't help to soothe my fears, but let's not dwell upon that for the moment – it tends to alter my mood dramatically.

"Yes, I was about to invite you," he reassures me, hastily and with a touch of grumpiness, his smile too swift and rigid to be real. "But the thing is, we will be away for about twenty-four days; will Ginnie be alright without you?"

This is a clever move on his part and I'm sure he knows it; knows I will worry; knows that no matter what Ginnie and I put in place it will be tricky for her with work and that they will miss me. I feel a mixture of things: a strong sense of doubt that he wants to take me with him; a gritty determination to go there anyway. I have never done anything like this before.

But still I bite my lip in uncertainty. That is a long time. I've never been away from our children or grandchildren, especially the older girls, for longer than nine days, and that was only once, on holiday in Miami.

What will we do about the pre-school and after-school care? I am almost as close to our granddaughters as their mother is; what will the girls do without me? My mind begins to problem-solve, in an instant.

The suggestion behind Mark's words is an unmistakable challenge that I cannot refuse.

I'm going.

"I'll have to talk to Ginnie, sort that out with her, then," I say.

I want to go. I know little about the place, to my shame. But I don't want to miss him for twenty-four days and, truthfully, there are other reasons for going with him, the earring being one.

Right up to the date in early November, when we depart, I know very little about St Helena. It is often said, but true in my case, that there is always too much to do to find out. I will know it, I suppose, once we get there.

Several things begin to conspire to prevent me from getting there. Our granddaughter's reproachful cries being one of them.

"But, Nanny, twenty-four days? Who's going to take us to school? Who will take us to ballet if Mummy is working?"

I make elaborate plans, both to reassure them and to keep Ginnie's life and family running smoothly. I also promise them kittens – not a wise move. Ginnie tells me off for this, says she isn't keen on cats and that they'll have to live with me.

Other difficulties emerge shortly before we are due to go.

After visiting the hospital with my sister and my mother, we are told that she has developed cancer of the colon. She will have to have an operation, and probably chemotherapy afterwards to remove the nasty little cancer cells that are left after they remove the vast majority.

"It will be alright," my sister Lucy says, "I've asked them at work for some compassionate leave."

But it won't be alright, it will be hard on them all, and guilt makes me snappy with Mark.

My dad is getting older; it now takes him ten minutes to pick something up when he's dropped it, and he forgets things that happened the day before. Most alarming is that he's forgotten the name of his favourite pub.

I begin to wish that Mark hadn't been given this marvellous opportunity; I'm scared about going away with him.

But he is already immersed in emails and telephone calls and things called threshold documents and interim orders. He doesn't even appear to notice that I'm snapping, finding it much easier to be objective, easier to turn his back on it all. He's going to save the world, or at least the island.

When he comes home after work each day, he talks casually about people on the island of whom I have never heard: Tessa, Rachel, Helen, whoever they may be.

In the meantime, I comfort Mum, set up practical support for Ginnie, and we re-write our wills. My mother-in-law tells me, rather too cheerfully perhaps, that we could be kidnapped by Somalian pirates like the man in the film; that the Ebola virus appears to be spreading across Africa. There are rather too many real situations for me to worry about, so I don't have time to be fearful about such things. I book injections for Mark and I and conclude my will by suggesting that some of the will inheritance be used for a fantastic party to be held in Cornwall, attended by friends and family. I also write three diaries in advance, for my mother and granddaughters to read whilst we are away, just to keep them going. Entertaining gobbledygook.

So, when it is time to go, I am apprehensive rather than excited.

Mum is in hospital, having had the operation. It has hurt us to see the physical and emotional changes in her. She has lost so much weight, resembling a tiny Margot Fonteyn as she leans back against the hospital pillows. Most upsetting of all is the fear in her eyes which she can't hide from us, though she smiles and even manages the occasional joke. I think, all of a sudden, that I can't remember her being afraid before this.

"I can't phone you very much once we are on the ship, and you can't send texts or use mobile phones in St Helena, but I will call you or Lucy, whenever I'm able to," I say, kissing her hand and then her forehead.

She nods slightly.

"It's all going to be fine. You'd better go now, or you'll miss the plane. Look after one another and don't fight," she murmurs as an afterthought, because Ginnie, our daughter, has told her that Mark and I have had a couple of arguments recently.

"How long will you be away for?" Dad asks, from the chair beside the hospital bed. He asks it not because he wants to make me writhe with guilt, but because he can't remember what we have already explained.

"For almost a month, Dad."

"Oh…" That's all he says.

I can feel tears welling up in my eyes. I pinch my palms with my nails, a tip given to me by a formidable head teacher in Cambridge, years ago, when I did my probationary year.

"I love you. We'll get Christmas started as soon as I'm back!" I promise, kissing his cheek, then kissing Mum gently upon her cheek. I want them to hold on to the thought of Christmas.

I couldn't do this without Lucy and my brother and sister-in-law; at that point I am feeling very, very selfish, but they stare back at me without blame, rising to kiss me and saying, "Don't worry, it will be alright."

I am quiet, right up until the time arrives to get onto the plane for the fourteen-hour flight to Cape Town.

Trundling our hand luggage through the airport shops, I gaze at the posters of women advertising perfume and make-up.

When I hit fifty-five, I became neurotic about my face, my hair, my body... No, that isn't true; when I found the earring... It was then that I changed.

Now I find myself thinking about the things and the people who are truly important. I don't want to leave them. But being with Mark is important too, isn't it?

We haven't really done many long flights over the years. The last time we did, travelling to Florida, I had our baby grandson kicking and yelling on my lap and I annoyed several passengers by singing 'Whose Pigs Are These?' until he fell asleep. Mark moved to another seat as I recall.

* * *

This plane is like a great silver tank. I can't be much of a science teacher. I still don't understand the science of how they get up into the air. I don't trust this idea any more than that the earth is a sphere. It is an airborne hotel larger than any plane I've ever travelled in. I'm really not a nervous type, but I don't want to get onto it.

The air hostesses are reassuring, not because of their manner with the passengers but because they do not, for a change, have sleek blonde hair and high-sheen lip gloss. A few of them are actually my age, post-fifty. That at least is reassuring.

I think of Mum and the children again. It will be hard, not to be able to hug them for a month, but I can't keep feeling like that, or Mark will wish I hadn't come.

There are films. I watch a very light one with Cate Blanchett, who is speaking in an unintentionally funny French accent. After all of this, and a ham sandwich, I am tired, but I don't think I'll be able to sleep as yet.

We have a glass of wine, and I take out *Mostly Men*, by Lynn Barber, which I bought at the local Cancer research shop. It is very funny and very perceptive.

I've read quite a few of her interviews, and now I've reached the interview with Sir James Savile. She puts it to Jimmy Savile that people say he likes little girls; his answer is that, because of his association with celebrity pop groups, young teenage girls flock around him. He replies, she says, in a flurry of funny voices, Jimmy Savile patter.

I think back to the '70s. Someone has described the island to Mark as, "Like Britain in the '70s."

I close my eyes and lean back in the chair. Reading about Jimmy Savile reminds me of something. My mind drifts to the chateau in France where, pre eleven-plus, my year group was taken for a couple of weeks on a residential visit.

At first, I remember the other children, the children who were with me then. I recall the brightly striped dress I wore (my mother made it) and then the lovely woodlands around the chateau where we used to play. But I know where my mind is really going to; it does, from time to time, not in fear but in a kind of surprised indignation that I have never voiced aloud.

It was an early lesson in sex that I didn't understand, that I shouldn't have had, not at twelve.

Silvia, Karen and I, the good girls, the ones who appeared to do their best in class, were playing hide and seek in the woods, leaping over the fallen logs, giggling and shrieking, when Mr Conway's voice called to us from the large open doors at the rear of the lovely, old French chateaux.

We went to him immediately, of course. He was a respected teacher. But on that day, he didn't resemble the teacher we knew. He wore trousers, but his chest was bare except for downy, grey hair, which I have felt repulsed by to this day.

The slightly flaccid waist was rather ugly to my twelve-year-old mind.

I had liked him though, trusted him up to that point. Afterwards, that memory of him turned him into a sinister, cartoon figure.

It was very hot, so I suppose we accepted that his stripping off was okay.

He was with another man, another member of staff with whom he was friendly, someone who smiled a lot, also respected by parents, also shirtless, a French teacher who we didn't know so well.

Mr Conway beckoned us into the room.

There was a sort of raised bed behind them, like a bed on which a doctor might examine someone. Looking back, I suppose the bed was something to do with sports injuries.

Mr Conway pointed out the tube of sun cream lying on a table. Would we mind rubbing it into their backs, because they couldn't reach around that far? Those were his words: "We can't reach around that far."

We looked at each other and giggled shyly. And we must have thought it was an unusual request or we wouldn't have giggled. We didn't move, didn't kick into action as we would have done in class, but turned our faces to one another or looked down at the floor.

I think we knew it was odd, but we were just twelve, just past the eleven-plus exams, had no experience of doing anything like that, not even for our fathers. So, we stood together, feeling awkward.

I have no memory of rubbing that sun cream in, although I remember Mr Conway lying on his stomach on the sunbed with his chin on his arms, a broad, contented smile upon his face, waiting expectantly.

I do remember my embarrassment and that I couldn't wait to get out of there, back to the sunshine and the woodland, and that it was Silvia, the most naïve of us all but most nervous about refusing, who picked up the cream and complied. Nothing more happened; if the men had erections, we didn't notice; they were lying face down, and maybe we wouldn't have known what an erection was.

It happened in the '70s. Things like that did happen in the '70s. The years pass and we wake to the fact that what once happened is not acceptable. My father, gentle, often anxious, feared the cane and the teacher's walking stick, frequently used during the war on the mildest of boys, but never used on the girls. These things leave scars, but I wasn't scarred by what happened, although I didn't tell my parents about it until a few years after. I watched Benny Hill like everyone else.

With these strange thoughts, I fall asleep.

When the intense, yellow light of morning in a different continent penetrates the windows, I wake once more. I feel a rush of excitement for the first time that soon we will be in South Africa. Then I experience guilt shortly after it.

I think of my mother, lying against the pillows in the care of strangers whom we must trust.

I think of her great patience as needles are thumped into her thin arms repeatedly, leaving bruises until any fatty tissue can be found. I think of Dad, who is lost and lonely without her, and of my sister and brother who will care for them both.

I'm in a kind of trance as we move very slowly in the dense sea of people for our passports to be checked. I've never been to Africa. It seems incredible to me that I'm here, now.

We trundle our heavy cases past the airport shops, filled with wooden animals and clothing with African designs. We wait in the intense, bright sunshine, close to the taxis parked outside.

I think of Nelson Mandela and am amazed suddenly that I am in his country.

An attractive blonde woman is calling us by our names in her pleasant, husky tone, and it is as if she knows us. I don't want to stop thinking about Mum, but all of a sudden I do. I am her and she is me; we are one person, anyway.

The woman walks towards us. She is here to collect us.

Chapter 3
Diary Two

She has a large, silver four by four. Beside her stands a tall man with a large, pleasant face and sun-bronzed skin, who reminds me of a genial pirate.

The woman is Sharon, whom I've never met but Mark has spoken to on the phone. The man is Jeremy, her husband, who is even taller than Mark.

She turns out to be a lovely and highly organised example of South African womanhood. If it is possible to be known by everyone in South Africa, then this person is Sharon, for everyone seems to greet her that morning, as she calls out to them in a warm, husky voice.

We shake hands. They are couriers for the RMS *St Helena*, which will take us to the island.

If Sharon is the sexy, husky blonde of a Tom Sharpe novel, Jeremy is a well-dressed and sophisticated pirate, with the most amazing accent I have ever heard. It isn't, as we are to discover, a 'Saints' accent, but the accent of Tristan da Cunha – weirdly West Country in the midst of Africa. But then, I suppose, no more weird than the accents of the Cornish tin miners would have sounded, having emigrated here a century and a half ago – the Jacks and Jennies who were forced to go elsewhere to mine for minerals. Maybe Jeremy is descended from one of them.

"We already picked up the judge and his wife yesterday," Jeremy explains, as he heaves the five cases into the boot of their large estate car; then, regarding me with one eye shut against the sun, "You brought some clothes with you, then?"

"They're not all my clothes!" I protest defensively. "Most of them are filled with files, and Mark's court clothes, of course."

"Know what happened to the lady lawyer we picked up earlier?" Jeremy asks, hastily changing the subject. "She got like, a gold bracelet on... Had it snatched clean from her wrist in broad daylight in Long Street. Course, she knew she shouldn't ha' worn in really, and she say it were her fault like, for forgetting to take it off in a place where there's so much robbery. But she were very good about it; said so long as it bought someone a good meal and not drugs, it weren't too bad a loss." He closes the boot as Sharon climbs into the passenger seat. "You been out here before?"

We tell him we haven't.

"There's a lot of good in Cape Town and a lot of bad – poverty and wealth, both. You know about the shanty towns of course? We pass some of them on the way into the city. You can visit some of them if you want to."

The car passes out of the airport and onto a broad freeway. All the time I think to myself, *Nelson Mandela was here*, like a hippie at a Bob Geldof concert. As though I can't quite believe that we are on this hallowed ground.

"I'm not sure I'd want to visit them, although there are plenty of places I do want to see; it's a bit like being a voyeur into someone else's misery, in a way," Mark says, in reference to the shanty towns.

"Yes, I get that," Jeremy agrees, "but they got these projects going now, the tea project and the art projects, so tourists can visit them and buy things, contribute themselves, see?" he explains.

We stare, mesmerised, at the vast, stark landscape of the motorway and the tall skyscrapers of the buildings ahead of us as the car tears past the frail buildings of wood and tin which stand precariously on the other side of a wooden fence, closer to the freeway than anyone might care to live.

They look as though they might collapse in a small breeze.

In their own way they are beautiful, individual; sometimes painted in bright colours, sometimes with the hull of an upturned boat for a roof, or with a hammock slung between them. People doing the best they can with their homes. But within these chaotic villages must be an explosion of humanity, I think; problems of every kind, layer upon layer and with no escape.

"Are there efforts to build proper housing here, I mean, to rehouse families?" I ask.

"Oh yes, sometimes," Sharon says, twisting around in her seat to get a good look at me. "But you know what they do? The problem is, the family moves into their new home and then they rent out the old one to a family newly arrived from Zimbabwe. So, it goes on and on. You meeting the others this evening?"

I wonder nervously what they are going to be like, the other lawyers. Mark knows them, of course. Some of them are from a practice in Birmingham and some from London. I've never met them.

Will they think it odd that I am travelling with him? I have never done so before.

Well, I'm here now, and the judge is travelling with his wife, so I hope to be excused and accepted. As for Mark, I think he probably felt compelled to ask me to come for various reasons, but at least he doesn't appear to mind it too much.

I watch his face in profile, contemplating him both inside and out.

He is good-looking, he has weathered time better than I, but then, generally speaking, men do, don't they? He is a good lawyer; he doesn't like to be crossed; that's what he's like as a husband and father, too. We have been married for almost thirty years.

No doubt Winnie Mandela had thoughts like that about Nelson, and God knows she had to endure far more than I ever have.

Mark is a very important person, in the estimation of others as well as his own. I am just the woman at home, to be asked with some irritation, "Who has eaten all the jam?" – as if it were me; or, "Where have all my socks gone?" – as though I am hiding them.

Sometimes it makes me feel fairly irritable when other women stare at Mark. Like the time we were in a restaurant and a young blonde girl fluttered her eyelids at him throughout our meal, despite the presence of the boyfriend sitting opposite her, which I thought vaguely rude and intrusive until eventually, after a long time, I turned to her and asked whether she would like me to organise a date with Mark. It was just the once – I usually behave with greater reserve – but I have to admit I felt better for voicing my thoughts, even if Mark was fairly furious with me after it.

As we drive towards the waterfront, an excitement and slight nervousness at meeting these new people takes hold of me.

Mark is excited too, because he gropes for my hand and squeezes my fingers.

It is all very different to the things I have seen before, although vaguely similar to the waterfront in Toronto, perhaps.

At first impression, the waterfront is a huge dockland, flanked by sentinel tower blocks and cushioned by the great, brown mountain. The air is hot, a little dusty, the roadways perfumed with fuel from the hundreds of cars passing by.

The mountain is Table Mountain, a smooth solid mass of boulder rock with a thin layer of cloud floating above it today.

"That's what we are going to do tomorrow, before the ship arrives," Mark said. "I've got tickets to go up in the cable car."

I am impressed. He has vertigo. Once, I had to lead him down the steps of Plymouth lighthouse by the hand. I smile, I want to kiss him, but he does not like to be kissed in public, unless it is before family or close friends.

"That's what you will do if the wind and clouds don't change, otherwise she'll be closed to the public and you'll have to hold your tickets over until you get back from the island," Jeremy laughs. "It's one of the windiest places on earth. They call the white clouding 'the tablecloth'."

We say goodbye, for the time being, to Sharon and Jeremy, thanking them for their help, and book into the Commodore Hotel, where the porters wait with wide, welcoming smiles and beautiful black and red suits.

It is large, old-fashioned; an almost European-style hotel. The walls are decorated with African wall hangings and paintings, and rhino heads.

Guests lounge about in the reception, an interesting group, as though they are about to take part in one of those staged murder mysteries. They recline in deep, leather chairs or teeter on the bar stools. It has an air of 'What shall we do before the safari begins?'.

I feel guilty, again. I am too excited about it all. Whilst Mark is checking us in, I close my eyes and pray that Mum will be okay, drawing some strange looks from the concierge.

I text my brother and sister, and our two children, who aren't children anymore and whom I'm missing already.

There are two Americans in the lobby, one about Mark's age. A tall, fair-haired man in a cream suit is standing with his cases as though waiting for something to happen. The other, his wife I assume, is a lady of about the same age. She's a large lady, and is sitting down on one of the leather chairs. She is well dressed, but her face is hot and flushed and she has kicked off a pair of high-heeled shoes that are totally unsuitable for travelling. She is seated beneath a fan in the high ceiling, which moves the air laboriously.

I smile at her, and she loses the slightly irritable expression for a moment to smile back. I don't talk to her then, but I've made a friend; her name is Julia.

Another guest casts me a half smile, a young woman seated opposite me. She is African in origin, wearing jeans and a tee shirt. She has a gentle demeanour and is fanning her face with a leaflet as though she isn't used to the heat.

"They've taken ages to get my room ready," she confides.

"Oh no, I hope we don't have a long wait too," I reply.

"You were on the plane this morning," the girl says, smiling.

"I was indeed." I don't recall her but don't wish to be rude.

"Don't worry, big plane. My name's Thadie."

"Hi... Stephanie," I introduce myself. "We've only booked in for a couple of nights; we're going to St Helena on the boat."

"Ah, me too. Holiday?" Thadie asks.

"For me, yes, but Mark, my husband, is working there. He's a lawyer. You?"

"Working there for a few weeks on behalf of an environmental agency," Thadie says, "attempting to save a turtle nesting ground from the new airport."

"There are turtles?"

"Didn't used to be that many, but since the building of the airport began they've started hatching on one of the beaches."

"Maybe it's a turtle protest?" I suggest, hoping she has a sense of humour.

Thadie grins. "Maybe, but it's a bad time to do it."

Mark calls me across to the desk then. The porter is stacking our cases onto his mobile golden cage. I said goodbye to Thadie and suggest we have a drink on the ship. Then I follow Mark to the lift.

We have a large, beautiful room with air conditioning and fridges and fruit and a grand double bed, but we don't hang about to admire it for long. I stuff an apple into my handbag as we leave the room. Then we step out into the quiet street in front of the hotel.

"Go towards the waterfront, but if you go that way," the doorman indicates to the left, "be careful; it isn't as safe as the waterfront." I clutch my bag tightly to my side and wonder whether we will be ambushed.

Mark takes my hand and we amble down the sunny street, passing the Springbok Museum, which I know he wants to visit, being a big rugby fan.

On our way, two or three young men hold out plastic cups to us, begging for money. I give the first one some change and, after that, Mark says authoritatively, and no doubt correctly or we will quickly lose our money, "No," shaking his head first at me and then at the second young man. The third youngster, he must be about seventeen, follows us along the street, his voice repeatedly asking, begging. My conscience clings to him like a magnet, until at last I pull away from Mark to give him a few rand coins.

Only one older man threatens us, hitting a bin with his fist and swearing; the younger men all look thin, scared, hungry and lost.

I think of my JJ. He's not really *my* JJ, but Henry's friend. He was one of the most artistic and able pupils at their school. He came from Zimbabwe as a child, and then one day, for no apparent reason (because the last thing he was, was a danger to the community), he was told that he had two weeks to pack his bags and return to Zimbabwe.

He was going to be sent to his country of birth, where he had a father. Having lost any trace of a Zimbabwean accent and with a totally British outlook on life, it was cruel to do that, unforgivable, and I still don't have a way to get him home.

He's been there for almost two years now.

Crossing the busy street, Mark holds tightly to my hand. This always gave me a lovely, protected feeling, until, some time ago, I realised that when he was very angry about something I had done he would not hold my hand. Presumably, this was so that I would get run over, which would serve me right.

Good job I am a big girl and can cross roads on my own.

We are going to meet Helen, the barrister opposing Mark, as well as a Jack and a Phil, the latter the lawyer supporting Mark. There's an Edward, too, who turns out to be a very posh lawyer indeed, and who has met the Queen on a few occasions and Robert Mugabe too, apparently.

One of the first things you see as you get close to the Victoria and Alfred Waterfront is the big fairground wheel. Next, you notice the bars and restaurants, and of course the harbour itself, the waters of which are smooth and black by night and painted with streaks of bright colour from the buildings that fence the harbour in. By day, the seals sun themselves on the jetties whilst gulls skim overhead. By night, the human animals enjoy themselves. Violence and bad behaviour are kept at bay by stern-faced security guards.

So, it is early evening when I first see it, the lights just beginning to reflect upon the water.

We are heading for a restaurant called Den Anker, which is right on the waterfront itself – a wooden building built upon decking, known for Belgian and Dutch cuisine. I think one of the lawyers has recommended it to Mark.

A group of people are seated on the decking outside; a large but immaculately dressed young man with a black beard rises from his chair to greet us. He wears an expensive and well-cut suit, beneath which shines a waistcoat of peacock feathers; he waves a hand in our direction, calling out to Mark, who grins back at him.

This is Jack, a criminal lawyer. I defy anyone not to like him. He is perhaps a couple of years older than our daughter, a mine of information upon every subject, trivial or serious, as well as a born story-teller. As I was to learn, he has the ability to remain genial no matter what shit hits the fan.

We climb the wooden steps to the restaurant and Mark introduces me to those he has met before, to Jack and Helen and Phil, and the remaining introductions are left to Jack.

It is Helen that I am most curious about I suppose, as the only other woman, because over the past couple of years I have woken up to the fact that a lot of women like my husband, a lot of women flirt with my husband and almost every lawyer I meet appears to be younger than me.

Total insecurity, that has forced my burgeoning, middle-aged figure into lacy bras and knickers that somehow never look right, and demanded I have my hair lightened and straightened, and forced me into make-up, and high heels I have never worn in my life. I was once a bluestocking, a flat-footed teacher, and rather too proud of it for my own good.

There is also the tendency to wonder, since finding the earring, whether the woman I am smiling at might be the owner of the other half of the pair.

Helen is dark-haired, at least ten years younger than me – neat, pretty and smart. I like her after roughly fifteen minutes in her company. She has a very clear, well-educated voice, but does a Mancunian accent which outdoes Victoria Wood for hilarity, and she can impersonate top female judges, too. Her skills are many and varied.

I decide that she is not the owner of one rather beautiful, dangly earring, on the basis that she is too nice a person and clearly happily married, and with children.

What reinforces the theory is a lack of artifice; she seems no more impressed by Mark's company than anyone else's. She is attractive, yes, but chummy to boot. Perhaps a bit of a tomboy inside, I conclude. The kind of person who would fearlessly have climbed trees as a child.

Phil is lanky and strikes one as a bit of a rogue, until you realise that he shares the same fears as everyone else. He reads avidly, which you can tell after a short time in his company. He's very quick to spot weaknesses in others, perhaps, but I can't say that he capitalises on them, except for a clear, Liverpudlian sense of humour which becomes obvious as the evening progresses. They are all a good fifteen to twenty years younger than Mark and me, except for Edward, rather the gentleman and a very nice man, I think. It is easy to imagine that in Africa he would wear a very British hat to protect him from the heat. There is certainly something of the diplomat about him; as time went on and the legal arguments grew more intense amongst this group, it was Edward who placed himself at the centre of things, risking the random shellfire.

Conversation, that evening, is innocent and often amusing as we feel our way carefully around one another. I think Mark causes offence on two occasions, but his charm is such that he appears to get away with it.

I had agreed with Mark that if topics of conversation arose about the legal cases, I would sidle away and do my own thing. Quite how much of 'my own thing' I would have to do has not yet become apparent.

I had also decided not to drink too much as it loosens the tongue, with sometimes catastrophic effects; it has this effect on me, anyway. Mark had suggested that I keep a 'low profile'. I felt that this was a tad paranoid, but agreed.

My resolve only lasts a couple of hours, not because of drink – because at that point I have only drunk sparkling water – but because I get a little bit, well, 'passionate' about things; perhaps Mark knows this, and is wary of it.

Jack, the young, bearded lawyer who could have successfully secured the part of Sir Francis Drake in an episode of *Blackadder*, and who is ferociously patriotic, had been speaking in loud, rounded tones about the heritage of the island of St Helena being part British Navy and part slave. We got onto the topic of the recently discovered bodies of slaves on the island. It was one of the few things that I had had time to Google.

The bodies, into their hundreds, were discovered by the construction workers who were building an airport runway for the island.

A team of archaeologists had travelled to Saint Helena from the University of Birmingham to examine them. These slaves were mostly adolescents, because these would fetch a higher price at the slave market. There were suggestions that some of them had passed away through dysentery and other diseases, but suggestions, too, that some had been killed, or rather murdered.

"Do you think there will be a memorial at the site?" I ask. "There should be something, surely, to commemorate their deaths? It's so terrible, such an atrocity, to be wrenched from your family and home, manacled in the bowels of a ship, then released only to be murdered..."

Jack looks at me in horror, his handsome face darkening. "Murdered? They weren't murdered, they died from their diseases," he protested.

I frown. "Not according to the articles I've read, suggesting that some of the bodies have gunshot wounds to the legs and that there are women buried with their arms about small children. The child and the woman wouldn't have died simultaneous deaths."

"It did happen," Jack argues indignantly.

"But it couldn't have happened where you have several women cradling children, surely? I mean, you are a criminal lawyer, so is that likely?"

"So, who are you suggesting killed them?" Jack asks passionately. "Look, the British Navy at the time had been ordered to stop slave ships and remove the slaves; they would simply have brought them to the island and dealt with them there, but they certainly wouldn't have killed them."

I think about the conversation I had recently on the subject with Henry, our son, a knowledgeable historian.

"But, so far as I understand it, the British Navy could be brutal at this period in time. They would have been told to deal with the slaves, probably without specific instructions as to how they were going to do this.

Mightn't it have been a convenient option, just to bump them off?"

Another young man has appeared before us, across the decking, close enough to hold his begging cup towards us without risking the wrath of the waiters. I think about JJ again.

"The British Navy would not have killed any of the slaves," Jack scoffs, his voice rising indignantly, with more patriotism than objective reasoning.

I lift my eyebrows, not hearing the loud squeal of my voice as I challenge him.

"But why not? They were ordinary men in an age where such things happen. Such things happen today, across the world. What if the sick slaves were just a bloody inconvenience and this was the most expedient way of dealing with the problem?"

Edward, who has been talking to Helen and Phil about some of his past cases, now looks towards us anxiously, shocked by my use of the word 'bloody', perhaps. Mark rests a hand gently upon my shoulder to remind me of the whole low-profile thing. As Jack's booming voice outdid mine for volume, it is rather unfair, but I dip my voice accordingly.

"What's your theory, then? Because gunshot wounds surely mean that some of them were killed."

Jack chews the top of his beard and reflects. "It's perfectly possible that a few of the islanders who were there at the time killed them," he concluded. "After all, there wouldn't have been enough food, enough provision. Maybe they decided they didn't want further burden upon their resources."

"But... I thought the island had a large population of freed slaves at the time?"

Jack shrugs, holding his hands out in a question.

"No," I say, shaking my head, whilst Mark and Jack expect me to say, *"Perhaps you're right."* "The guns would have had to have been there at the ready. Soldiers would have had guns, wouldn't they? No matter that it was two hundred years ago. It was a crime, Jack, and the dead deserve a voice."

As we walk home later, Mark rebukes me. "Could you keep your opinions to yourself? Or maybe mute them a little? I don't want to fall out with people."

I twist my face towards him, my mouth falling open as I carefully step over the outstretched legs of yet another poor bloke with a plastic pot, half asleep in the street.

"Well, I'll try," I agree uncertainly, but I can't keep the doubt from my voice as I say it. This trip might be more demanding than I had thought; and anyway, that was rich coming from a man who used ridicule to corner people in court, I think dryly.

As Mark goes to the hotel bar to buy a drink, I wander through the open doors to the courtyard beyond to explore. The small garden is surrounded by high, vine-smothered grey walls. A circular swimming pool lies at its midst. I drift through the ornate gate to dip my fingers in the warm, blue-green water.

The voice floats towards me from a private place somewhere beyond, and after seconds pass I realise that it is Thadie, the young environmentalist.

"It will all be alright, Maya, try to stay calm. Relax and listen to the CD I gave you. I'll be back before you know it, and I love you. I'll look after you; all will be well…"

Her voice is so gentle, so intimate, that I rise from my crouching position next to the pool and retrace my steps, returning to Mark and the gin and tonic. When Thadie appears in the same room a few moments later, I pretend not to have noticed her.

Chapter 4
Diary Three

Once before, many years ago in Paris, he did this to me. Mark is merciless when it comes to travel. Every hour must be utilised. Knowing that we won't be here for long, he doesn't want to relax for a moment.

On that occasion in Paris we had left our children with my mother-in-law for the weekend. We must have visited every monument, walked along every street, as well as visiting every bar and café and following every metro route, until, at about eight o'clock in the evening, to the disgust of the adoring French audience, I fell asleep, exhausted, upon his shoulder. Snoring with abandon in the home of the Comédie Française, I risked the guillotine.

I was in my late twenties then. Teaching, raising a family, supporting Mark's career. I am in my late fifties now and it's getting much harder to stay awake. But of course, this isn't something I want to tell Mark, who is surrounded by attractive, enigmatic young female lawyers. So, I determine to keep up with his schedule whilst feeling like a flag being dragged after him in a wind.

There is no wind on this day, at least on the low ground beneath Table Mountain. The sun scorches our pale skin, a frighteningly different sun. We scarcely have time to breathe let alone notice that our noses have burned to a crisp on the top deck of the bus. I am grateful for a glass of wine and some lunch in the pretty courtyard of the Stellenbosch Vineyard.

We have travelled all around Cape Town on a red bus at this point, headphones screwed into our ears giving a potted history of the place. The commentary is brisk but informative, and apologetic when it makes reference to historic racial discrimination.

We are seated on the sunny but windy open top deck with other tourists, including three old ladies whose Corsa is lovely to listen to, although I understand not a word. They are clearly enjoying a day out. I would love to know what they make of Cape Town and what they say to each other. Each of them wears a crocheted woollen hat as protection against the fierce sun; one yellow hat, one green and one blue.

The Kirstenbosch Botanical Garden is stunning. A little like being on the set of the film, *Gorillas in the Mist*. Although, disappointingly, there are no gorillas, no monkeys or zebra either, as we climb the path that winds through the gardens. Mark declares that we won't see everything at this rate, so we race back to the bus stop.

We cover much of the Constantia wine route on the marvellous red bus, passing the hectic shanty towns which topple in higgledy-piggledy frail disarray.

I smear cream into my face; my cheekbones and nose now look like the flag of Switzerland in reverse.

We hear about the Portuguese and Dutch settlers, and about the people who lived in the area before them, along with lion and zebra, now long gone. The story of the Khoikhoi, from whom the land was taken, their chiefs imprisoned after they argued with futile, primitive, honest rationality that the settlers might be a bit upset if the Khoikhoi moved into Amsterdam, taking Dutch land instead.

We hear about the Dutch farmer, Wolraad Woltemade, and his valiant horse who ploughed into the sea again and again to rescue the drowning sailors who clung to the horse's mane and tail, until the crashing waves drowned them all on the last desperate attempt at rescue.

"And if you turn your head to the right," the female commentator says, her voice dipping conspiratorially in a rather sleazy tone, like a deviant schoolgirl at St Trinian's, "you will see the vast beaches of Camps Bay, where you can drink in the sunshine and do a bit of celebrity spotting and perhaps admire the many beach babes."

Her voice is suddenly better suited to an advertisement for a Benny Hill programme. Perhaps she is a lesbian, because I don't think the beach babes would appeal to me. This is clearly aimed at the men.

The sea this time of the year is icy cold, and the sharks are searching for beach babes in vain, whatever the environmentalists say about the sea being their territory, not ours, so they snack on the limbs of surfers instead.

Recently a surfer made an on-the-spot decision to lose his arm, rather than his life, thrusting the limb into a shark's jaws before rapidly swimming away with one arm remaining. I mean, fond as I am of belly boarding, I would find these dangerous waters a little too 'high risk', but mountains are there to be climbed, I suppose.

I put a hand upon my hot forehead – I haven't worn a hat, as most of the people on the top deck had thought to do, so I am no more intelligent than the intrepid surfers – then I gaze towards the luxurious looking Camps Bay Hotel. We are informed that Prince Harry stayed there not long ago, possibly to get a good view of the beach babes.

There is a group of seven black African children performing in the road below us as the bus jolts toward a bus stop. The eldest child can only be about ten, the age of our granddaughter. The little group appears to be unescorted by an adult, until I see a plump lady standing back between two parked cars and I realise that she is escorting them. The children are performing a lively song, wearing homemade African costumes for the entertainment of tourists seated at a bar. A little boy from the group is holding out a cup to collect coins. It is the first day of their summer holidays. I can't see my grandchildren doing this by choice, not on the first day of their holidays.

Further down the street, a woman, possibly in her late thirties, is sitting on the pavement with her thin back to the wall. She is holding a crying baby on her lap. The child is swathed in shawls, for the sun is bright and intense but a fierce wind has started, strong enough for the sand to whip and sting the legs of the beach babes. Beside the mother there is an upturned hat to collect money from tourists. The woman doesn't resemble an alcoholic or a drug addict. She looks like a woman who needs milk or nappies.

As someone passes her, dropping coins into her battered sunhat, she turns her face upward and I see her humbly mouth the words, "Thank you, my madam."

What a mixed-up place Cape Town is, a place where human homes are as flimsy as Coke cans but stabling for horses is an expensive, solid shelter; where wealthy young women sway along the pavement like Californian girls, and black mothers beg for money.

I wonder whether there are social services here, or family lawyers, whether the police have the power to pick children up if they are found on the streets, begging.

What were Nelson Mandela's words? Something about there being no keener revelation of a society's soul than the way it treats its children? I've no answers, so I shouldn't criticise and, really, although I know so little about this place, there is still something strongly good about it – a story begun, with an elusive ending.

The bus passes on and we head for Table Mountain, which has beckoned to us and followed our journey all morning – a great, smooth-edged sequence of boulders, which cradles Cape Town, set against a vivid blue sky and ethereal clouds. I would like to paint its browns and greens and golds.

Table Mountain is home to a wide range of creatures, but no longer to the big game animals. Last night, Jack told us that one of his favourite classic films, *Zulu*, was filmed on the mountain.

The bus winds its way past white and yellow villas in sunny streets lined with palm trees, their fronds waving gently like green ribbons in the sunshine.

Our bus stops for a chattering group of black schoolchildren to cross the road, luckier than the ones begging for money, excited at the prospect of their summer holiday.

At the corner of the street, as we start to wind our way up the hill towards the foot of the mountain, two men stand with homemade Christmas bells and angels carefully fashioned from tiny beads of glass or plastic.

There is no one around to buy them just now, but they smile patiently as they sit upon a low wall, chattering to each other.

Tiny beads of glass...

My thoughts suddenly return to Mark.

I look at him in profile, so handsome, such a complex person. All I ever wanted.

I think of the earring, also made from tiny beads of glass, caught in the cloth of his shirt some while ago. I wonder again who it belongs to, what she looks like, and how it came to be there.

It caused a massive row between us, and when we were quiet once more he refused to answer questions about it. He had no idea how it came to be there, so he said.

Rubbish, of course. But I didn't want to raise the issue again. That was when I realised that all of the time he had been going to legal dos and dinners, he hadn't been alone. That was when, after he told me about the job he'd been invited to do in St Helena, I told him I would go, too.

I have never travelled away with him before this. I work, I take care of the family, whilst Mark takes care of his career.

We alight from the bus, dismayed by the queue for the next rotating glass elevator to ascend Table Mountain. It is comparable to the queues at Disneyland, even though it is now late afternoon.

We stand behind a gaggle of American girls with skinny jeans, tiny bums and backpacks. They are more suited to our son in age, I muse, but that doesn't stop several of them from smiling over their shoulders at

Mark. I've become quite used to being totally invisible by now, I think petulantly.

As the cable car swings away from the foot of the mountain, the ground moves beneath us. Below lies the vast city, a city like no other, spread-eagled and chaotic, reflecting the bright rays of the sun. I search for wildlife in a safari of my imagination, for zebra galloping in a herd, but find only two human hikers who have made the journey on foot.

The motion of the car can scarcely be felt as we rise to the summit, skating high above the tufts of foliage and crevices in the rock, and we draw closer, the mountain becoming a shining grey, granite wonder, patched with grassy knolls, pin-pointed by sunlight.

I feel a buzz of excitement, a small rush of happiness and elation as we are lifted through the air, to have Mark away from the office, to myself, and reach up to kiss his cheek.

We wander with other tourists to the opposite side of the mountain, along a winding path, to take photographs of the vast ocean sparkling below us and the sheer drop towards the beautiful villas far, far below. All that there is to prevent a tumble down the side of the mountain is a low, and seemingly inadequate, wall. As we stand with other tourists, the woman beside me squeals, "Look, aren't they cute!" to her companion.

I look down to the rocky ledge a few feet below, to the place at which she is pointing.

They are cute indeed, a little family of, of... I don't know what they are. They are a mix of plain, short-haired, buff-coloured small badger and large guinea pig. They snuffle across the rocks, three or four of them, happy and well fed on crisps being tossed over the wall by the mostly Japanese tourists. Cute rats. Creatures of Lewis Carroll's imagination, perhaps.

Are they carnivore, herbivore or omnivore? I wonder, as I watch them amble right up to the foot of the wall. The fattest of them is followed by tiny babies. She lies down to sunbathe upon a patch of rock, and they make a beeline for her nipples, gorging themselves contentedly on milk.

"There's a sign here about the wildlife," Mark points out to me. "They are called rock hyrax, apparently."

I'm impressed; he may be a good lawyer but he's not big on nature. Once, when we took our children on a walk in the woods, I pointed out the names of the trees.

"What's this one called?" our son asked.

"Fred," Mark replied with a derisive snort.

"Sit on the wall," Mark says now. "I'll take your photograph."

I twist my lips reluctantly; the wall doesn't bother me, it's low enough to sit on, but I hate having my photograph taken.

There are so many younger, prettier people to photograph. Once, about five years ago, Mark had hooted with laughter, saying that I looked like Kenneth Williams. The comment was really caused by my attempt to hold up my head so than my neck would be taut, not saggy with the loose skin of the middle-aged.

I wriggle my backside onto the wall, trying to look moderately attractive in the face of the wind which has grown considerably stronger, now blowing my hair across my face.

I stare at the camera I bought him for his birthday, a contrived, self-conscious smile upon my lips, until a sudden, violent gust of wind catches at my chest, almost like a soft push from an unseen hand. It rocks me backwards towards the sheer rocks, which descend, tumbling below us, thousands of metres above the sea level.

I flounder, then panic in an instant, my fingers gripping at the stone wall as I fight to keep my balance in the wind.

But a woman comes rushing towards me, one of the Japanese women whose eyes widen with horror as she predicts my backward fall. My eyes lock with Mark's in alarm, appealing for help. The camera removed from his face, there is a smile creasing the corner of his lips which is darkly amused.

Rather too slowly, his facial expression changes, as though he hadn't realised the peril I faced. Perhaps a delayed reaction, but uncertainty is already gnawing at me. Then he reaches out to take my arm, helping me down from the wall. He and the Japanese woman.

I feel upset, I feel indignant. I don't know what I feel.

I thank the woman but look away from Mark. I stand perfectly still until the horror of a fall and certain death pass over me and I return to the present. For some while I remain deep in thought.

When I have recovered, I look up at his handsome face and frown. "Take your time, why don't you?" I say, without smiling.

He laughs quietly then, putting a hand upon my shoulder.

"Come on, let's go and get a cup of coffee."

I am confused now, rather than frightened, confused and hurt, but there is no anger left, where, perhaps, there should have been.

He loves me, he tells me that quite often, and yet there was the sadistic smile of a schoolboy torturing a small animal upon his face, just as I rocked backwards and forwards in the wind.

I can't quite bring myself to hold his hand as we amble towards the shop with the other tourists.

Chapter 5

Diary Four

On the bus top on the way back, I text Lucy.

'How is Mum? How are you? I miss you.'

They would never suggest I sit on a wall, thousands of metres from the ground. I never doubt their love.

The reply returns swiftly, as though she is in another street, not another continent.

'Mum's feeling weak, but all being well she has chemotherapy in two weeks' time. The drugs she's taking are making her a bit delirious, so she's had to go back into hospital. She didn't have a good night and is afraid of the nurses at night-time, when they have a change of staff. I put a big tin of Quality Street and a note to thank them next to her bed. Bill is coming to see her this evening. She sends her love and says you aren't to worry. She will be fine. I'm fine, x.'

Thank God for my sister. I would tell her anything, but I don't tell her that I wondered whether my husband was waiting for me to fall off a mountain top. She would say that I was being fanciful and that she had more urgent things to think about.

I text our two children then, reminding one to feed the rabbits which belong to our grandchildren but which we now care for, and asking the other to get a job, as being a DJ is unpaid work.

There is time, before we meet the others again, to have a swim in the hotel pool. Whilst I swim up and down with leisurely strokes, Mark lounges back on one of the sunbeds, resembling a Hollywood film star rather than a lawyer. Perhaps ego is the link.

He swims every day. His skin is brown, his chest broad, his hips small and his legs long. He is far too good-looking.

I am almost three years older than Mark and more aware of it than ever. I am not merely imagining that every woman who walks past him stares, or drops something, waiting for him to retrieve it, or merely loiters for no obvious reason.

I think of JJ again, in Zimbabwe. Perhaps because, geographically, we are so much closer to him now and because it helps to divert my attention from Mark and the women, to mull over something far more meaningful.

I have done some research on Harari, where JJ is living, where he was expelled to, actually.

You don't have to read very much to understand that, beautiful as it may be, it is not currently a very good place to live and certainly not what JJ, who had lived in the UK from childhood, would be accustomed to.

I close my eyes as I swim and see JJ's face. Jonathan, our son's friend, loping towards our house at the foot of the hill, wearing the black hat pulled down over one eye and bearing some resemblance to a young Wesley Snipes.

I watched him loitering outside Isuru's house, hoping to catch a glimpse of her at her window. She was a very beautiful young woman, but he didn't stand much of a chance because, although I knew she liked JJ, her father was the local pastor. Her father was Nigerian and believed that JJ should attend his church more frequently, and that hip hop, which JJ and Henry wrote and performed together, was the music of the devil.

I remember watching a scene from an open window at the front of our house one summer's evening, recalling Catherine, the pastor's wife, at her kitchen window, smelling the lovely sugary warmth of the cakes she was baking with Isuru's sisters. Then I saw her purse her lips in a prim line as she noted JJ in the street.

Perhaps JJ noted the thin line of her mouth, too, as foolishly, rebelliously, he took a cigarette from his pocket and lit it, then stood between our two houses to smoke it.

It wouldn't have helped to impress Isuru's mother.

JJ had achieved an award for excellence at the school that he attended with Henry.

They had done their A-level exams. JJ's mother had wanted him to go to college and study Business, whilst JJ had said he *would* go to college… to study Media. They were at loggerheads most of the time and, although he wasn't aware of it, it would have serious repercussions for him.

He had loitered for a long time outside our house, hoping to have a word with the lovely Isuru, whilst I went back to the kitchen to grapple with a different problem.

The dead bantam, plump and floppy, lay upon a board on the kitchen table.

I kept chickens then, and this one had been molested by a cat; and though she had been very healthy up until that point, the sudden attack must have stopped her little heart. I had found her half an hour or so before, shooing the cat from the garden whilst the other hens cowered in their coop.

I was not going to waste her, even though I had been extremely fond of her. She was the 'boss chicken', if there is such a thing, and the boldest of them all.

She used to leap up from the ground, exactly like a rocket, to retrieve worms from your fingers.

I had never plucked a chicken and I didn't know where to begin.

Thus far, I had removed the dead bantam to the kitchen sink and yanked at a fistful of dry feathers. Not one of them had come away in my hand. Clearly this wasn't the way to do it. Help came from an unexpected quarter.

JJ knocked at the door. I wiped my hands upon a kitchen towel and went to answer it.

"Hello, Stephanie, is Henry upstairs?"

I nodded, smiling at him. "He is, but before you go up there, I don't suppose you know anything about plucking dead chickens?"

He took off his jacket and 'I'm the man' hat, hanging them on the hall stand.

"I know quite a lot about it. I used to watch Dad doing it when I was young. He keeps chickens at our home in Harari."

He followed me into the kitchen, staring down at the hen, nonplussed.

"Boil up the kettle,' he said. "You have to pour boiling water all over it, then it'll be easy."

He rolled up his black shirtsleeves, taking the apron from the back of a kitchen chair to protect his shirt and pulling it over his head. I watched him pour boiling water over the feathers, watched him grab the tail feathers with a hand, yanking them out with ease. "There y'go," he said, turning to me with a smile.

"JJ, why didn't I think of that? I'm so stupid... Of course!"

He shook the feathers that had stuck to his hand into the sink and nodded his head for me to try it. They came out with ease then, popping away from the pink, pockmarked flesh until, within minutes, the chicken was featherless.

"You are a Renaissance man, JJ. You can paint and draw, make music and films and pluck chickens."

"Why, thank you, ma'am," he grinned.

He boiled the kettle to make a cup of tea, knowing our kitchen well, and then, as I bagged up the sodden feathers, he took the large chopping blade from the rack and said, "Okay, so now we have to chop off its head. Would you like me to do that?"

I winced and nodded, more of a coward than I'd thought; watched as he took the heavy chopping knife from the rack, raised it to head height and, with one sweep of his arm, brought it down with a thwack, severing the neck and hitting the wooden board.

"Now you joint it..." He raised the knife again to cut through the belly as I stared down, fascinated by his butcher's work, to admire the most beautiful piece of nature's art I have ever seen. I will never forget it, for it was lovelier by far than a Faberge egg.

Smooth, fragile, never hatched, the shell as translucent as porcelain, and all surrounded by a perfect ovoid of yellow seed and green grass which was the undigested food, all of it shining like wet marble in the hen's stomach.

"We should get ready now."

Mark's voice, calling me from the sunbed, wakes me from my dream state. My mind is capable of drifting away entirely, so much so that recently I walked into the swimming pool area with only a towel across my arm, having drifted so far into the depths of my mind that I had forgotten to don my bathing costume. Not a mistake to make here, not if I was to keep a low profile.

The picture of JJ and the chicken fades in an instant as I climb out of the pool to join him.

In the hotel room, Mark makes love to me. His fingers are soft and slow, his fingertips caressing the base of my spine. When it is over, I remember the incident on Table Mountain and think about my stupidity. He loves me, of course he does. It was a mean thought.

I used to initiate lovemaking, but now, an 'older woman', I feel almost grateful to him, as though he has chosen me over younger women. We have been together for more than thirty years and I have only felt this way recently. Only since the earring.

Afterwards I lay quiet in his arms, my head resting upon his broad chest, and he says, "Are you alright?"

So, I ask it. "Do you still want me?"

"Of course I want you! Don't ask stupid questions!" he pleads, and I realise there is guilt in his voice. I know Mark very well, that he is silently begging me, *"Don't make me feel guilty about doing whatever I want."*

"Was there something wrong with my performance?" he asks, as though at a loss.

"No, of course not, you are a wonderful lover and I love you," I answer him, for this is genuine.

The first stars have appeared in the dark blue sky when the taxi arrives to take us to meet the others. We have avoided them quite deliberately in the day, because Mark says he needs to keep some distance at the start of the case.

We are driven through Cape Town to a meat restaurant called Nelson's Eye, which is almost completely full upon our arrival. After the impressions of the day, black schoolchildren or white, never the twain shall meet, I feel reassured, somehow, by the fact that this restaurant has quite a few black guests. South Africa is a beautiful, vibrant but disconcerting place, still not the place that Nelson Mandela wanted.

We have dressed up for the occasion. Helen looks lovely in a black dress with a simple white cardigan thrown about her shoulders. Maybe because are the only two women there, we sit opposite one another, at first appraising one another once more, but relatively soon we start talking about our families. Her husband is also a lawyer, presently working in Argentina.

Conversation comes easily with Helen, as we go from French food (her husband's family is French) to how I once believed I had gout in my right leg from drinking too many pina coladas in Cuba (it turned out to be a trapped nerve).

I like Helen a lot, conversation is easy, but perhaps I am so comfortable with her because, although she laughs at Mark and enjoys his company, she doesn't seem to feel the need to keep touching her hair, or the jewellery at her bosom; she doesn't keep trying to attract his attention as so many other women do.

The conversation turns to the case, which I know little about, and as I am not one of the lawyers involved I am not meant to know.

I am merely on holiday, the camp follower that Mark doesn't need because he has so many of those. It's a joke between us, but I wonder all the same.

Mark and I had discussed that I should remove myself from the group when the real nitty-gritty of legal discussion began, but we are hemmed in by tables on every side in this packed restaurant and the food is just arriving. On the one side, I have Jack's rather impressive form leaning towards me; we are at a corner table and I am slightly squashed by the chair behind me.

I say nothing and sip my wine as they begin to talk of the twin girls involved in the case, Teagan and Kaysha, and their American–Scottish mother, Cara, who would not, or could not, tell the social workers who the father of the girls was, other than the fact, clear to everyone, that he was black.

The lawyers here are representing different people in the case.

Helen and Phil represent the parents who have fostered one child and now wish to adopt her legally, whilst Edward represents the second set of parents, who are gay but wish to adopt both children. Mark represents the children themselves.

I am aware of his views, that the children should remain as close to each other as possible as they grow up, and that they should have access to Cara, the mother, in later life, if that is what the children wish.

I didn't fully understand the reasons that they had been taken from Cara in the first place but knew she had lived on St Helena for a little while and that she had come from America where she had lived with her mother, who had returned to the island.

She appeared to be a savvy young woman, but for whatever reason she didn't want to take the children back.

Mark had become angrier and more indignant as the story unfolded, by way of emails and Skype from his contacts on the island. The proper legal channels seemed to have been overlooked; there were no family lawyers there to advise on the case, and children were fostered and adopted without efficient paperwork, or so it appeared.

And the two babies were now almost nine months old.

This, apparently, was just one of the many cases they would be attending to.

From the conversation going on around me, there are many peripheral issues to deal with, not least of them who should carry the can, ultimately, for decisions about the two girls. It does sound a little like the casual sale of two Labrador puppies.

"What is important here," Mark is saying, "is what is in the best interests of the two children, not what is in the best interests of the prospective parents."

Helen raises her eyes slightly, as if to say, *"Yes, I am perfectly aware of that."*

"Who, in the case of one of them, has now settled in very well with the foster parents, who are showing themselves to be loving and devoted to the child. They have already formed strong bonds," Helen insists.

Mark makes no comment. Instead he says, "Do you realise how badly Cara herself has been treated? Shunned by some of the older islanders for her sexual behaviour and, because they don't see her as an islander…"

"I've heard some of it," Edward agrees. "One wonders why they couldn't have arranged for her to have a taxi on her visitation days, rather than having to descend the six hundred and eighty or so steps of Jacob's Ladder to Jamestown, not to mention the ascent when she returned home for the day in the dark. People have been killed in the attempt to traverse the steps at night, apparently."

I had seen pictures of Jacob's Ladder in geography textbooks, a sheer ladder of steps ascending the reddish-brown volcanic rock.

"Even so," Helen says, her gentle features altered by the grim smile which indicates her alter persona in court, "I don't think that my clients are going to give in on any of this. As you said, Mark, the interests of the child are paramount, and one of the girls, at least, has been in a happy, loving environment for some while."

The conversation ends abruptly then, leaving an uncomfortable silence like invisible volcanic dust, and I'm sure I'm not the only one to be grateful when one of the actors in *Scarface* passes our table, handing us a new topic of conversation.

Chapter 6
Diary Five

The next day we wake a little later than usual, hastily repacking our suitcases and giving Lerato, the maid, whose language is Swazi and who speaks little English, a tip.

After breakfast, waiting for the taxi to take us to the harbour, we sit beside the pool in the shady courtyard and I ring various members of the family. I have been told that mobile phones are redundant on St Helena; you cannot make calls or send texts. In every way, you are very isolated from the rest of the world.

I call Lucy first. Mum has returned from hospital and Lucy is caring for both our parents. I feel very guilty about it and very grateful to her.

"Mum is feeling a little better. She hasn't eaten very much, and she complains that the pro plan drinks are slimy and disgusting. I'm making her some chicken soup which we can keep in the fridge."

"Oh, thanks, Luce. I'm so sorry about not being there."

"Don't be silly, the school has been very good, they've given me several weeks off, and Emma and Bea are being very helpful." There is a brief pause. "Dad has deteriorated a lot, you know. I hadn't realised just how bad his memory had become. You know Mum was getting frustrated because he kept asking the same questions? I don't think she was exaggerating it. He has asked me three times in the space of half an hour whether the hospital says if the cancer has gone away now, and twice in less time if he should boil some eggs for her..."

I chuckle. It isn't funny, not funny in the slightest, to see your father, who could converse on any subject, who had taught you so much, become so dreadfully confused.

"He might be asking you about the cancer because he's afraid. He lost his mum, didn't he, years ago when he was only in his late twenties. Maybe he's thinking of that time too. He was very lonely when I stayed with him, missed Mum so much."

"Mm..." She laughs then. "He never forgets to fetch the paper from the shop and his beer for the evening! But seriously, I think we should try to get another appointment for the Memory Clinic."

We agree this is a good idea, then she says, "Doug turned up on my doorstep, by the way."

"Doug? Really... after all of this time?"

Mark is mouthing at me that the taxi has arrived. I get up, following him to the hotel's entrance, with the phone to my ear. Doug is Lucy's first husband, and we are all very fond of him, punctuated with spells of extreme frustration when he takes off to work in Thailand for a year at a time without telling anyone where he is going, or Iceland or anywhere the mood takes him, really.

Before Lucy met her partner, John, she and Doug had been married for three years. She discovered that Doug was fooling around with an art student, and left him. They had two young children at that point; Emma was now twenty-seven, the same age as our own daughter.

"Yes, says he's had enough of travelling around, says he wants to be closer to the girls. So he's bought a flat in the Iffley Road."

"What a cheek. Pity he didn't get a bit more involved in their lives earlier."

"Absolutely my thought, but Emma is over the moon; he's taking Emma and her boyfriend out for a meal this evening. Bea says she's not going…"

I have to say goodbye to her then; I have other calls to make. Mark is glaring at me irritably from the back seat of the taxi. I climb inside and smile apologetically.

The taxi lurches forward to the sound of African hip hop resounding from the car's stereo system, driving fast towards the harbour.

When we have handed over our cases to go on board, filling in forms saying that we don't have Ebola or a variety of other diseases, we stand in the shadow of the RMS *St Helena* on dry dock, looking up at the large, white ship.

I can feel Mark's excitement and squeeze his hand as he laughs at something Helen says. He will be working hard, focussing everything upon this case, but it will be a great adventure for him too – for us both, I suppose.

We are standing with our new friends and a large group of passengers waiting to board, having been called up by name in alphabetical order. Further back in the queue stands Thadie, who resembles one of the turtles she seeks to protect, with a large haversack weighing her down. I wave at her.

I don't know what to expect, which is all part of the excitement. I have no way of predicting the bond I will feel with some of these smiling strangers before we arrive at the island, but I hope, somehow, to have Thadie as a friend.

SEE YOU AGAIN, ONE TIME IN SAINT HELENA

A ship adrift upon the ocean is like a floating village; you are forced to share living space with a multitude of characters; in the case of the RMS *St Helena*, the spaces are sometimes small. Many of the passengers are 'Saints', not literally, or perhaps they are, but that's what the islanders call themselves.

There are people returning to their home, some of whom have been away for a long, long time, others taking employment on the island, and a few tourists, because it's expensive to travel by ship, which, as there is no airport yet, is the only mode of travel. The journey takes five days. In the case of two charming French men, Sebastian and Philippe, they are devoted fans of Napoleon, off to St Helena to visit Longwood, Napoleon's last home. But there is also a large group of mostly younger men, all from Zimbabwe, recruited to do the building work on the airport; and as I watch them queue to board the ship, a crazy plan half formulates in my brain. What if I can get JJ to St Helena?

We climb the iron stairs to the ship's living quarters, a difficult climb for the older folk, I reflect, before heaving myself upwards with my haversack on my back and the required sensible shoes upon my feet.

We are met by smiling, white-uniformed stewards, both male and female, and mostly, I understand, from the island itself.

The islanders have lovely faces, at least most do. There seems to be no such thing as ugly, and their friendliness and gentleness is endearing. This is the first occasion on which I encounter the islanders' unique accent.

"I tought I tore you on the plane," greets a middle-aged man called David – in the way of Sylvester the cat saying, *"I tought I tore a puddy cat."*

We collect the keys to our cabin, which is small but very comfortable. A musical welcome resounds from the sound system, a succession of '70s hits: Boney M. singing "Ra ra Rasputin... lover of the Russian queen," went immediately into 'Car Wash'. The music of my youth, but a little grating after a while.

We can't be bothered to unpack, so go went up on deck to watch the ship leaving the Cape Town dock. Passing the desk, I hear Jack asking civilly, but firmly, why he has to share a cabin with two other men, when he'd asked for a cabin to himself.

"I wouldn't mind so much," he hisses as we pass him, mopping the sweat from his brow with a white handkerchief, then mouthing at us, "but one of them was a criminal client of mine – hardly appropriate!"

Helen is also queuing to request a change, on the basis that she has highly sensitive material in her cabin connected with the case and has been forced to share with another lady. The ship's purser says they are fully booked and changing cabins isn't possible, but he gives her an empty cabin on the bottom deck with a desk and chair where she can work and keep the files locked up; and eventually an amicable 'swop' is arranged for Jack.

Mark and I are in a cabin next to the judge and his wife, which I am rather worried about. It's not so much Mark's snoring, as the fact that, since I found the pretty, dangly earring in a pile of his shirts on his return from a visit to London, I've been a little unsettled at night. I've taken to getting up at odd times to make tea.

I don't want to disturb the judge and his wife with my nocturnal wanderings.

Chapter 7
Diary Six

It's as though the whole ship, passengers and crew, are on the sun deck, mostly waiting for the ship to depart, watching the activity in the dock. I'm nervous about the boat being top heavy, keeling over like a toy boat in a bath. We watch the ship's progress until we are a long way out to sea, and until Cape Town and Table Mountain are distant images upon the horizon.

Everyone is hungry. The staff prepare a feast of sandwiches and cake.

After beef tea, which settles the stomach nicely, I take two anti-seasickness tablets whilst Mark goes to find the ship's doctor to have an injection for the same reason. But I feel very well, not at all sick, as the ship sweeps steadily and majestically through the navy- blue water beneath a bright blue sky.

The ship brings provisions to the island, as well as people: food, of course, including things like powdered milk and baby food, all to be sold in the shops there; medical provisions, including expensive new equipment for the hospital, when it can be afforded; livestock – chickens, pigs, the occasional bull – and all, incredibly, housed away from the passengers in containers behind the bridge. On occasion I'm sure I can smell hay in the middle of the ocean.

Items as large as cars, as compact as teaching materials for the schools, anything and everything that is needed. How they manage all of this on such a small ship is as much of a mystery as a pregnant woman with an almost flat stomach carrying a sizeable child, but it also works.

After we have been on the ship for a very short time, we are called back to the sun lounge for a Health and Safety talk about what to do if the ship capsizes and how to don our bright orange life jackets correctly.

"Wear any warm clothing you can find," the attractive lady purser says.

"But if we end up in the sea, won't that just get very wet and drag us down?" Marianna, a French lady of senior years, asks me.

I shrug and pull a face. I will be just as I am on an aeroplane; in other words, I'm not going to think about it.

"When you have tightened the belt of your life jacket, you will see that there is a whistle as well as a light for attracting attention…"

I have a mental picture of myself bobbing up and down in the sea in layers of jumpers, desperately hunting for my whistle and torch. Other people are thinking similar thoughts from the vacant expressions upon their faces.

"The links on your belt are so that you can join with other people to make a chain; you are far more likely to be seen if you are bobbing up and down in a long line than as an individual."

"You are far more likely to be a sitting target for a shark, surely," I whisper to Marianna, and the lovely purser glances sharply at us for talking in class.

I stop talking, imagining instead a shark, moving on down the chain of people, munching on limbs like a child choosing pick-and-mix sweets.

I have enough trouble with the loops and clips of the life jacket belt without having to deal with them in an emergency. As my fingers fumble at the belt, Thadie steps forward to help.

"Oh, thanks!" I whisper gratefully, hoping that I'm next to her if we all end up in the sea.

When the talk is over, we disperse, then store our life jackets in small cages beneath our cabin beds. The piped music has stopped. All seems quiet except for the throb of the engines and the creaking of the boat, until we hear the pretty little melody singing out across the ship that we were told to expect. It's sung in a country and western style, which is the music favoured by most of the older generation of Saints. An unofficial anthem, the song is played at the start of every journey.

The captain, who is from St Helena and is so handsome and authoritative that when his voice announces, "Stand clear of the watertight doors," strong women quiver, has his own fan club. Not long into our voyage, he announces that there is a whale shark on the port side of the ship. Those too excited for rest rush up the staircase to the sun deck to scan the seas.

The Saints, in the main, stay put, sleeping, or lounging in easy chairs whilst they catch up with friends they haven't seen in a long time. I suppose that, to them, seeing a whale shark is rather like seeing another red bus.

I would love to see the whale shark, but all you can really see is the spurt of water rising from its spout and a blackish shadow beneath the distant waves. After that excitement, because it is so very hot, I go for a swim in the tiny pool on the deck, which cools my sweating skin, but it is impossible to do lengths as it's the size of a jacuzzi.

I am joined by Meryn, a lively occupational therapist who has been recruited by the lawyers to advise upon one or two people with multiple disabilities on the island. She tells me that she has a mere four days to gather information on people whose ages range from six to eighty, and has to return home then to write her advisory reports.

Later, walking across the sun deck with a towel wrapped around my costume, I yank at the sun lounge door. Two young black guys leap up immediately to hold it open for me, something I have been training our son to do for many years but to no avail.

At least a dozen young, black African men are seated in the sun lounge, munching on sandwiches, with cake piled high upon their plates. They do not, somehow, appear to be tourists. I thank the two young men profusely and ask, "Are you on holiday?"

The younger of the two stares blankly at me and clearly speaks no more English than I speak Matabele or Shona, but his older companion chuckles and shakes his head. "No, ma'am, we work for Cecil Thomas; we are going to work on the airport," he explains.

"Ah… Are you all from Cape Town?" I ask.

"No, ma'am, from Zimbabwe."

"You had better eat all you can on the ship to build up your strength." I smile, knowing that this is probably their sensible plan.

I wish them well and go to change out of my costume, and all the while I think about the many workers leaving Zimbabwe to come to Saint Helena. I can't really imagine JJ doing the hard labour involved in building an airport. My kneejerk plans about encouraging him to come to Saint Helena are silly. JJ is too physically slight and academically inclined for that kind of work.

When I return to the deck after my shower, the sky has turned a deeper blue and the sea is vast and smooth, streaked with silver.

I stand against the rail, marvelling at the smooth, steady passage of the ship and gazing out at nothingness but sea to the horizon. Not even a seabird in sight.

Mark joins me at the ship's rail, a cigarette held between his fingers. "There's a gin and tonic for you on the table," he says, before a slight, conspiratorial jerk of his head towards two men sitting at a nearby table, deep in conversation.

"They are journalists," he explains, in a hushed 'don't-look-now' voice. "Be careful what you say to them; avoid them if you can."

I nod. It is like being in Lisbon in the Second World War, I contemplate, with spies everywhere.

We wander towards the table where Helen and the others are sitting. She is wearing a pretty, large-brimmed sun hat and rather resembles a character in a Merchant Ivory film.

"Has anyone seen the judge yet?" Jack asks, sporting a pipe between his teeth and resembling a young sea captain more than ever he did.

"No. You know them well, Phil, do they keep themselves to themselves as a rule?" Edward asks.

"Oh God no, both the judge and his wife are very friendly, tremendous fun, good sense of humour in both cases. But this case is a bit of an issue, isn't it? Perhaps this time, they are waiting till we get closer to the island before they socialise."

Mark and I each pull up a heavy, plastic chair to sit beside them.

Phil, who has forgotten his hat, has a white handkerchief tied to his head, bandana style. He and Edward are very friendly, but the white handkerchief is almost a class-conscious statement, in direct conflict to Edward's background, I muse.

"Come and sit by me, princess," Phil calls to me as I jostle for a space. I glower at him without a trace of humour.

"You are in your late forties, I am in my late fifties; it is an insult to call someone of my age 'princess'," I say.

Yes, it did sound pompous, I suppose. But really? Some men lack any sense. Either that or they are being deliberately provocative. Calling me princess at my age is offensive.

"I've been told that the judge and his wife are very popular on the island," Mark says hastily in case I have caused any offence. Perhaps it is fair. Phil appears to be a nice person; maybe his rudeness was unintentional.

In the midst of various anecdotes about the judge, a sixth person comes to join us – a large-bosomed lady of Jack's age, very tanned, with a blonde bob and sunglasses. Jack introduces her as Sally, a fellow criminal lawyer in the St Helena court.

Edward pulls out a chair for her and offers her a drink. Stupidly, I stare at her earlobes to see whether the other earring in the pair might be dangling there. It has become a fetish. I look at Mark's expression; he is smiling, but there is no tell-tale hint that he knows her.

She has beautiful hands and red nails like polished talons. I suppose female criminal lawyers might need those from time to time. Helen has already told me she never goes into battle in court without being armed with fresh lipstick.

"Have you heard what's happened about the court opening?" Sally asks, before the introductions.

The lawyers stare blankly at her.

"There may be a bit of a panic when we embark..." she says, dipping her voice.

"Why?" Edward asks. "Surely the stress of the case will be panic enough."

Sally drums her sharp nails upon the table.

"The court opening will be two hours after the ship gets in. We are going to have to disembark, get through customs, book into The Ambassador Hotel and then get straight into our court robes, apparently."

"That's a bit of a tall order." Mark smiles, but the smile is languid, charming, relaxed. It never fails to confuse me that, in his own home, a mark on the wall or a stray sock can make him so cross. Whereas amongst his fellow lawyers, a terrible disaster can be faced with humour. A bit more of that at home would be nice, I reflect.

"I think the judge is going to help, I had a word with him earlier; he's going to ask the purser if we can be allowed off the ship first. We can take whatever we need in the way of robes and such out of the luggage the night before we dock, and they'll keep our cases at customs for us; the Customs House is only along the street from the hotel."

The conversation ceases for a moment as we stare in astonishment at the Bishop of St Helena, a sprightly man in his eighties, jogging around the deck, followed by two of the lady therapists. The Bishop wears his ecclesiastical purple top and has his trousers rolled up to the knee.

"It wasn't very well organised, then," Helen comments, bringing us back to the issue of court robes. "Who organised it?"

Sally raises her eyebrows at Jack. "I think it was Fiona, the public solicitor, who asked Mairead to do it. She's a lovely lass, has a heart of gold, but she's so disorganised, she probably put the wrong time in the diary."

"Is she the one who couldn't find the threshold documents?" Helen asks critically.

Although I'm not familiar with their names, most of the lawyers from St Helena have communicated with their counterparts from the mainland via email, by now.

"That's the one." Jack grins. "Ah, I can't find them anywhere, me filing system is good but I can't recall whether I put them in 'T' for threshold or 'H' for Helen. I tink the fairies have probably carried them off to give them to the pixies. I'm sure they'll bring them back later."

When the laughter stops, because it was a very good Irish accent apart from anything else, the conversation turns to how many knots the boat is travelling at and what the depth of the ocean is. It is a conversation for dedicated trainspotters, so I decide to get changed into a frock in lieu of a cocktail party in the ship's lounge, and Helen and Sally rise from the table to do the same.

The harsh blue light of day has softened to evening. I pass a tall man and his pretty, fair-haired wife, accompanied by a little boy of about eight.

There is nothing remarkable about them, except that the little girl the woman holds in her arms is less than a year old and is darker skinned than her parents. Cute, bonny and black with soft curls, not resembling either parent as the little boy does, but she is pulling at the woman's fair hair with confidence.

As they pass me, the woman smiles, but there is almost a challenge in the father's eye.

"What a beautiful baby," I say, for want of something to say.

"Yes, she is, and we love her very much," the mother says, kissing the baby's plump cheek. "Her name is Teagan."

And of course, that's when I realise. The parents are Helen's clients, the baby is Mark's. I should have known immediately. I ought not to have smiled at them, should have ignored them, but it isn't my way. I feel certain they had decided who I was and were perhaps trying to influence me so that I might influence Mark. It is a clever ploy, forged through desperation.

I pass on through the door, which the man holds open for me, knowing that I must retreat quickly, and Helen catches up with me then. "It's rather difficult, isn't it?" she says, "being on the same ship, I mean; they are such lovely people."

I feel guilty of a sudden, realising how hard this decision is, this judgement about the lives of two children and good people who have begun to love them.

At the door of the cocktail lounge, we shake hands with the handsome captain, the purser and the chief steward.

Drinks are served on silver trays by the staff. These people, mostly from St Helena, care for the cabins, clean the cabins and serve us at dinner time. They are amazingly hard working, with five-week shifts on the ship, late to bed, early to rise; and, as I was later to discover, they often have jobs on land to go to. They smile as they work in a friendly and generous manner.

I find the high heels I bought before our travels extremely uncomfortable and impossible not to teeter in with the sway of the ship, but I manage… well, most of the time. I scan the room for Thadie, disappointed when I can't find her amidst the melee.

Most have worn formal attire, except for Phil, who wears smart jeans and a tee shirt and receives a look of disapproval from an old lady of St Helena, to whom I have been talking about the island.

Her name is Edith Walters, and she knows the name of every islander on board. I like her from the start because she smells of Max Factor and lavender, which remind me of my own grandmother.

Tentatively, I ask her, "You wouldn't happen to know a lady called Justine Hudson, and her husband, Nigel?" For these are the names of my cousin's parents.

"Justine and Nigel, of course! They are my next-door neighbours but one on the island. How do you come to know them?" she asks, eyes shining.

I explain, whilst watching Mark with a cryptic eye, as he is deeply in conversation with an attractive redhead in a sleek blue dress.

When I have told her all about my connection with the family, Edith looks very pleased. "You know," she said, "everyone knows everyone else in St Helena. It's very difficult to get an unbiased jury; ask your husband. I'm sure he realises that. My husband was a lay advocate – he's passed away now – but the problem has always been that it is impossible to find jury members who are not in some way related, even distantly, to the defendant."

Mark catches my eye then, his expression filled with surprise, a smile upon his lips that says, *"Oh, there you are, darling."*

But what he actually says is, "Stephanie, come and meet Tania; she's a teacher, like you…"

Chapter 8
Diary Seven

The ship's dining room is small and very beautiful, although the paintings on the wall of passengers being rescued from the *Titanic* are an unnecessary reminder of what might happen if we hit an iceberg.

It isn't grandiose, but it has a certain kind of gentility about it, with white cloths on the round tables, and heavy chandeliers.

Each table sits between four and ten people, and the lawyers are split between two tables, giving us a chance to converse with others.

I see the judge and his wife for the first time. They are, of course, seated at the captain's table. I do not stare, that would be rude, but catch a glimpse of them. I think they must both be about my age, which is to say mid to late fifties.

He is a lean, handsome man with a rich, deep voice that carries to our table. He likes to laugh, I discover, sometimes in a loud guffaw. She is tall, has blonde hair in a long plait running to her shoulder blades and is attractively sun bronzed, as though they spend much of their life abroad.

Mark, Edward and I sit at a table with four others. The chief purser, Keith, is amusing, although I am a little embarrassed at some of his loud and patronising comments about St Helena, as a very nice family of 'Saints' are sitting at the table behind us.

The Saints can be a bit too laid back, is his opinion, and their wine is rubbish, another critical opinion. I wince each time, not the only person there with a strong urge to turn to the family with an apology.

Clive is a small, thin, nervous kind of man, but very nice. He works for British Heritage and has a cottage on the far side of the island, near a bay in which it is impossible to swim, or so he tells us, a place called Sandy Bay. His job on this occasion is to rescue the East India Company cannons which have pointed out to sea there for over two hundred years. Now, they must be moved as they have corroded.

"Why has it taken two hundred years?" I ask him.

"No one has bothered about them," is the simple answer.

I am starting to believe, from the apparent lack of concern, that this is the answer to everything. No one appears to have 'bothered' about St Helena. I think of *Brigadoon*, the old film, a mysterious island that could disappear and reappear.

At our table is a large, very jolly but occasionally intimidating woman called Jennie, whom we recognise instantly, from Helen's description of her, as her cabin fellow. She is a lovely lady, very kind and caring. To be fair, Mark isn't the only one to compare her to a walrus. It gets a laugh from Keith, but had she been a man would it have been so funny?

She has jutting teeth and spits quite a lot when she talks, so that her fellow diners get into a tactful and subtle rhythm of moving their soups a few centimetres away every time she opens her mouth to speak. She is, more importantly, a tour guide with a great deal of knowledge. Perhaps people also find her intimidating.

The ship's doctor, who gave Mark his anti-sickness injection, is tremendous fun and tells us that he has only lost one patient on board the ship, which is a mercy.

After dinner, we remove ourselves to the deck, beneath the stars, with the huddle of lawyers, and drink wine and smoke and laugh and joke.

And then the judge, Judge Tom, and his wife Georgia (who Helen and I felt bore a close resemblance to Ivanhoe's Rowena because of her fair skin and the long, fair plait running down her back) emerge on the deck also. Judge Tom smokes roll-ups which, along with many other traits, make him very human indeed.

I don't know how the others feel about them, but soon my nervousness dissolves. I feel very comfortable in their presence, as the others appear to be.

Advocates are braggarts, for the most part. Before long, as the dark sets in on deck and the wine flows, so do the tales from court, of unnamed clients and witnesses and cases, each story outdoing the last.

We go to bed very late that night.

I have never slept in a bunk at sea, in the middle of the black ocean, to the drag and pull of the boat upon the waves.

I find it hard to sleep at first. I keep thinking a little anxiously of the sea creatures beneath me – the whales, the dolphins and sharks. But I also wish, as I always wish when we are away from them, that our grandchildren could have the excitement of these experiences. They will one day; I will take them, I resolve.

I think of our parents, of my siblings and their families and of our children and grandchildren, and I think of the little girls, Cara's little girls, and the case ahead of Mark.

I am very glad of the crew. I have drunk rather a lot of wine and am not convinced that I could get the life jacket over my head in an emergency, let alone do it up.

The five-day journey to St Helena is a happy time. I grow fond of everyone around me, although I sorely miss my family and am frustrated by the snatched conversations on the ship's phone with them.

I can do nothing for Mum but talk to her; when my grandson becomes sick, I can only suggest treatments that our daughter might give him.

The lawyers work every day, mostly in their cabins, in a frenzy of activity.

"Where's Helen?" Jack would ask.

"Working," I would reply. At which Jack would race off again in a flurry of guilt, to do the same.

They hold advocates meetings in our cabin, for confidentiality – after I have tidied up the room of course.

On the last night, we stay up late with the lawyers and drink quite a lot. The judge and his wife have been friendly company. They know the crew by name, having travelled to the island so many times to work. I don't think I meet one single person who is shy or reserved with them, other than the little boy on deck in the sunshine in his blue paddling pool who turns his back on Georgia when she tries to hand him his rubber duck.

Perhaps it is the wine, on that last evening before we dock in St Helena, which disturbs my sleep. Perhaps a dream about the ghostly owner of the earring which

Mark has refused to discuss. I toss and turn for a long time before having the most dreadful nightmare in which I am trying to rescue my baby grandson from the waves.

I wake in a state of panic, whilst Mark sleeps soundly in the bunk opposite me.

For some while I toss and turn as I try to return to my slumbers, listening to the distant throb of the ship's engines.

Eventually, I pull on a pair of jeans and a jumper and leave the cabin, closing the door softly behind me. It is so quiet that I can't believe anyone else is awake, but I'm sure they are, including, of course, the officer of the watch.

I steal into the small kitchen where Nora and Violet and Grant and the other ship's staff make tea, taking a carton of milk from the fridge and an apple from a bowl.

I trundle along the quiet corridor in my dressing gown, munching on the apple, until I reach the staircase to the upper deck.

The dream about my grandson had been so real that I have an overwhelming urge to go to the ship's phone to check that everything is alright.

Reason begins to take over.

I have been like this since the overwhelming fear that my husband has a mistress.

That is also nonsense. He doesn't. Mistresses only ever happen in the case of politicians, and in stories, I tell myself.

So, then, why has the feeling that we are drifting like pieces of flotsam, after such a long and happy marriage, crept over me of late? Why the earring, which I carry like an evil omen in my handbag?

I don't want to go back to bed just yet. I finish my midnight snack and creep along to the library, where we have also joined in with the hilarity of quiz nights.

As I pass the phone booth, I see her. She has her back to me. She is wearing a towelling dressing gown belted over her thin figure, but it is unmistakably Thadie. I wonder who she is calling in the middle of the night, crouching over the mouthpiece. I've been in the phone booth and it is quite soundproofed. I creep past her, carrying on to the library.

I switch on the light and kneel before the books on the lower shelf.

The first book I lay my hand upon has a blue, sparkly cover. It is called *The Other Wife*. I put it back in a hurry, as though the cover is contagious; I do not want to read that.

I pull out *To Kill a Mockingbird*, one of my favourite novels, making me think of Mark once upon a time, before I had asked myself whether he was cheating on me, which Atticus would never contemplate, I think huffily.

I turn it over in my hand, and as I do so I glimpse a blue folder at the very bottom of the bookcase.

I draw out the folder and open it, turning the loose pages slowly.

The notes have been lovingly compiled by someone, printed off and secured inside.

It is a slave log – that's the only way to describe it – list upon list of the 'freed slaves' on the island of St Helena.

Jack had told me that the people of St Helena were descended from slaves in the main part, many of them from the union of British naval men posted there from the days of the East India Company and women who had been slaves or were freed slaves.

He had told me about the young children, who, according to records, had run about the town with no supervision because, in the first instance and cruelly, although they had been given their freedom their parents had not.

I read the start of the log with eagerness, forgetting I have to rise early and that it is the middle of the night.

'... each slave owner was paid, by the Crown, compensation of between one shilling and one hundred and twenty pounds per slave, but then the slaves, once freed, had to repay that compensation to the Crown. The following lists set out how much of that debt each slave had managed to pay.'

Given the historical attitude towards class and slavery of the time, I am still appalled. You can't, I suppose, impose modern laws and viewpoints upon situations in the past, but if ever a people deserved compensation from a government these people did.

I read on:

'Yeo, Anne... amount of the loan, twenty-five pounds... amount repaid, ten pounds... has a large family, sickly, and has not been able to earn more than will support them.

Jacob, Charles... amount of loan, fifty-eight pounds... amount repaid, fifteen pounds...

Has a large family, bad character, whipped frequently.

Gurden, Benjamin... died without liquidating loan.

Rift, Dolly... a common prostitute, conduct very bad, left the island without paying loan.

Hudson, James... cannot at present afford to repay anything, his wages being too low.

Reynolds, Thomas... of such a bad character that he is rarely employed

Anthony, Fanny... washerwoman, character good, has repaid half of her debt.'

There are many such accounts and so many thoughts going through my head. I had thought that I knew a lot about the injustice and horrors of slavery, but this log is such a revelation, making the slaves real to me. These poor people had to pay for their freedom.

My maiden name is there; and although we come from very different places in the world, Camilla's, my cousin's wife, maiden name is there. Were we descended from slaves or slave traders? I know which I would prefer.

The gentleness and modesty of many of the islanders I have met on the RMS now makes a kind of intangible sense to me. From the very start, they have been disadvantaged; perhaps the laws and ethics of the island have not kept pace with the mainland.

In the middle of the night, I feel frustration welling up inside of me, but at least not frustration with Mark any longer.

Eventually I return to my bed. I sleep this time, waking too soon to the authority of the captain in the early hours of the morning.

* * *

I groan, desperately longing for more sleep, but Mark, excited at the prospect of being able to see the island for the first time, showers and dresses in a hurry. He wants to take photographs.

I join him on the deck before we have eaten breakfast. Holding a cup of tea in my hand and a little bleary eyed, I wander with other people to the rail.

My first impression of the island is slightly intimidating, but awe-inspiring too – a landscape I have never known before.

From the sea, as the ship cruises around the starker, more isolated parts of St Helena, you are met with huge, craggy, brown volcanic rock and nothing else.

It is an illusion, of course, for the island contains the greatest variety of ecosystems I have ever known; the island is verdantly green for the most part. But gazing at it from the ship's rail, I scan the skies for pterodactyl and listen to the thump of my heart.

It is one of the most awesome sights, to borrow the phrase from my new American friend, Julia, who is travelling on the ship.

I feel sure that the first sight of St Helena must have scared the pants off the Emperor Napoleon.

Whilst Mark is taking photographs, Julia and husband lean against the ship's rail with me.

"I may stay on the boat…" she drawls, in a gruff whisper, having already decided that St Helena is rather smaller than the USA.

We stand at the rail for a long time before going down to breakfast and packing up our last things; and when we have thanked Violet for cleaning our room, we go back up on deck to be met with a more reassuring sight, for here is little Jamestown, the capital of St Helena, just as I have seen it on a postcard in the ship's boutique.

The yachts and boats bobbing in the harbour, the little street climbing to its neat and pretty and colourful town of Georgian houses, all held behind the fortified entrance of pink and brown stone and the archway entrance, rising to the white castle buildings and the

Union Jack fluttering in the breeze. The frontage is lined with trees; there are no pterodactyls, there is only birdsong.

Thadie appears at my elbow. "Amazing, isn't it? Little Britain in the land that time forgot!"

I laugh at her description. "Where are you staying?" I ask.

"On the wharf, at an inn-cum-guesthouse called The Jolly Sailor, all expenses paid. You?"

"The Ambassador Hotel, with the lawyers."

She grins. "Expenses didn't extend to that, but I'm looking forward to it. The landlord is quite a character, so I've been told. They're both in Jamestown anyway, so make sure you come over for a drink."

I nod. "I certainly will. I'll probably be on my own quite often; Mark will be working all day, so some company would be great. So long as you don't ask me to go diving with you."

We wait on deck, to be called off the ship with the friendly people we have come to know.

"Nice talking to you, see you round," the Saints say, and at the time I have no understanding of how true this is, for Jamestown is tiny, the island a few miles by a few miles. I will see them all again before very long.

We stand a while beside Judge Tom, who smokes one of his cigarettes whilst we watch the little boats arriving to ferry us to land.

One of them tows a platform which will carry the luggage. The barge carries the cargo men, whose job it is to take the heavier cargo from the ship, which includes the machine, worth thousands of pounds and delivered by Sharon, to test women for breast cancer.

The men on the cargo boat resemble colourful parrots in their yellow protective hats, sporting flotation jackets in red, yellow, orange and green. They smile up at us as they get closer to the ship.

It is our turn to leave the boat first, so that the judge and the lawyers will make the court opening on time.

We carry our bags on our backs because we have been told our hands must be free to hold the rails in case of a choppy sea. Sam, one of the stewardesses, helps me on with my flotation jacket and we leave for the landing craft, helped by the stewards and boatmen to make the little leap onto the boat.

We cross the water to the Customs House and I wonder whether my few South African shells, collected on the beach for my grandchildren, will be confiscated, as Jack said that the officials are quite strict. But they are not detected by the Customs men or the sniffer dog, a springer spaniel called Monty.

The process doesn't take long, and over the little bridge we are greeted by a smiling reception committee, Saints of all ages, who say hello as we pass them. They await their relatives and friends, but it is as though they are waiting for us. Although I don't know any of them, the welcome they give us is heartening.

One figure, small and neat in a black skirt and white shirt, with slim brown legs ending in a neat pair of court shoes, steps forward. The people surrounding her step aside respectfully so that she can reach us, and I feel instinctively that she is someone who is well liked. I feel sure that this is Mark's email friend, the lay advocate, Tessa, of whom he has spoken to me.

She has a pixie face and soft, curling brown hair, and she could be the same age as me, or ten years older. It is hard to tell. She has a kind of enviable, ageless beauty.

"Mark?" she asks, for they have never met, and her smile is very genuine, as though she is saying, *"Phew, what a relief, you have come at last."*

She stretches up to plant a kiss on his cheek and he is forced to stoop.

"We are so glad you've come," she says. Then Mark introduces her to me, and I like her instantly for all sorts of reasons, including the spontaneous hug I receive.

She introduces herself to Helen and Edward and Phil, and holds up a hand in greeting to Jack, whom she knows well.

"You've all had breakfast?"

We assure her that we've had plenty.

"You must borrow my car, you'll need one. Some of your clients live a long way from the court. If you've brought your driver's licence, Mark, we'll go over to the police station to sign the insurance forms later."

Gradually we get through the dense crowd.

"Patrick from the hotel will bring your cases later. He has a truck. We'd better go on up. You just need your court clothes. I'll just introduce you to Rachel, the attorney general. Aha, there she is..."

A tall lady with straight, blonde hair, broad shoulders and the tan of an Englishwoman abroad is striding towards us. She is handsome rather than beautiful. She too is dressed for court, in a black suit.

As I understand it, Tessa and Rachel were the first people to draw the attention of the government to the island's long overdue need for an experienced team of family lawyers.

Rachel smiles broadly and seems equally happy and relieved that we've all arrived in one piece. I am naïve then, about this overwhelming relief; it takes a while to understand that the Saints are floating, hundreds of thousands of kilometres away from the mainland, like a beautiful, vulnerable piece of driftwood.

We follow Rachel and Tessa, as our cases are taken ahead of us in the back of a truck. Before we reach the archway, I glimpse the white-walled public house where Thadie is staying. The Jolly Sailor watches over the bay, as official looking as the Customs House, despite the cheerful hanging baskets outside. It stands sentinel, as though it has the same right to refuse entry.

Chapter 9
The Jolly Sailor

The Jolly Sailor was the oldest Inn in Jamestown, proclaiming itself king of the harbour at the time that poor old Napoleon arrived to finish his life in Saint Helena.

Standing upon an outcrop of jagged brown rock, its windows reflected the waves. To the fanciful or the drunk, the front door was a gaping mouth and the beam running above that a severe moustache.

A previous governor in the 1880s was advised that The Jolly Sailor had become known to Queen Victoria, at a time when it was still called 'The Victoria'. She did not approve at all when she became aware through her own sea captains of the wild, drunken behaviour there, and, so the story goes, declared that something must be done. So, they changed the name of the popular inn and closed several others of a similar reputation.

The Jolly Sailor had belonged to the Jessop family for over three hundred years. Henry Jessop was a slaver who had saved his ill-gotten gains to purchase the inn, then, marrying a freed slave woman, had settled down in St Helena.

On the morning the RMS *St Helena* arrived with the lawyers, Alan Jessop, a descendant of Henry Jessop, was cleaning his bar. He had a headache. Friday was always a busy night, sometimes with a fight or two. Nevertheless, he moved about the place with his usual efficiency, long practised, in harmony with the mop and bucket, scrubbing the beer-sticky floors clean until they shone.

Molly would never do the job in a million years. She was still in bed. Alan didn't really mind, for Molly had her uses. Cleaning was a job that reassured him, put the world to rights once again. His father had done it and his grandfather before that.

What wasn't reassuring were the united, self-righteous voices of the church congregation. If it hadn't been so swelteringly hot, Alan would have closed the heavy pub doors, remnants of a ship's timbers from an ancient naval vessel. He rested his broad arms upon the mop handle for a moment, to survey the smooth, clean ocean of the shining pub floor, then lifted his head to look through the open doorway. In the distance, beyond the smaller fishing boats and yachts, the RMS *St Helena* was moored.

The hymns often made him feel bad, making his headaches worse. On occasion, when they sang songs about the sea, it brought tears to his eyes. Both Alan's father and grandfather had fought for their country in the two world wars. In 1982, Alan had volunteered with the rest to join the RMS *St Helena*, that grand ship now moored in the bay, to fight in the Falklands War. The ship had been requisitioned for that purpose. Every able man on the island had volunteered to fight and those who had not been killed had returned to a hero's welcome.

It was exactly in Alan's peaceful, reflective moments that she would come to him like a ghost, and so she did now, the vision of a young woman in a nightdress, barefooted. Her sad, moony face brought about a terror in him. No, not that, it brought a savage loathing of her, of himself; a panic akin to standing on the deck of that ship and waiting to be blown to pieces or burned alive, a panic like the fear of hell which made his skin itch so that he scratched at it to be free.

Not Molly, whose large, motherly body made him feel safe, who would have punched him till he was out cold if he so much as laid a hand upon her, but that first wife...

There had been times over the past thirty or so years when Alan had believed that he could actually see her, usually in the bar. She looked like a child, a small, waiflike creature with long black hair that reached her waist. Sometimes she wore it in a plait. She would stand and stare at him like a ghost, frightening him. He could see her as though they were still married, as though she lived here, still. Beneath the white nightdress he saw her well-shaped breasts. The image could still turn him on, along with the fear. The days before her mad mumbling set in.

What came first? Her madness, or the violence inside of him that turned its full force upon her? It was her own fault, but she could still make his broad forehead sweat with the guilt of what he had done. When her ghost silently trod the wooden staircase he would touch the heavy gold chain at his chest, even though it lacked a crucifix.

It was her own fault. Stupid, addle-brained, dull-witted bitch. He ought never to have married her; his mother had said it and she'd been right. But in the end he had gone too far, beating her over the back with the broom handle when she came to him. How could he care for the bar and her? When the baby was born, she couldn't even care for that. She had to go back to England. He wanted to keep the child, but the brainless social workers had sent the baby with her.

She had brought out the worst in him.

Not Molly though, Molly was warm but tough. It was Molly who sorted out the drunks, throwing them out on occasion. Her breasts and forearms had the weight of a sumo wrestler behind them. They didn't care, those Friday night revellers who spent half their wages in The Jolly Sailor; they loved her sarcasm, respected her strength.

Richard, their boy, was a fine lad, "a chip off the old block" as Molly said.

Her lilting voice bought him back to earth; a large woman, she had a voice like an opera singer.

"Alan, you finished yet? I need a hand with the bins. You want one cup o' coffee?" The words floated down to him from the kitchens above.

"Sure," he called back, relieved to be brought back to earth.

There was a light knock on the open door. Alan turned to see the small black girl with the elfin face and skinny body, framed by bright sunshine.

He shaded his own eyes and allowed her a full-lipped smile.

"Come in, sweetie," he called, before going to her to relieve her of the heavy rucksack. Molly's idea, that they should do bed and breakfast. It had brought in a tidy bit of money.

The girl entered. She wiped her forehead with the back of her hand and handed him the rucksack before bestowing a half smile, regarding him in a way that took him back to his primary school teacher.

"Thadie, right?" Alan asked, heaving the bag onto his own back and telling himself that Molly was right, he should drink less, or he'd get dementia like his own dad.

Thadie nodded. "That's right. You're Mr Jessop, yes?"

"I am. Welcome to The Jolly Sailor. I'll show you to your room."

Thadie followed him towards the staircase, pausing to look at the large, polished turtle shell displayed on the pub wall, a remnant from the days when the Americans farmed them on Ascension Island to make turtle burgers.

Chapter 10
Diary Eight

As we follow Tessa and Rachel through the archway and into the town, I glance over my shoulder at the hundred or so small fishing vessels on a dazzling blue sea which reflect the sunlight.

The sun is also shining on the massive volcanic rocks that embrace Jamestown. They are covered with a thin, grey mesh – a spider's web, to prevent rock fall – and lined with layers of dried lava, chocolate coloured, a great layer cake fashioned by nature.

The smell of the sea follows us across the black stones on the shore and then beneath the banyan and tamarind trees outside the archway; and in the background, the gentle waves break upon the shore.

Once through the arch, the first sound that you hear isn't human, it is the sound of the birds chattering in the trees. They are an incessant cacophony of sound from the early dawn to the last thing at night. The rock-birds, the wirebirds, the pigeons and doves, and the host of birds whose names I do not know.

We are walking quite quickly, there is no time to explore just now, but the others are looking about this unfamiliar place as I am.

The inside of the Jamestown archway is painted yellow and decorated with plaster reliefs of arum lily which grow all over the island. The wirebird, the national bird of the island, is painted on the wall above the arch.

To the left of us are the white castle buildings. To the right, across the street and the car park, is the town's museum, the tiny prison and the tall grey church with its square battlements and four spires – St James Church, Tessa tells us.

The police station and the courtroom are on the left, beneath the trees. There are two menacing black cannons facing the town. We pass these buildings and the little library and the castle gardens too – a beautiful, well-tended burst of bright flowers in neat flower beds beneath giant trees indigenous to the island, also filled with birdsong.

In the main street we pass square-fronted, Georgian buildings of lemon yellow, cream, powder blue and turquoise. Some of them have balconies decorated with shrubs in brightly painted pots.

We follow Tessa, who, proud of her island, points something out to us every now and then. She is greeted by many people; "Mornin' Tessa," they say, or "Mornin' Miss Tessa."

The pavements are neat and clean; older people sit on benches placed all along the main street. They chat to one another and almost all of them greet us with a friendly, "Hello." Not so far along the street, we arrive at the Napoleon Hotel, one of the few hotels, we are told, in Jamestown.

The Napoleon is a tall, colonial-fronted building reached by stone steps and flanked by black, wrought-iron railings.

On the balcony flutters the St Helena flag next to a rather grand, painted effigy of Napoleon, who stares a little sadly at the shoppers in the street. He has big brown eyes set in a gentle face, and over time I grow rather fond of him.

I follow Mark into the front entrance with its heavy silver and crystal chandelier and walls adorned with paintings of white arum lilies – modern paintings, the lily heads too heavy for the yellow-green stalks. The heat recedes a little as we step off the street.

I pause to admire a painting of General Sir Thomas Picton, whoever he is. I determine to research him on the internet when I can. He has the appearance of an older Mark, a handsome man with a longish face and resolute jaw. But I have to follow Mark and Helen, who are mounting the staircase behind Tessa and Rachel; there isn't time to stare dream-like, admiring portraits.

We leave the dark green marble of the corridor, glimpsing a leafy courtyard with wrought-iron tables through the open doors.

Tessa and Rachel ascend a winding, carpeted staircase to the next floor.

Every inch of the walls here is adorned with paintings, every room filled with antiques from around the world. There are African tribal spears poised above French writing desks, as though we have entered a massive emporium, a vast antique shop.

When I look up at a reproduction of Vermeer's 'Girl with a Pearl Earring', something catches in my throat.

I am thinking of the earring, I suppose.

I try not to, but it seems suspended in my mind, as though it is something very real and poignant trapped in the upholstery of a chair and my frustrated fingers can't reach it. Suddenly, stupidly, I feel hot tears trapped behind my eyes, for I do love Mark so very much. I want to throw something at the painting in the absence of the cheating husband, Vermeer.

I take a deep breath. Mark turns to me, pausing, suddenly aware. He frowns, staring at me in a very odd way. "Are you alright?" he asks. It's more of a criticism than a sympathetic enquiry.

"Yes, of course I am," I lie, walking past him to catch up with Rachel's long strides, because I know there is too much to be accomplished today and the other days, and the earring must wait.

We reach a wooden landing which continues outside, suspended above the courtyard and the hotel bar, and the lush, tropical garden of reds, greens and hothouse pinks, following Tessa into the reception room which is also the hotel office.

Briefly, we are introduced to Emma, the attractive South African lady who owns the hotel. She understands the hurry that the lawyers are in, hands out keys to our rooms and explains the telephone system.

Tessa and Rachel say they will order coffee and wait for us in the Napoleon's courtyard. So a young woman follows Emma's instructions, showing us to a large and very lovely white-walled room that is hung with tapestries. It looks down upon the main street and, oh joy, there is also a fan to cool us down.

I stifle my older-woman-in-life-crisis moment, changing hastily into a slightly creased, flowery dress and a cream jacket before helping Mark to prepare for the court opening.

I do up his shirt at the neck, the wing collar gold pins which are attached to the shirt being quite fiddly. He shakes out his black gown, putting it on, and finally dons the advocate's wig with its little pig tail. I wanted to kiss him for luck, but feel that he wouldn't want this, so don't.

Lastly, he shows me how to take photographs with his new camera. "You look great," I assure him, and we go to join the others.

We walk down the street together in what I think is an impressive, or in the case of the advocates among us, slightly intimidating, group. Once again, almost every stranger says hello to us, even the police wave from their car.

It comes to a point in St Helena, I discover, when if a person doesn't greet you, you think they are being rude.

Within a couple of minutes, we are back at the courthouse.

On the stone steps, which are flanked by black cannons, various people are starting to gather. Mostly lawyers, but two lovely older ladies, the island's golden girls, and also the court clerks. Then there's the chief of police and his wife, the chief magistrate (who has a permanently grim expression, but seems nice underneath it all), and the other lay advocates who work with Tessa. Three of them are from Saint Helena and one is from High Wycombe.

Tessa holds her gown across her chest in a sterner fashion than we have seen her so far, as if she is preparing for battle. She has a determined look upon her face.

The mayor, in his ceremonial regalia, appears to be watching her with a wary eye, or maybe that is his usual expression.

Whilst Mark converses with the lawyers, and is introduced to those he hasn't yet met, the two older ladies say they will invite me to coffee, which is very kind of them. They tell me a funny story about George, one of the older lay advocates who was a teacher here. It concerns a stolen sheep. Stealing sheep and goats is a common crime on the island, apparently. Not so long ago, George brought a sheep into the courthouse so that the jury could discern whether it was stolen. It had missing teeth, and George held the creature's mouth open as evidence.

"Mark, Stephanie, this is Clive, the public solicitor..." Rachel says, introducing us, "and his wife, Catherine."

"How do you like the Napoleon?" Catherine, a small woman in her early fifties, also from Yorkshire, asks me; whilst Mark converses with Rachel.

"Oh, it's beautiful, and our room is lovely," I say.

"Emma is quite an incredible woman; but apart from two ladies, who have been with her for years, she finds it difficult to keep her staff, especially the chefs."

"Why?" I ask.

"I think any chef worth his or her salt runs off to the UK in the end, to develop their career, I suppose. It's a small island and people tend to come and go."

"Perhaps," I venture, "the new airport will bring more tourists and the chefs will stay."

There are two young policemen outside the court, standing on ceremony, like the guards at Buckingham Palace. They are both Saints. Their mothers must be very proud of them, I muse. They stand against the backdrop of the small, white courtroom, beneath the bird-filled trees and a hot blue sky. There are mauve flowers in the flower beds on either side of the East India Company cannons which face the town square.

There is something surreal about all of it; I feel as though I am in a dream state.

In the street, a group of tourists, fresh from the ship, has gathered to watch and to take photographs. I also take as many as I can with Mark's camera. There is a young man, mid-thirties, shorn-headed. His shirt sleeves are rolled to the elbow. He is taking photographs with a large, professional-looking camera – click, click, much faster than I can. I guess he must be a journalist.

Suddenly he turns the camera toward me as though to take a photograph. I jump back as though he has turned a water pistol on me.

"Hey!" I object, genuinely. "That had better not be of me; I don't even allow my family to take photographs of me, not without written permission."

He laughs dismissively. "Just testing for the light," he says, "honest. You got in my way."

He has a South African accent. I stare at him for a moment, wondering whether he is genuine; the accent seems genuine enough.

He lets the camera hang about his neck and steps forward amidst the hubbub to offer me his hand. "Matthias," he said, "or Matt if you prefer, journalist for the *St Helena Post*."

I shake his hand.

"Not much point in taking my photo anyway. I'm only married to one of the lawyers, not one of them. Stephanie, or Steph. Pleased to meet you. Is your accent South African?"

"No. I'm originally from Zimbabwe, but I've been here for five years." His smile seems genuinely friendly, but you never know what you're getting with a journalist, do you?

"So, you are married to...?" he asks, his voice trailing away as he looks over my shoulder.

"Mark Tremaine, the tall one." I nod my head towards Mark, now deep in conversation with Mairead, the young, blonde, Irish lawyer. There are quite a few blonde lawyers here. Sometimes I wonder if the blondes just give him a bit of variety, me being a brunette.

"Ah..." There is a pause. The 'ah' suggests he's heard of Mark, but then news travels fast, even when you live on an island five days from a mainland. I experience a filial jolt of pride, although almost everyone on the ship appeared to know who the lawyers were before we had even set sail. Matt points to a place beyond the courthouse. "Look, my office is over there; if you are ever at a loose end whilst your husband is working, feel free to come over for a cup of coffee."

I smile and nod my thanks. It would have been nice to believe that I was being chatted up, but whilst there were gorgeous girls like Mairead about, I hardly think that this was his intention. I certainly have no intention of visiting his office or yapping about the lawyers.

Judge Tom and his wife arrived then, in their chauffeur-driven car. The chauffeur is a celebrity in Jamestown; he's a respected, local character who everyone seems to like. He wears gold-framed sunglasses; and although his real nickname is 'Loose Change', I think he should be renamed 'The Boss'.

"Don't tell him that," Tessa says, "you'll make him big-headed."

Georgia, the judge's wife, had worn tee shirts and shorts on the boat, but she looks very pretty in a pale blue dress and heels, whilst the judge is resplendent in his red robes and full, curling wig.

The judge speaks to various dignitaries and disappears into the robing room. The lawyers and visitors follow suit. Of a sudden, the throng presses through the doors of the courthouse and I am left alone, until one of the lovely, vivacious, golden girls grips me by the arm, saying, "Come and sit with me, dear." It is so kind of her, as though I am a stranger arriving at an unfamiliar church and she would put me at my ease.

I had heard that the courtroom on Ascension, also the robing room, is decorated with turtle shells, inscribed with the names of previous judges. This courtroom is quite different to anything I have ever seen; though small, it carries with it an impressive simplicity. Over the subsequent weeks, it saw good use from six in the morning until late into the evening.

The ranks of the judiciary fill the seats towards the front of the court, the visiting lawyers seated behind them, and finally the lay people take the other seats.

The two young policemen thump on the door with their ceremonial maces for the judge to come forth, and the judge emerges in all his splendour.

After this, firstly Rachel, the attorney general, greets the judge, making her speech of welcome and presenting various items, including a reminder of recent legal events on the island, along with good wishes for a lay advocate who is retiring.

Then Judge Tom addresses her in reply, welcoming Mark and the visiting lawyers whose expertise, he hopes, will benefit the island. He thanks the magistrates and lay advocates for their hard work. He makes a special point about Tessa's friend George, saying that he hopes he will slow down a little towards retirement, after his recent operation.

It isn't a very long ceremony, and when we come out into the sunshine I kiss Mark upon the cheek and say goodbye. His work with Tessa and Rachel will begin immediately; he must visit the young woman, Cara, whose twin girls are to be fostered.

I am left in the sunny Jamestown street, alone suddenly, to my own devices. I will visit the museum, I decide.

Chapter 11

'A Hunting We Will Go...' 1819, Saint Helena

"Doxie, Dor-othy, Doxie, Dor-othy..." the little girl chanted distractedly as she walked towards the harbour, mixing the sing-song chant with half-remembered tunes her grandmother had recited when she was younger. She could just recall the old lady's voice.

Her granny was buried in the town cemetery now, so her mamma didn't get much help but for Doxie. Doxie was nine, skinny-limbed, with a long dark plait, now wound beneath a battered sun hat. She had been christened 'Dorothy' after the English lady in the white house up on the hill who had left the island now, but who was kind to her mamma when Doxie was born.

Not many called Dorothy by her full name, 'cept Mamma if she cross.

Mamma worked for the minister's wife. She not kind. Mamma say she one nasty old lady. The minister's wife had a face like granite with stiff curls beneath a lace bonnet.

Now, Doxie worked too; she worked in the big house for Mrs Redbush; but Mrs Redbush good to her. She gave her food for Mamma and her sister and brother, so they got more food than most. It was a big help as Doxie's pappa gone over the sea for some while.

He come back, but they don't know when, and sometimes her mamma sad and hug Doxie hard.

Mamma hold Doxie's chin up and say, "You gettin' pretty. You mind the boys; you stay with the other girls." Doxie did that, for the most part.

Mamma had to pay half her money back to be free; she worked hard to do it and she use Doxie's pay too.

When Doxie was through with the chores for Mrs Redbush, she'd go find her lil sister and brother, George and Eliza. Take some food for 'em that Mrs Redbush give her.

She got pastry and bananas today, but she'd have to call them 'way from the others, cos they all want some, and never enough.

Her apron needed mending, Doxie mused, as she pushed a small finger through the hole. She had small green banana in one pocket and pastry in the other. She had already eaten some pastry. If the child'n begged food in town, they sometimes got whipped for it. Some people kind, mind, like Mrs Redbush, and gave the leftovers away.

She lucky working in the big house; some of the others worked in the fields getting flax, doin' hard, hot work. Or they work in the mill or the mule yard.

Doxie pushed past a grey mule near the water pump, smelling hair and sweat from the animal, to pump the handle with her right hand, scooping up water with her left. She dropped the iron on her foot yesterday and didn't burn none, but there was one bright red bruise on her bare foot. She splashed some water on it.

Doxie crossed the bridge to the harbour, passing the soldiers in their smart red coats with the shining gold buttons and white trousers. They had muskets in their hands. When the officer in charge came, they stood stiff like toy soldiers. When it was as hot as this, they slouched and laughed loudly.

Doxie was afraid of the soldiers but lil Georgie weren't. He grinned at them one time, so she hit Georgie on his arm, hard, to warn him. They do nothin' to him that time, but once they stick Georgie's friend Daniel in a tree and leave him there nearly all the day for being sassy.

Doxie just walked straight ahead, brown eyes fixed on the sea, hurrying past the soldiers at the town wall.

Once she saw the governor and his wife in a fine carriage. He had one red coat too, and a fine lace ruff at his throat and gold 'paulettes on his shoulders. His wife looked very fine. She wore a black dress. Mamma said it silk.

The sea smelled strong of salt today. It whooshed in against the ebony rocks and sucked back again on the smooth boulders. Sometime they all played on the rocks but Georgie was afraid of the crabs nippin' his toes if he weren't afraid of the men.

Far out in the bay the *East Indiaman* was moored, a fine cargo ship bringing goods to Jamestown; she made the fishing boats look so small. When the ship first came, the town were full of sailors. There were thirteen alehouses in the little street, Mamma said, though Doxie never counted them. There were sailors in the town now, coins jingling in pockets, smokin' on their clay pipes. Doxie never saw Mamma smokin' but she wondered what it was like, what it felt like to draw in the smoke.

She passed the mule yard where the poor mules stood, dopey in the sunshine, their heads hanging to the floor as though they longed for sleep. They were loaded with cane baskets filled with green leaves for the flax. Doxie made for the far side of the moat.

No water in the moat now, dried up for years, but it was where the children be safest playing. Safe, mostly, playing hide and seek in the bushes. Georgie once fell off the ladder on the side of the moat; he was smaller then. But now he had learned to climb it like the chatterin' monkeys the sailors brought to port.

Sometimes Doxie felt so tired now, and wished she could be little again, in the moat, just playing. But Mamma said she'd be a woman soon. She didn't want to be a woman if it always meant work.

The doves always seemed so happy, she thought, looking up at two now. The blue sky seemed to shine through their translucent wing tips as they hovered overhead. The doves happy, and the mynah bird and the lil' sparrows all happy, 'cept for cats. Town filled with cats.

One time, she and Eliza found feral kittens in a crate with the mamma cat, at the side of the warehouse, and Eliza tried to pick one up; but the mamma cat scratched Eliza bad, so now they were careful.

Doxie saw her brother down in the moat with some other little boys. His hair stood on end, thick with dust. His grey shirt, too big for him, hung from his little sloping shoulders, revealing the chest, still a baby's chest.

Doxie looked for Eliza, shading her eyes, and saw her at last, hanging from a tree branch, kicking her legs beneath the grubby, white smock. No one mind if the little ones grubby. But Mrs Redbush say Doxie must look clean every day.

She waved her hand at Eliza till the little girl saw her at last and dropped out of the tree, springing upwards on her bare feet. She came to Doxie straight away, out of hunger rather than obedience, pulling Georgie out of the tangle of bushes and hawking him by his arm towards the ladder to climb up.

Some of the other children called after them but were ignored. They would fight for the food, so Doxie led her brother and sister quickly to the shade of a tree, and they sat on the rough, curling roots. Her own mouth filled with saliva, but she'd eaten her share. She broke the pastry in half, watching them eat, putting a hand on Georgie's head like she'd seen her mamma do. He was very hot, his skin sticky.

"You go get a drink from the pump now," she advised him.

The food took seconds to swallow. After that the crumbs in their lap were picked, one by one.

Doxie got up, intending to lead them to the pump, when a hand came down upon her thin shoulder making her heart leap into her gullet.

The red-coated soldier had stepped out from behind the tree.

For a moment or two the fingers held her by her bony shoulder blades. Then he let her go when he felt sure she wasn't about to run, staring down at her, a slight frown on his long face, the lips thrust forward in a pout. Her heart thumped as she waited. She held her breath until at last he reached into the leather purse on his belt and pulled out a coin, holding it before her.

It was some treasure to behold and she was momentarily mesmerised by it; Doxie bit her lip nervously whilst her brother and sister moved closer to her skirts.

She looked up at the man, stretching her chin upwards in a taut line, for he was very tall.

One eye squinted against the sun, then she waited, the breath rushing out of her at last in a sudden rush of relief. She'd thought he wanted to scold them.

Doxie had seen him before. He had a face like a fish with the full lips that curled out; his big, goggle eyes; the face as translucent as a jellyfish washed up on the rocks.

He was sweet on Fanny Hudson. All the men were sweet on Fanny Hudson. Ugly fish face only stood a chance 'cos of his money.

Eliza and Georgie began to lose their nervousness and fidgeted from foot to foot to be back in the moat.

"Take this to Miss Fanny, along the Narrow Backs," he told Doxie. "Tell her I'll be coming by later." His voice was dry and dull as cracked mud in heat.

Doxie felt a rush of disappointment. For a moment, she'd half believed the coin was for her, but he knew she'd have to run the errand anyway. Few children were brave enough to disobey the soldiers.

She threw him a half nod of the head, then gave her siblings a little push towards the moat. They ran away happily, for this was nothing to do with them; they had a child's loyalty to her. The soldier gave her one last look, wondering whether he could trust the urchin; then, deciding he could, he returned to his duty by the castle wall.

Her shoulders fell. She didn't want the task, because her legs ached with the day's work and because to get to Miss Fanny's house she had to pass the back of The Jolly Sailor, and her mamma said never to go near the place, the men always drunk there.

She gripped the coin in her hand and started off with the long, weary sigh of her grandmother towards the port archway, whilst fish face watched her progress. Then she walked across the cobbles towards the prison and the mill.

There were men working here, not from the mill, for they were busy on the other side of it. These men were building a great ladder up to the sky, up to the fort anyway, a ladder of stone steps which would take a long time to complete because the brown rock was hard to hew. When it was finished, it was said that there would be more steps than stars in the sky. It would be a quicker way to reach the fort above for the soldiers who would no longer have to climb the winding road above Jamestown.

These men, stripped to the waist, ignored Doxie. She was just one of the hundreds of nameless children in the town; and anyway, they were listening to their engineer at the foot of the new staircase, standing for the most part with their backs to her.

She raced barefoot past them, and past the foot of the stream they called The Run; it ran down the hill to the mill and the sea, beneath the mill bridge and past the tunnel. Doxie walked briskly, the coin locked safely in her fist.

She had intended to run past The Jolly Sailor to avoid the men in their cups, shouting lewdly. But once close to the inn, she saw it was too early in the day and heaved a sigh of relief. Relief passed quickly. Her heart began to beat painfully fast beneath the small ribcage.

The landlord's son and his thin friend were seated high on the lane wall. Doxie didn't really know the lad, who was plump but handsome. She'd heard stories about him though. Like the story of the cat whose tail he'd tied burning brushwood to and set alight. He was a bad lad, by all accounts, and liked to torture small girls.

She carried on along the Narrow Backs, her bare feet oblivious to the rough pathway, neither looking left nor right. Certainly not looking at the boys. She heard their laughter, to the accompaniment of her own heart thumping. But to her relief, when she glanced back, they had not followed her. They were leaving her alone, or so it seemed.

She sped quickly to Miss Fanny's house then, which was little more than a brown shack with faded material hanging at the door, hardly a house at all, any more than her own home. She leaned against the wall for a moment in order to catch her breath.

"Miss Fanny?" she called softly then, and waited for an answer. Maybe Miss Fanny wasn't there, for no sound came from within. She heard a small noise, the creak of a bed or chair, and called once again.

"Miss Fanny, you there?"

She stood back as the curtain was drawn aside.

The young woman looked down at her quizzically, bestowing a half smile upon her. She was exceptionally pretty, just like a princess, in her white, muslin dress. Like an angel, Doxie thought wistfully. Miss Fanny reached out and stroked Doxie's cheek with the tip of her finger.

"The soldier at the castle gate? He told me to give you this. He say he come by later," Doxie explained.

"Ah." Miss Fanny patted her own soft brown curls as though the soldier was already there before her, reaching out to take the coin from Doxie's sweaty palm. She held it to her breast for a moment in a languid movement of the long, slim fingers, then stared toward the distant sea, smiling thoughtfully down at the girl before nodding her dismissal.

Miss Fanny turned away, pushing the curtain aside then letting it fall – not before Doxie had glimpsed a man's large, hairy brown leg in the dark interior of the shack.

Her task, at least, was done and the narrow shoulders fell in relief.

She walked back along the lane, trailing her hand along the wall and singing the old song in her head. "Oh, soljer, soljer, won'ya marry me, with your musket, fife an' drum..." She mouthed the words in a happy whisper, feeling brave and clever. The task was over. Doxie was a shy little girl; she hadn't savoured the idea of interrupting Miss Fanny.

Then she stopped. She stopped and listened again, once more, to the noise, accompanied by the beating of her own heart.

There had been no sound in the lane but the voices drifting up the side of the mountain from the town, and birdsong. But she heard something coming from the break in the wall made by a rock fall, heard something amongst the plants which grew wild there, clinging to the rock face.

Maybe a wild goat – there were several around. They escaped the ship then bred, then ate all the plants until there was only rock. Mamma said that was why the rocks were so bare. Maybe, though, if it were a kid, she could catch it and carry it down to the town! Keep it for milk. Nervousness was replaced by excitement at the thought of the smile on her mamma's face.

She went forward cautiously, her bare feet hot on the stone floor where the pathway was most exposed to the sun.

She heard muffled laughter. Her heart thumped in its narrow ribcage. Excitement quickly turned to terror and realisation... them big boys from The Jolly Sailor...

He sprang out in front of her, the bigger boy, the landlord's son, grinning at her. They'd followed her.

When he lunged at her, she tried to run back to the shack in panic, to Miss Fanny, but the thin boy, his friend, came out from behind the bushes and caught her in two easy leaps.

Now the thin boy held her wrist easily, though she twisted and pulled until she thought her wrist would break. Her battered hat fell off her head and her long plait swung down. The big boy wound it in his hand, like a hank of rope, and dragged her by it towards the break in the wall, dragging her backwards as though she were a large doll made from stuffing.

Doxie whimpered and then screamed, but the thin boy clapped his hand swiftly over her mouth. Half pulling, half pushing, they shoved her through the gap and onto the bank, dragging her to a piece of the cliff where there was an overhanging rock and where the ground was almost flat. Desperately, Doxie tried to clamp her teeth into the flesh of his palm. She nipped the skin by his thumb and he let go with an angry yelp, rewarding her by slapping the back of his knuckles across her face, stunning her into silence.

The fat boy went first whilst the thin one held her ankles down so she couldn't kick.

He ripped at her skirt and wrenched at her bloomers as he held her mouth to stop her screaming, ramming her head onto the rough rock as though she were a pig to be butchered.

At first, she screwed her eyes up tight against the horror of it, whilst her mouth tried to scream again. Then, as her body stiffened instinctively, she opened her eyes once more. She saw him unbuckle his belt and caught sight of his thing, before closing her eyes tight against it, revulsed and terrified by what she felt would happen next. The fat boy laughed.

The hot tears burst forth, clouding her vision, till she had no choice but to be somewhere else – to force herself to be somewhere else.

Beneath the tree, she looked up at the blue-tipped doves above his shoulders, trying to glimpse the birds beyond the pain and the anger and humiliation of her Hunting.

Chapter 12
Diary Nine

"Hello."

I have been wandering about the Jamestown Museum for about half an hour, a large and interesting museum for such a small island, impressive in its information and artefacts. Until that greeting, I had lost myself in the history around me.

The greeting comes from one of the two South African men on the ship who had insisted upon buying a drink for us – two tall men, in their late fifties or sixties, very self-assured. They were charming conversationalists, even if Helen had insisted they were gunrunners.

I remember laughing at this. "Why do you think that?"

"One of them claims to be a banker and the other was rather illusive about his profession, don't you think? He said he'd been a lawyer and skipped over the rest. He didn't say why he wasn't a lawyer anymore, or what he did now. I don't know; I just don't feel as though I trust them…"

"So, what do you think they are?" I had asked.

"I don't know, visiting the island as a potential tax haven?" She had stared at me mischievously, grinning. "Gunrunners perhaps?"

On the ship, they had worn dark, formal suits every evening. Now the slightly younger one of the two, having changed into light trousers and a short-sleeved shirt, was staring down over his sunglasses at me.

"Hello." I smile. "Did you take some good piccies this morning?" For he was one of the people outside the court.

"Yes, I saw your husband there. It was fascinating to watch. Have you had a good walk around the museum?"

I nod. "Not finished yet." I wonder why he is here. It doesn't appear to be his kind of place, certainly not the natural destination of a gunrunner. "Where are you staying?" I ask.

"At the Napoleon. That's where you are, isn't it?"

"Mm... I think we were all rather lucky to get rooms; it's fully booked from the sound of things. This museum is fantastic, isn't it? Have you seen the model of Jacob's Ladder? That's rather good fun. And the exhibition relating to the street children in St Helena, from years ago? There are so many things of interest."

His lips twist into an apology. I think, We are both acting out a part.

"Actually, I've not been here for long. I think I'll have to explore it properly on another day. I simply arranged to meet a friend who's been living on the island."

And as he says this, a tall, elegant blonde in a linen trouser suit wafts through the door and beams a lipstick smile at him, removing her own sunglasses to kiss him on the cheek.

He doesn't introduce us, which surprises me, but seems in rather a hurry to be gone. "We must meet up for a drink at the hotel," he calls back over his shoulder as she links her arm through his. It is odd, as though he has gone from being relaxed to receiving a piece of unwelcome news, and yet she has said nothing to him beyond giving him a kiss and a smile.

I wonder if she is a gunrunner too.

I have my own plans, anyway. I formed an idea on the ship. The RMS *St Helena* is of historic interest, a kind of floating Orient Express, and will, I believe, make the setting for a great murder story, which I intend to write. So, I don't ponder on the two South African men for long.

Firstly, however, there is the incredibly steep and daunting Jacob's Ladder to climb.

I do not really have the footwear for it, I think, looking down at the toes of my sandals.

The ladder is about seven hundred concrete steps high, in volcanic cliff. No wonder there isn't a queue of enthusiastic people all waiting to climb it. It is sheer; I have to tilt my head back so my chin points to the sky to gaze at it.

I rub my neck, turning my face towards the town which I would have preferred to explore. In the distance I see Jack, crossing the square with a local policeman. He waves a hand encouragingly in my direction, whilst the expression upon his face seems to say, *"You can do it. I've never bothered, but I'm sure it's possible…"*

After only one hundred laborious steps, I have to sit down to catch my breath and drink from a bottle of water.

Immediately below me is the stream they call The Run and, beyond that, the prison, housed in what looks like two or three separate buildings that have been linked together. It is certainly recognisable by the iron bars set in the stone window frames. One of these buildings appears to be propped up by a remnant of the old East India fortress; there is a thick-walled buttress to the side of it.

Close to the prison is Saint James Church, a fine, tall structure, the colour of sombre, grey mink. Clustered around it, the buildings stretch higgledy-piggledy towards the road, curving high above the town. When I say that all the rooves are corrugated, it sounds ugly. But the buildings aren't ugly at all. In fact, there are many beautiful houses, with well-tended gardens, for the houses are painted in shades of white, pink, blue and peach in contrast to the dull, reddish brown of the rock.

Looking down, the ladder is incredibly steep and daunting; heaven knows what the descent will be like.

I look toward the sea beyond. Three white doves fly across the rocks below me. I take a deep breath and decide not to stop again. I will never get to the top if I keep stopping. Then again, although I am not fat, neither am I as fit as I would like to be.

I climb again, passing an inscription in the concrete with the names of two lovers. I wonder whether they are old and together now, or if an earring drove them apart.

After counting another hundred steps I stop again. I have climbed to the first floor of the Eiffel Tower; I have climbed the twisting steps to Tintagel Castle. Perhaps it is the heat, but I feel daunted by this never-ending climb and wonder how on earth the old people of the town do this, or indeed Cara, trying to reach her fostered children.

I sit down again to take a swig from my bottle.

This time I have a panoramic view of the sea beyond the archway, and of the rectangle of light blue water which is the impressive, Olympic-style swimming pool that I determine to swim in each day.

I can see the two or three bars on the seafront: Mori's Bar and the bar which spans the old mule yard. I see the tiny figures of some of the lawyers outside the court, including Mark's, as he converses with a client.

If I trip in these sandals, it will be a painful fall, I tell myself, determining to ask Tessa, who told me that as children they used to slide down the rails of the ladder, whether anyone had ever been killed in the process.

The first thing they should spend any tourist budget on is a funicular.

At that point, feeling very weak, I give up. I am not going to reach the old fort after all, or buy a milkshake from the bar at the top. I am going back down.

The town is filled with people now, quite a few tourists but mostly those who live and work here.

There are very few shops. I go into The Star, which is a supermarket, because I've been told that the bar at the Napoleon closes at seven thirty, and I want to buy a bottle of wine. Later, I discover that Emma has a splendiferous choice of mainly South African wines in her cellar.

There are one or two gift shops, and I buy four tee shirts for our grandchildren.

The staff in the shops, indeed in many of the town's offices, are mostly women. I feel sure that the men work hard in other situations. There are fishermen, there are local men building the airport, there are men who work hard, but today they appear to be mostly spilling out of the pubs: The Standard, The White Horse and The Jolly Sailor.

The older gentlemen sit on one of the town's many benches, or with a pot of tea outside the hotel.

I, too, sit on one of the benches to watch the town go by and am quickly joined by George, who is a gentleman in his eighties.

"What do you think of our little town?" he asks.

"I think it's very beautiful," I say, as it is.

"Some people come off the boat and say that it's dirty."

I laugh at this. "Really? I think they must be jealous. I come from Oxford, which has lots of lovely buildings, but at the end of each day the streets are littered with plastic food containers and all sorts of things. I think that your streets are very clean indeed."

It's true. There are hardly any dogs, no dog faeces. There are feral cats who seem to keep themselves to themselves. But the streets are immaculately clean and cared for.

Saying goodbye to George, I meander back to the hotel.

It is a strange thing to have all this time. At home, I am generally in the company of at least one grandchild.

There's no hope of being alone in the courtyard of the Napoleon Hotel.

It was very quiet when I left it this morning, but it is lunchtime now, and you can hardly find a spare chair.

There are doctors, lawyers, journalists, social workers, tourists and Saints taking a lunch break, all packed into the long courtyard area.

I quickly realise it is a hotbed of gossip and conversation, some of it inappropriately loud.

I head for the shade of what Raymond, the barman, calls the frangipane tree. I've never heard of a frangipane tree. It has lovely little flowers on it, with five white petals around a yellow centre. As I am walking towards it, a rather red-faced young man in his thirties stops in front of me. He is with a brunette in a black skirt and white blouse.

"Where's Helen?" he asks, his voice frank and rather brutal, devoid of any politeness, like someone brought up by snappy, non-communicative parents. The brunette smiles apologetically; she looks almost embarrassed, but also in the man's thrall.

I am momentarily perplexed. I've never seen this guy before and am confused as to how he knows that I know Helen. He has the abrupt manner of some journalists, so I assume that is what he must be.

"I've no idea," I state, with equal stroppiness. "Working, I suppose."

For a moment I stare back at him. He appears to be upset about something. Then he marches past me, followed by the brunette, and I carry my coffee to the tree and sit at a small white table. Almost immediately I am witness to a conversation between two men who are very obviously journalists, seated at a table a few feet away from me.

"I didn't get you here to pussyfoot around; you need to get to the point with them. I need some kind of a story by tomorrow," the older man says to the younger.

I look down at my coffee and long for a cigarette. So many people are smoking. I reach into my handbag for a piece of nicotine chewing gum. Our son, who is very healthy, has told me that I must quit this unhealthy and disgusting habit by the time I come home.

A young woman who I spotted earlier, someone who works at the hotel, comes to sit close by me. She lights her cigarette.

"Hello. Is this your lunchtime break?" I ask her. Then I feel guilty. I am longing to talk, when perhaps she is longing for silence.

But she's very friendly. "Yes, ma'am. You come off the ship?"

"Yes. I'm very lucky; I'm having a bit of a holiday whilst my husband is working." I feel guilty in that instant. I should be working, too. I am just a voyeur.

"You stayin' in room fourteen, right? Is your husband a lawyer?"

"Yes. He's at court right now."

"Ah. I think he representin' one of my friends."

"Well, they've got a lot to get done here." I mustn't ask about her friend, of course. I'm not allowed to know.

I hold out my hand. "I'm Stephanie, Steph. What's your name?"

She says that her name is Tina. She has two little children and works at the hotel till three o'clock, then fetches them from her childminder, who isn't a qualified childminder but her next-door neighbour.

I tell her about my grandchildren and we talk children for a while. Then we talk about the island.

"Everyone know everyone's business here," she says with a rueful smile. She has a nice face and a nice smile. I think she is probably in her early twenties. I imagine it can be hard for the young, here on the island. It's hard enough for the young in any situation.

When Tina is gone, I take an exercise book from my handbag, thinking that I'll draft out the ideas I have for my murder mystery.

But I don't get very far; there are too many interesting people here. When I look up, there is a paunchy man with a surly, pock-marked face, standing nearby. He has darker skin than most of the Saints and sways a little as he drinks from his can, but I think that's his way. I don't think he's drunk. He is wearing a Liverpool football shirt that has seen better days and dirty jeans. Every now and then he mumbles something to himself. He doesn't appear to be very typical of the other hotel customers. I change my mind a little; he might be semi-drunk, if there is such a state of being.

There aren't any chairs available in the crowded courtyard but for the one opposite me, which Tina recently vacated. I notice one of the young, blonde lawyers at court in discussion with a man a few tables away. He appears to be glancing up at her every now and again, droopy eyed, like a silent puppy waiting for a dog treat. Sickening. I preferred the company of the semi-drunken Saint.

"Would you like that chair?" I ask, feeling a little sorry for him. "No one is using it."

He frowns at me. "I like to stand," he growls. "Never sit down, always stand." For a moment I think he might be giving me advice, but I realise he is referring to himself.

"Ah. Okay, then." I smile. I go back to my note-taking, and the next time I look up he is sitting in the proffered chair, staring at me with large, slightly protuberant dark eyes.

"What you writin'?" he asks.

"Oh, just a few notes, about the things I've seen on the island so far. But I only got here today, so I haven't seen very much."

"Huh," he scoffs. "Could be writin' anything, could be writin' 'bout me."

"Well, I'm not," I assure him truthfully.

"Everythin' on this island expensive," he says; "ain't gonna change. Nothin' change. Everythin' bad."

I purse my lips sympathetically. "I'm sorry about that, that's not fair. I'm sure not everything can be bad, even though sometimes it feels that way. I think there are people who live on the island who will try to change things; some of the lawyers would like to change things."

"Huh!" he says dismissively. "Lawyers change nothin'. Nothin' gonna bring down the prices."

I feel a bit like Flora trying to reason with Urk in *Cold Comfort Farm*, but I feel genuinely sorry for the poor chap; it's just that I can see we aren't going to make any progress this way.

I hold out my hand. "My name's Stephanie," I say. "What's yours?"

He glowers at me then. "You don't know my mamma!" he growls, rather loudly, with a sour curl of the lip.

"No, I don't," I agree, completely at a loss and unaware at the time that this is the ultimate Saint insult.

He rises from the chair with his can of beer and prepares to leave in a huff, just as Tina walks past us with a tray of teacups.

"See you later, Danny..." she calls casually to him, but we both wait until he is out of sight before we laugh together.

Chapter 13

Diary Ten

Mark and the others weren't too late returning from the courthouse after that first evening; it had been a very long day. In the following days, the court lights could be seen from way up the street at ten or eleven o'clock at night. From the first day of their sitting, people brought cases to them; the human rights man brought his list; and with dogged determination, they ploughed through these things.

For that first evening, and on many subsequent evenings, we were invited to Tessa's house.

Both Tessa and Rachel are very generous with their time. Both work a full day in court, deal with phone calls from local people in their evenings, care for their families and manage to prepare sumptuous meals for the visiting lawyers. I have yet to meet a man who can do all of this and yet still smile.

Mark drives the car that she has loaned us up to Half Tree Hollow, where she lives.

Helen, Phil and I squeeze into the back and, from the front passenger seat, Edward twists around to stare quizzically at me.

"You're keeping some interesting company." He smiles, good-humouredly.

"Why? What do you mean?" I ask him, genuinely baffled.

"Emma says you were in conversation with Danny today. As a matter of fact, he was hiding from Emma. He's banned from the hotel for drunken behaviour."

"Oh, really? Well, I didn't know that." I grimace apologetically. "Maybe he's learned his lesson; he wasn't drunk and disorderly today, just a little on the rude and argumentative side."

"You probably didn't know that he was one of Jack's clients? He's a surly fisherman who once attacked a man with a nineteenth-century sword that was left in a trunk in his grand-pappy's house. It was removed by the police. Jack says that when he becomes drunk he volunteers himself to the lock-up."

"I don't suppose they have any Alcoholics Anonymous on the island, eh?" Mark smiles.

"No, or family mediation or a Citizen's Advice Bureau either..." Helen adds with a wistful sigh.

"Which reminds me," I remember suddenly, "a very surly, pushy man with no social skills came to find you today, Helen. Short, bit of an angry face, yellow-tinted glasses perched on the top of his head. He asked where you were. I thought he was a journalist."

Helen flushes pink. "That wasn't a journalist," she says. "That was one of the social workers."

We fall rather silent then, because we have entered Disney World, or so it appears. Or perhaps the *Pirates of the Caribbean* ride. Through the dark, our passage takes us along winding, hilly roads, flanked by tall rushes and the gnarled and twisted trunks of trees that are ancient and beautiful. And although it is becoming dark, and despite the fact that the road leading out of

Jamestown is high and winding, with a very low barrier at its edge, there is absolutely no street lighting at all, only the light of a rising moon. We have left the brown volcanic rocks and are entering a landscape of lush, tropical plants, of banana tree and cactus, yucca tree and exotic bushes.

Tessa's house stands at the very highest peak of the valley, at the end of a short yellow dust track. A lovely, low bungalow and a carefully tended garden of assorted plants stands before us and, below that, similar houses, some of them built long before the land laws came into being.

There are two or three cars already parked in her driveway. We alight from the car to the delicious smell of roast lamb, fresh from the Falklands, and are met by Rachel with a glass of wine held in her hand, standing on the open veranda where a porch swing and a small dining table also stand.

Around the side of the house, two children are playing and arguing about a ball.

"What a lovely house!" Helen says as we join her.

"It is, isn't it? Just wait until you see inside."

"It must be lovely and quiet in the evenings." I smile, realising that the tall youngsters with their sandy blonde hair, a girl and an older boy, must belong to Rachel.

"Tessa says it's so quiet and secluded that she sometimes sleeps on the porch swing there at nighttime. It's cooler at this altitude too, so she gets the pretty little lizards without getting cockroaches – a great advantage."

She calls her children to her and the girl throws her arms about my waist, and then Helen's, in such an open and affectionate way that we are both taken aback. The boy, a little older at eleven, says hello but casts a critical frown at his sister for her enthusiastic welcome.

We follow Rachel into the house, with Deborah, the girl, running ahead of us exuberantly, whilst shrieking, "Aunty Tessa, your visitors are here!"

It is a pretty, well-loved house, covered from wall to wall with photographs of Tessa's own grown-up children and with older photographs of her Saint family.

Hanging on the wall are framed documents commemorating her many awards. She has clearly worked hard on behalf of her island.

Through the interior, long, glass-panelled window, we see several people seated at Tessa's dining room table. I recognise George, who, like Tessa, is one of the older lay advocates and someone who has done much for the island. Then there is Mairead and the other lovely, blonde lawyer, Amy. We greet them and Rachel introduces us to a young lawyer, a native of the island, Sam. He is soon to qualify. Jack is there too.

Tessa emerges from the kitchen wearing a blue apron over her court clothes; her sleeves are rolled up and she looks gorgeous and dynamic despite the duties of the day. I realise quite suddenly who she reminds me of. She has the eternally youthful look of Josephine Baker, I think.

"I cooked one joint of lamb for you..." she begins. This doesn't imply that she might have cooked two joints of lamb – I am gradually picking up the Saints' way of speaking. We might say, in the UK, "I've cooked a joint of lamb," or, "Here's a pot of tea." Saints say, "Here's one pot of tea."

Helen and I help her get the succulent lamb out of her wood burning stove and set the table, whilst Mark and the men pour the drinks.

When I go through to the dining room to find the cutlery for Tessa, I can't help but note that a perfectly rational conversation about some point of the law between the two blondes has degenerated, since Mark's appearance, into a giggled conversation about 'stripper shoes'. He has that effect upon so many women, no matter how good a brain they might have.

We sit at the large, polished wooden table whilst Tessa emerges with a huge plate of lamb, and roasted vegetables which she has grown in her own vegetable patch, although, apparently, growing your own vegetables is not a common thing to do on the island.

Dinner is a noisy affair with lots of wine, including a couple of South African variations produced by Jack with the non-PC title of Fat Bastard.

The conversations around me are noisy and diverse.

"I had an interesting chat with Father Patrick today," Tessa says, looking at Rachel across the table as she helps her children to their food. They are going to be allowed to watch the television whilst eating it, something which, I must admit, I allow my grandchildren to do.

"On no, Tessa, you haven't fallen out with him again!" Rachel raises her eyebrows to the ceiling in mock dismay.

"Well, I don't know what he getting paid for. Keeps himself to himself, writes that old history of Great Britain, don't know any of the local people's names, don't get interested in their problems and hardly a soul turn up at his church. Not like Father Piers and the old bishop, and they much older."

"So, tell us, what did you say to him?" Rachel asks.

"Tell him that, and more; tell him he need to do something to help all the unmarried young mothers we got on the island... He say it none of my business."

We laugh. Tessa and some others like her, the elders of the island, have the freedom to say what they like. Perhaps it is why the government in Britain only give those who work here short-term contracts, so that they are careful what they say; and if they aren't, they are packed off in a hurry.

But Tessa is an 'elder'; she has free range to express herself.

"Tell them that story, Tessa, the one about the first time the Cecil Thomas building company came to the island to build the airport. Tell everyone what you and Rosy did," George urges.

Tessa gazes coyly from one to the other of us. She has such a girlish expression, and a way of cupping her hand over her mouth to disguise her mirth.

"Well, first we had one public meeting see? About whether or not the airport was a good idea, and I guess it was split fifty-fifty. Half of the people wanted it cos it would make things cheaper to get back and forth; the others say no, it will change the island too much…"

"It's not going to be that much cheaper, at least not to begin with," Jack interrupts, "and it's probably going to mean the Saints have to fly to and from Johannesburg."

Tessa glares at him for the interruption, and the man who represents hardy criminals assumes an expression as meek as a lamb.

"Well, anyway, so after that meeting they decided on the airport and the government took on a South African company, because no British company could see the way to getting all the materials here from Britain, and Cecil Thomas was cheaper," Tessa continues; "and one day the Cecil Thomas men come to Jamestown and they set up a booth so they could take on recruits to work on the runway, but not enough men here of course, so they start bringing in men from Zimbabwe on the RMS."

I remember the men we met on the ship, and their foreman, Joshua, who was very pleasant to talk to.

"So," Tessa continues, "I say to Rosy, come with me, we going to join the queue for work, and she say, 'Why for?' You see, I say, just come up with me. And we stand in the queue with all these younger men and get some funny looks. Then at last, when we get to the man with the clipboard doing the recruiting, after 'bout an hour, he say to us, 'Well, what you think it is you can do for this island?' So, I look at him and I say, 'We was thinkin' we could set up a gentlemen's club, with a bar and a pool room, a sauna and so forth, and I could be the madam.'"

It isn't the first story I have heard about Tessa. A lot of people love her, most respect her, but very few can beat her for straightforward honesty. The laughter following this is so genuine.

It is George's turn to entertain us then; he is quietly spoken, but a force to be reckoned with, as is Tessa. He is a trade union man who has travelled far afield for the benefit of the islanders, as has Tessa's husband.

He starts by talking about the cases of kidnapped goats and sheep on the island, which makes us laugh. But these cases, though not considered trivial by the people who bring them to court, seem to disguise so many underlying problems concerning families, and there are no experienced family lawyers working here permanently.

From what George says, the economy is very poor and the benefits, for families and working people, negligible. They do not receive child benefit or allowances as we are used to in the UK.

"Many of the Saints have a touching loyalty to Margaret Thatcher; the reality is that she tried to take away their citizenship before the Falklands War," Phil adds.

George smiles thoughtfully and nods his agreement. "Over two hundred men volunteered to fight for their country in the Falklands War, leaving the island, and leaving their families at a very difficult time, when the ships couldn't get through with provisions."

After dinner, we sit in groups with our coffee to talk – Saint Helena coffee, grown on the island.

Rachel, Tessa, Helen and I sit in the cool evening air beneath her veranda, and Tessa and Rachel tell us about the ghastly 'sport' of 'Hunting', which was practised right up to the time when Tessa was a young woman, in the 1970s; and which, along with other family violations, drove her across the sea to London and the Foreign Office, some while ago, for help and support.

'Hunting' is the term that some young men use to describe the practice of chasing a young woman, usually under the age of fifteen, for sex in an isolated place where her screams for help cannot be heard.

"How horrible, how dreadful." I shudder. I was a teacher; I'm not a stranger to the ways in which abuse can happen, but I'm stuck at the stage where I want to put my fingers into my ears and cry, *"No, please don't tell me,"* and I'm not proud of this.

A family lawyer can't do that; they don't have that choice.

Finally, for the sake of a child, they have to make decisions.

"That's why we need your husband and Helen here, and the others." Rachel smiles.

"I had thought he was here for the twin girls and the fostering of them," I say, feeling very stupid.

"That's one important thing," Tessa says, nodding and kindly dismissing my stupidity, "but there are others."

I get up at last to find my own family lawyer, who is competing with Phil, Jack and Edward for the 'most amusing court anecdotes of my career' award, for the benefit of Mairead and Amy, the two young blondes.

Amy has thrown her head back, revealing a swan-like neck. Blonde tresses cascade down her back. Mairead is looking into Mark's dark eyes and laughing in her husky, pleasant, Irish tones at the fact that the judge's car says 'BONC 101'.

Then Mark looks up at me suddenly with the expression of a little boy caught with his fingers in the sweetie tin.

"Ah, Steph, there you are!" he says, as though he has been looking for me for hours.

I smile benignly and wish I was at least twenty years younger.

"Let's go into the garden and look at the stars," Mark suggests. "Edward says he's never seen a display like it before."

He grabs my hand, picks up his wine from the table and pulls me after him, as the other boys cast him a look which clearly says, *"You should have left your wife at home, mate."*

Chapter 14

Thadie and Sanele

At breakfast on the morning after she arrived in St Helena, Thadie ate hungrily. First bacon and egg, then toast, jam and tea. She stifled a burp; her breakfasts weren't usually so large.

Breakfasts were served in the bar area; there were two other tables that were occupied, and five guests staying at The Jolly Sailor, in all.

Close to the window sat a visiting cleric and his wife. Between their table and Thadie's was an interesting young man, black African, who had consumed more than Thadie and washed his breakfast down with large mugs of coffee. The breakfasts couldn't be faulted; the bedrooms were clean and comfortable. Sanele, sipping his coffee, would have liked to have been staying at the Napoleon, but this wasn't a bad alternative.

The only interruption to the morning had been caused by a mistake. The visiting vicar, a tall, aesthetic man, his fair hair receding from a wide forehead, had asked the landlady not to bring eggs in any shape or form. "They make my wife feel very sick," he explained, gazing with sympathy at the younger woman opposite him. Perhaps she was pregnant, Thadie wondered.

But Molly, the otherwise efficient and smiling landlady, had forgotten the instruction about the eggs, her mind temporarily upset by her son's school report, and delivered eggs to both parties, boiled eggs in little egg cups. The vicar's wife turned her head away and the vicar rose, his bony frame stiff with indignation. He snatched the brown eggs from the table and placed them on an empty table close by, saying nothing to Molly, who apologised profusely and sucked on her lips, mortified by her own mistake.

"Can I have them, if no one else wants them?" the young man seated close to Thadie asked. There was a slight grin upon his face which erased when Molly glared at him, but she handed him the eggs anyway.

Thadie returned to her own thoughts. She had been trying to recognise the pub from Maya's description. But the memories of someone who had last seen the place aged three years were not much to go on. What Maya had told her, frequently, was that the inn stood upon a harbour wall that reached the rocks which jutted out to sea like an old man's fingers.

All that Maya really remembered was standing in a river of sunshine in the otherwise darkened bars and toddling towards her mother, who was very beautiful then. Maya remembered playing with her mother's long, dark hair. Often, she spoke of this – happy memories trapped beneath the sad.

How much Thadie loved Maya was difficult to say. Other than the times when she was engrossed in her work, Thadie thought about Maya every moment of every day. Before Maya, she believed she had loved none other, not even the foster parents who poured so much love into her, who had been so generous with their time and gifts. Maya was not just a lover. She was the sister Thadie had never had.

It was Thadie's sole objective to comfort her on the nights she woke, often crying, after some bizarre and terrifying nightmare. She wanted to protect her, above everything. Maya was fragile, and whether it came from an unhappy life – for after her mother was taken into the mental hospital, Maya was adopted by a family who cared less, far less, than Thadie's had – or whether Maya had inherited some weakness of the mind from her mother, Thadie didn't know.

Each week, twice a week, they went together to visit the mother. Sometimes it was alright, but at others Maya returned depressed, listless, hopeless. Then it was Thadie's job to restore Maya, taking her to the cinema, for walks in the park; holding her small, skinny body in her arms until the spark returned and she was rewarded with smiles. Thadie wanted to buy Maya a puppy, but the small flat they had shared since university wouldn't allow it. One day, one day…

Maya was beautiful, inside and out. Her mother had once been beautiful. Maya's most treasured possession was a dog-eared photograph of her mother holding her in her arms when she was an infant – the woman with the long, shining black hair and the baby with a fluffy head and a gummy smile.

Maya's mother looked nothing like that now. The woman looked twice her age. She didn't speak, she dribbled and had to be spoon fed. Her hair was brittle and white, her eyes hollow and distant, a tunnel into which you would never find the light, no matter how hard you searched for it. There were ancient bruises on the thin bones of her scapula, as though life had been beaten out of the woman.

Thadie was dragged back to the present by the sound of someone softly clearing his throat. "Do you mind if I sit here?"

She glanced upward at the interesting young man who had been breakfasting nearby. He spoke with a musical African accent which was hard to define, and yet the words were pronounced in familiar and perfect English.

She smiled back at him, disguising mild irritation. She was good with people, rarely allowing her true feelings to show. She had, though, been enjoying the solitude.

"Of course, please do." She smiled.

He pulled back the slight wooden chair and sat opposite her, stroking the small, silky beard on his chin in a practised habit before holding out the fingers of his right hand.

"Sanele Bhengu," he said, smiling, "interpreter. I saw you on the boat. What are you doing on the island?"

"Turtle conservation," Thadie said. "Who are you interpreting for?"

"Some of the Zimbabwean men who've been employed at the airport," Sanele explained. He leaned in close, then, speaking in a rapid whisper. "Hardly surprising that they are in trouble if the islanders are as xenophobic as the landlord."

Thadie raised her eyebrows at his description. "Really? Alan is xenophobic?"

"Ah, well, you weren't here in the bar yesterday evening."

She wasn't, it was true. She had had a busy day, meeting several people and being driven all over the island, so she'd retired early and left her bedroom window open to the cooling breezes from the sea. There had been quite a lot of noise coming from the bars, but it had lulled her, rather than keeping her awake. She shook her head.

"Why, what happened?"

"Three men came in, dusty from laying the runway, thirsty, doing nothing wrong, just quiet and peaceable. Jessop, he was so rude to them, aggressive. Told them he wouldn't serve them in his pub. I felt so bad for them. The conditions in which they work are terrible; do you know what they are paid?"

Thadie shook her head.

"Fifty pence for each hour's hard labour. Fifty pence!" Sanele grimaced in disgust. "They are separated from their families, from wives and children, and they are paid fifty pence an hour for their hard labour!"

"Is it a British company?" she asked.

"No, South African, but it's a British island."

Thadie nodded. "They left the place without a fuss?"

"They left as meek as lambs. It was wrong; the man dismissed them as though they were vermin."

"Are you sure? I mean, had they been in the bar before and been a nuisance?"

"No. I don't believe so. They didn't appear like that at all."

She pursed her lips in thought, then said, "There's nothing you can do about it. You're being paid by the British; you can't kick up a fuss or they might get rid of you."

"Ha!" Sanele gazed into her eyes. "A good job Madeba didn't think that way."

"Who? Oh..." She dipped her head slightly. "Mandela, yes, I suppose that's true. But, Sanele, I think you should keep out of it. You aren't here for long. What can you do?" She smiled at him, liking him for his empathy with a group of strangers.

"I have to go now, or I'll be late. Maybe we could talk some more later?"

She rose from the table. Sanele got up too, drawing a packet of cigarettes from the small holdall he had hung on the chair and wandering towards the open door.

As they passed the staircase, he looked up at a picture of Alan Jessop with a group of divers. They were seated in a small boat in the harbour.

"Do you dive, in your job?" he asked her.

"Sometimes, yes."

"I hate it. I never got over the sense of claustrophobia, but my parents insisted that I do every kind of sport, rugby, football, and for a time they paid for me to dive with my school. I haven't done it since. I think they believed that sport would keep me out of trouble."

"Did it?" Thadie grinned at him.

"To an extent." He laughed.

Chapter 15

Diary Eleven

Mark's alarm goes off at six thirty, as is his routine at home. He has slept like a log, but I have been fidgety all night.

Despite the window being open and the whirring fan, the air clings to my skin with a sticky warmth. I fell into a wine-induced sleep, then woke several times in the middle of the night to the lights of Jacob's Ladder piercing the window, mounting the cliff face.

I drink some water from the glass at the bedside table, trip over a case on the way to the loo and then get back into bed and kiss Mark's shoulder. He smiles at me but rises to face the day and the bathroom, whilst I drift into a happy half sleep, dreaming, remembering when Mark and I were younger and had small children. This is just before the orchestra of birdsong, which pursues you everywhere in Jamestown, wakes me once more; and, used to rising early, I shower and go down to find the breakfast room to join Helen and Jack.

It is a lovely room, large, with rough stone walls that are painted white. It is like a farm kitchen with oaken doors and old polished wood.

Emma knows a thing or two about antiques; this is the collection of a lifetime.

The dresser is heavy with blue and white willow-patterned plates. The walls are covered in paintings and prints of ships and the sea. There is a lovely and poignant ebony sculpture of Napoleon, staring into the flames of a large fireplace, contemplating his past campaigns.

Emma tells us that unscrupulous tourists from the visiting yachts come up here for memorabilia, if she isn't vigilant when they enter the hotel. She shows us a gap on a shelf, where there should have been a set of antique binoculars.

Beside the umbrella stand, which holds some rather menacing African tribal spears, stand Jack's and Helen's briefcases.

There are only two other people there because it is so early – a couple from South Africa. He is working for the British Government whilst she works temporarily in the Human Rights Department. But, then, everyone but the Saints themselves work here temporarily. The first person to rise and have breakfast, apart from staff, is Joshua, the Cecil Thomas airport foreman. He leaves with the company bus from the main street at six thirty.

Mark and I say good morning to everyone, then go to the table in the centre of the dining room, which is laden with food.

"Have you had your invitation?" Helen asks Mark, showing him a white card embossed with gold.

"To what?"

"To Plantation House... with the ambassador and his wife. Emma handed these to us as we passed the office."

A small Saint lady, so unassuming that you would hardly know she was there, in a neat black skirt and white blouse, comes to the table. This is Laurie. She is Emma's housekeeper and the subtle jewel in the hotel. She has managed all the years she has worked for Emma never to be cross, never to 'lose it' like ordinary mortals, according to Emma. But she has the slightly pinched expression of someone who has held a lot in over the years.

She asks us whether we would like tea or coffee and emerges a few minutes later with a light snack between that and the cereal – a huge plate of banana fritters.

I'm going to have to make full use of the pool I saw yesterday, I decide, discreetly clamping my fingers on the fatty bit around my middle whilst gazing with love at the fritters.

"Is there a correct way to address an ambassador?" Helen asks.

"Edward says you are supposed to greet him as 'Your Excellency' at formal gatherings," Jack says; before adding as an afterthought, "We might get to meet the giant tortoise too."

"The what, now?" I ask (my granddaughter's influence).

"Jeremy, the giant tortoise who was around when Napoleon was alive; bet he could tell you some stories. He lives in the paddock at Longwood House with his three younger concubines."

"Lucky old Jeremy," Mark says, with some feeling.

Jack dips his voice to a whisper. "There was a bit of bad feeling on the island when the ambassador referred to him as 'our tortoise'. The comment spread like wildfire and the Saints were quick to point out that the tortoise belonged to them…"

"I can't think that is their only real concern." Helen smiles wryly. "There are a few other outstanding issues to be resolved."

Valerie, Laurie's assistant, another Saint who has worked here for years, brings us our breakfast. She is a little hesitant, as though previous guests have not always been nice to her.

Outside, through the open doors of a private courtyard, a third lady, slightly younger than Laurie and Valerie, is taking down the washed sheets. She carries the huge bundle through the breakfast room to the kitchen and is immediately rebuked by Laurie for coming through the wrong door. She turns to go back by the other door and looks at us with twisted suspicion on her face as though it is our fault.

Later, we come to realise that although the people of Saint Helena are generally blessed with lovely faces, Gladys is not one of them, and that twisted suspicion is her permanent expression.

"Who else will be going to this dinner?" I ask, turning away from Gladys.

"Oh, the judge and his wife, the lawyers and some of the people who work in the courts, the deputy governor and his wife," Jack replies.

"Will Janine have arrived by then?" Helen asks casually.

I listen carefully, having no idea who Janine might be. I look towards Mark, to whom the question has been addressed. Is it my imagination, or has his face reddened?

"Oh yes, I would think so. Doesn't the ship arrive from Ascension Island on Saturday? So she will probably get an invitation too."

"Who is Janine?" I ask lightly.

"An independent lawyer, like me, but her office is in London. We've worked together on any number of cases. She's coming via Brize Norton to Ascension and then to St Helena." Mark smiles. His response was speedy.

He's told me all about the others, why not her?

As though to skip over the subject, he rests his hand over mine. "I'm going to be rather busy this week, of course, but maybe Tom will let us all have a bit of time at the weekend to do some sightseeing. It would be nice to visit Napoleon's home, and perhaps go up to High Knoll Fort, too. They say that the views from there are fantastic. But this morning, after court, I have to make a few visits with regards to these children. Will you be alright?"

"Yes, of course I will." I smile, hastily putting Janine out of my mind, grateful for his love and concern.

During the day, at least, he will be working his socks off; I have no doubts about that.

Edward and Phil join us then, coming out of the intense sunshine and into the darker, cooler room.

Conversations become hushed and private as they discuss the cases they will be handling during the day. I am about to bid them all goodbye, when there comes the sound of flip-flops marching heavily across the wooden floor towards the breakfast room. Rachel appears at the door, looking smart above the flip-flops but slightly flustered in her court attire, and with her two children in tow.

The boy, David, looks embarrassed. I am used to that expression as over the years my own children have frequently told me how embarrassing I am.

Deborah, the little girl, beams at me and asks, "Can I have a banana fritter please?" She is younger – no self-consciousness there.

"Hello everyone," Rachel greets us, a little breathless. She draws up the chair to the left of me and leans towards me with her chin on the heel of her hand, showing beautifully painted fingernails. Her large, expressive eyes fix upon me.

It is the look of a desperate woman who requires some help; I know it well. I've been there, got the tee shirt.

"Stephanie, I'm very sorry to bother you with this on your first full day on the island, but do you have any particular plans? Tours booked... anything like that?"

I tell her I do not, and wait, smiling. These people have welcomed us so readily, I'm not about to be churlish or defensive about my time.

I notice the children have backpacks on and predict what she is about to ask me.

So, I find myself on the front porch of the hotel a few minutes later with an enthusiastic Deborah, hopping excitedly from foot to foot, and a reluctant David, who has told his mum in no uncertain terms that, in the light of her babysitter letting them down at the last minute, he is quite capable of caring for his sister and doesn't need anyone else.

"Well," I begin brightly, in my most enthusiastic Mary Poppins voice, "if we have four hours, you can show me the pool first. You are both swimmers, aren't you?"

David rolls his eyes to the bright blue sky. I retain my smile, practised as I am in the assumption of children that I am an idiot.

"Well, I'm in the island diving team and she's one of the best swimmers in the school," David says, managing to stifle a 'der...' which I'm sure he would love to have added.

"Yes, of course you are. Okay. So, if you guys wouldn't mind waiting here for a moment whilst I pop upstairs to get my costume?"

The task can only have taken two minutes, but when I return they have both vanished.

I look up and down the street anxiously, calling their names. Teacher loses lawyer's children.

Roger, the barman and versatile hotel person, is along the corridor, a little way behind me, putting a shine upon the dark tiles with a mop and bucket.

"Hey, Roger, don't suppose you've seen Rachel's children?" I ask nervously.

"Ees gone down the street towards the pool," he obliges.

I thank him and start a brisk walk down the Jamestown road, trying not to panic or look disordered as my sandaled feet slap soundly on the neatly tiled pavement, urging me to break into a run. I am watched by several old ladies who have placed themselves on the benches for a morning chat, leaving the bench beneath the tree, which is covered in bird poo, vacant for the tourists.

I return my "Good morning" to each of them, with the certain understanding that when I bump into them later in the week they will certainly ask me why I was in such a hurry today.

The children have not gone to the lovely pool. The nice lady who says "There you go" a lot, and the lovely elderly gentleman who sits in the shade and eats chocolate biscuits whilst waiting for tourists to take his photograph, have not seen them either.

My heart begins to beat quickly. I have lost them, or rather David has deliberately lost me.

And then – and my relief is so great that I almost do a little dance – I notice a tawny head popping up from the sea barrier, David climbing the steps to the top of the harbour wall.

I march towards him and take a few deep breaths at the same time. They are just kids; no matter how old he considers himself, he is just a kid.

Deborah throws me a sunny smile as she emerges from the stony black beach where the small ebony crabs scuttle across the rocks.

I smile, and in my best reasonable teacher voice I speak as I look from one to the other of them.

"Now look, guys, I wasn't more than two minutes, and I did ask you to wait for me. I didn't know where you had gone to," I say reprovingly.

David shrugs, cool and nonplussed. "We've been here since we were little; we know every bit of this island," he says, tossing his head and not quite meeting my eye.

"*You* might, but I've only just arrived," I remind him. "I don't know whether the rocks are safe, or which coves are dangerous. Have a bit of sympathy for me, David."

He grins at me then. The first smile he has given me, the first glimpse of friendliness.

And after that we have fun, not just them but me too.

Yes, it's true, David leaps dangerously close to me as I attempt to do lengths in the pool, as though he will drown me, and Deborah demonstrates her diving technique from the board so many times that I grow dizzy. But they are nice kids; and when I suggest we get a milkshake from the bar at the seafront, they warm to me even more.

It is as we sat in the sunshine, discussing their schools and their likes and dislikes and looking at the boats, that I understand a little more about what David must have been feeling for some time. Why, perhaps, he has formed an invisible turtle shell of his own making.

"Our daddy was killed in a boating accident." Deborah says it suddenly, blurting it out in the way children do, without any intention to shock, whilst her brother looks away towards the sea, averting his face, angry, perhaps, at his sister's open honesty.

I don't know what to say. My face puckers as I stare at her, biting my lip. I look away then, towards the calm, silver-blue sea.

She has said it in the way of a generally happy little girl who has grown used to the idea.

"Oh. I'm so sorry." I feel hopeless, lost for words. Then, "How long ago was that?" I venture carefully.

"About three years ago," she says, whilst David remains silent on the matter. "His boat didn't have a kill cord on it and he hit a rock. The rules say that all of the boats have kill cords on them now. Mummy says it's Mr Jessop's fault; he sold the boat to Daddy cheap."

I don't know who Mr Jessop is, neither do I ask any more questions of them. Instead I ask that they show me around the town, suggesting we go to the sweet shop. This we do, showing great attention to the chocolates. We buy some. Danny was right, I think, they are very expensive compared with the chocolate bought at home.

Then Rachel catches up with us in her car and says that her next-door neighbour is happy to keep an eye on David and Deborah for the remainder of the day.

It is as I am waving goodbye that I remember I have another date.

SEE YOU AGAIN, ONE TIME IN SAINT HELENA

I have arranged to meet my cousin's parents in The Standard public house at twelve thirty.

Tessa had said that during the time of the East India Company, there were twenty or so pubs in Jamestown, an incredible number for such a small place, and that Queen Victoria's own disapproval of this had meant that now there were only two or three.

I hasten to The Standard before it, too, is closed.

I find myself before a small, whitewashed building, very simple in the way that Harry's Bar in Venice is simple. It is a local for the locals, not glammed up for the tourists.

The walls are covered with pictures of warships and pub teams, swordfish heads and photographs, and above the bar there is a display of trophies.

The air cools inside as it blows through one door and out through the other.

What makes it quite unique are the photographs of the locals which adorn the walls – a collection of loved people, some of them remembered with affection but no longer alive, some, quite frankly, pretty ugly, whilst others not so bad. But the nicknames beneath them, although quite insulting, generally match the faces.

Where in the world would you find people who are happy to be called Hatchett, or Dumb Boy? Not to mention Fart Egg?

"Hey, Fart Egg, what'll it be, the usual?"

I recognise a photograph of the judge's chauffeur in his younger days.

Then there's Piece-a-cake, Pie, Pretty Boy, Bubblegum, King George and Tanky, to name but a few. It sounds a little like the listing for the Grand National.

I wonder, as I admire them, whether he minded being called Fart Egg.

I think I might have objected.

I have, until that afternoon, only ever passed The Standard on my way to a shop, and usually you see men rather than women drinking in the Jamestown pubs. Today, there are eight men standing at the bar, including Camilla's uncle, Nigel, and his friend, also called Nigel, which makes conversation very confusing.

Sitting at a table is Camilla's mother, Justine, and her friend, Ivy.

I kiss Nigel on the cheek and hug Justine, whom I haven't seen for a long time, and they introduce me to Ivy and to all the people around the bar.

Nigel One buys me the biggest glass of wine I have ever seen, and what it lacks in finesse it makes up for in spirit. We stand at the bar for a long while, chatting about our families. Justine says how sorry she is to hear about my mother and that she hopes she will be better soon, and asks after the rest of my family. Then she talks about how much she misses Camilla and her grandchildren.

The other Nigel, and Harvey, tell me how hard it is to be away from their families and, although St Helena is carved into the heart of everyone who has ever lived or been born there, how hard it is for young people to stay on their island without the frustration of employment and high prices and the economy generally, because of the lack of a university, because of so many things.

Not only that everything is so hard to reach, not only the prohibitive cost of the ship (completely beyond the salary of the ordinary Saint), but there is no higher education. The prospects of a career are small for everyone, whilst the cost of living is astronomical.

It is, as they put it, like having a foot in one country and a foot in the other. You leave St Helena with your heart constantly longing to return. I've not yet seen the wonderful scenery that I've been told about, beyond the drive up to Tessa's house, but I hope that Mark and I can explore the island a little bit at the weekend.

Before I know it, I have finished one gargantuan glass of wine. Harvey's daughter, Sarah, comes to join us. She is living in England permanently but has returned for a few weeks to visit her father. She is full of fun and I think it must be my turn to buy a round, so I do.

Justine, her friend Ivy, Sarah and I leave the main bar to chat together.

The women of Saint Helena have a lovely, gentle, musical and very feminine lilt to their voices which I envy. I wonder whether this is because of the high peaks and the low valleys. My aunt, who was a nurse for many years, says it is so, that the voice is formed by the landscape. But I'm told that the accent changes dramatically from place to place across the island, although I am not familiar enough with St Helena to discern it.

By the time I am halfway through my second glass of strong wine, I am unable to discern anything. So I thank them all for their company, particularly Justine and Nigel, arranging to go up to Justine's flat on another day for coffee. I descend the steps of The Standard very carefully and wobble a little down the sloping, cobbled street, grateful that I wore flat shoes and not heels, and trying hard to keep a very, very low profile in the circumstances; hoping very much that the lovely golden girls who sit upon the town benches are not saying to one another, *"Look at the lawyer's wife coming out of The Standard. Do you suppose she's half-cut? There you go..."*

Chapter 16

Diary Twelve

When I arrive at the Napoleon, I sneak past anyone who might recognise me and head for our bedroom. I lock the door behind me and collapse against the pillows into a rather heavy and slightly drunken sleep.

I wake, roughly an hour later, to the sounds of the street, to human chatter and birdsong and occasional bursts of laughter, and to a car stereo blasting out hip hop music in the street outside.

I shower. Mark won't be back from wherever he is for another couple of hours.

As I leave the room, I notice that a note has been left on the dresser by Emma or one of the ladies who clean up. It is from Simone, who I met briefly at the court opening.

It says that she will collect me at ten tomorrow from the hotel for a weaving session.

It is very kind of her to think of me, but I'm not sure whether she means 'weaving', or whether this is a keep-fit term, like 'spinning'. Should I wear Lycra shorts? I don't work out as a rule.

I don't have any suitable gym wear. But I will go, I suppose; I should not reject kind invitations.

I decide to visit some of the little shops to buy tee shirts for our grandchildren. Roger the barman is now putting a high polished shine on the wooden stairs in lieu of a ship filled with European tourists – they say about two thousand tourists. I am perplexed about it; after all, where will they put two thousand tourists in a town no bigger than Clovelly?

I wave to the lady in the office downstairs and wander out into the sunny, late afternoon street.

The Star is one of the main supermarkets in the town and is close to the hotel. The tinned chocolates on sale for Christmas are ten pounds per tin. In the UK, the same tin is on sale for five pounds. This is upsetting as they are usually an affordable Christmas present for people; it is upsetting because wages are so low here.

I contemplate writing to Cadbury to point out that they started as a Quaker company, caring for people, so should reduce their prices in Saint Helena. Then I wonder whether the famous director has received my letter yet, asking him to offer JJ a job (that's if I can get him back from Zimbabwe). It's a long shot; no doubt he receives many such letters every day. No doubt my letters often end up in an office bin.

I purchase two bottles of water, needing to dilute the two large glasses of wine, and also a packet of nuts. The water in the hotel is drinkable, but the quality of water can be variable from place to place. In this hot, sunny climate, water is as precious as anywhere, and once, so I have been told, the reservoirs became so low that in some areas there was only enough water for six days, before, miraculously, it rained.

From what I understand, private swimming pools are not permitted; there is only the large pool in Jamestown.

As I stand at the checkout in the supermarket, the busy cashier, a young woman in her twenties, serves

SEE YOU AGAIN, ONE TIME IN SAINT HELENA

people quickly and efficiently. A short, red-faced man comes to join the queue behind me. He has a grumpy, mean expression and sways a little with drink.

I put my purchases in a bag and hear him say gruffly to the checkout girl, "You fat, you eat too much," as he waits.

I look at her, embarrassed and hurt on her behalf. But she is so cool and calm that I'm sure he must have spoken like this to her before. She is nonplussed; I admire her. Her dignity makes her as beautiful as a prima ballerina. Sad to know there are rude people everywhere, even on the friendliest of islands, but I am so indignant on her behalf that I can't stop myself from defending her.

"You must be the rudest man on earth!" I snap at him in disgust.

"Don't worry, ma'am, just look straight ahead and ignore him. Name Gappy; he go if you ignore him."

Her smile is beautiful too.

Ignore him? I want to slap him.

But her plan works, whereas mine would have caused an international incident, and he shuffles off, declaring "Ees, you fat, you fat…"

"Can't you ask your manager to ban him, refuse to serve him?" I ask.

The girl shrugs. "Been coming in here for all the time I worked here," she said. "Where he gonna get his food from? Poor old devil."

I leave, wondering whether there is an Alcoholics Anonymous on the island.

There are a few gift shops, a few supermarkets and a hardware store. The shops have Christmas lights around the windows and some of them have Christmas trees. I am not very well travelled, and it feels strange to behold them in the warm sunshine.

In one of the gift shops I buy tee shirts with a globe painted on the back and 'Where in the World is Saint Helena?' emblazoned upon the front.

One of the shops has a strange and unusual Christmas display – everything you could need for the toilet, from loo rolls to toilet ducks, all surrounded by fairy lights.

In the arts and crafts shop, next to the Tourist Office, there is a range of locally made things, from paintings to jewellery and woven flowers made from flax. Flax grows all over the lush parts of the island. There is a Christmas tree too, from which little paper tags hang. I turn one over in my hand.

"The idea is that you take a tag and donate a gift to a child on Saint Helena who mightn't get very much. We collect the gifts here," the woman behind the counter explains.

It sounds like a good scheme, so I take several, thinking that the other lawyers might like to donate. As most of the gifts for younger children have gone, I take the remaining ones, which mostly say, 'Gift for a twelve- to fourteen-year-old boy' or 'For a ten- to twelve-year-old girl.'

Then I meander thoughtfully through the shop, wondering about gifts for the girls. That's not too hard – they like pretty things for their hair, painted false nails, a bracelet maybe, and to my knowledge they still appreciate coloured pens for school.

The boys prove difficult, though. There isn't very much to inspire in the shops, and boys often prefer expensive musical equipment.

There are footballs, but not all boys like football.

SEE YOU AGAIN, ONE TIME IN SAINT HELENA

The sports tee shirts are twice as much as anything you might buy for a girl. I wonder what else they might prefer – a packet of cigarettes and a pornographic magazine maybe, I mull, thinking of our own son.

So, in the end, just as the shops are closing for the day, I choose deodorant and chocolates.

Crossing the quiet street, I see Mark, coming up from the court with Helen. They are walking side by side, heavy court bags slung across their shoulders. But I don't think it is a companionable silence; it is a weary silence, edged with some hostility. Their body language is stiff, as though they resent one another.

As I get closer, I register the hardship of a long day and a long battle in Helen's face. She is exhausted and perhaps a little frustrated.

I am not used to it all. I am not a lawyer, but a teacher. I just know that Helen has been so kind, welcoming me into this strange legal world, when before I was always too busy with kids and my own job to understand it.

I decide not to ask, *"Good day?"* of either of them. Instead, I suggest a gin and tonic.

Helen smiles wanly. "Maybe later," she says. "I ache all over, and I need a shower."

It is only as I follow her small figure up the staircase that I realise that in court, at least, she and my husband will sometimes have to be tough opponents.

There is no food available at our hotel in the evening, so, on Jack's advice, we book dinner for four people at Corrine's Place.

Edward and Phil have things to discuss with one of the lay advocates, one of Tessa's colleagues. The lay advocates usually work long hours, on a voluntary basis. They have been invited to dinner at his home.

By the time Helen has had her shower and a brief nap, she appears more refreshed, and the weariness has been replaced by a light application of lipstick and a smidgeon of positivity.

Mark has told me little about the day's work. All his cases, including the family ones, are highly confidential, but from his relaxed demeanour I guess that they might have found other foster parents capable of looking after the two children on the island, rather than removing them. That would presumably be the ideal, so they can keep in contact with the mother as they grow up.

Mark and I, Helen and Jack walk down to Corrine's Place at about a quarter to seven.

The street is dark now, except for the stars and the lights from the shops and the string of gems stretching up the rock face that is Jacob's Ladder.

Corrine's Place is at the end of the Castle Gardens. It reminds me of a surf shack.

The restaurant is open to the air, except for a wide roof festooned with flags from more than a hundred countries and decorated with memorabilia, shells and wind chimes hanging from the ceiling.

It is set with enough chairs and tables for a large party, a simple arrangement but fun. The chairs appear to have been rescued from a high school some while ago.

The fare is simple but wholesome, the menu often including freshly cooked fish. My frequently eaten favourite is spiced fishcakes with a Greek salad. It is also inexpensive.

I tell them about the Christmas tags as we sit down, the presents for teenagers, joking about the fags and pornographic magazines.

There is a definite, bleak silence. I stare at them without comprehension. No, it isn't the funniest thing ever, but not that terrible either. Helen, who is a ready laugh, does not look amused.

"What have I said?" I ask fearfully.

Jack pats my shoulder, comforting me. "They've had to watch gratuitous adult porn this afternoon," he says, "as part of another case."

I understand then, and vow to shut up in future, waiting for them to do the talking instead. It is a holiday for me, but not for them.

They begin a conversation about the medical records kept by doctors on the island, which, apparently, have been few and far between in some cases but often needed by the court, to the frustration of the lawyers and the judge.

I sip my Jamestown gin whilst we wait for our supper. It is very strong. The ordinary human stomach can only tolerate two tablespoons in a tumbler of tonic.

The conversation between the lawyers is muted compared with the buzz of noise from various families who have arrived to eat.

Our two South African acquaintances from the ship are sitting at the far end of the restaurant with the tall, willowy blonde woman I met at the museum.

"Have you seen them taking any tours yet?" Helen asks me.

I tell her I haven't. Mostly I have seen them having rather lengthy discussions at the hotel.

"Perhaps," Mark suggests, "in the light of the airport, they are looking at opening up another hotel, or some other business."

"No, they're definitely gunrunners." Helen grins, shaking her head slowly so that I wonder if she has had cause to oppose that kind of person in the past.

"Whatever. They've got good taste in wine, anyway; they didn't get that bottle here on the island," Mark says, clearly unconcerned.

After our meal, we walk along the dark street to the hotel. It is very quiet except for the occasional young person speeding through the town, windows emitting loud music.

Jack has bought a bottle of wine and we sit on the balcony to quaff it. It is relatively early, but they have a lot of work to do tomorrow, so this is one last drink before bedtime, or so they say.

The balcony is very pleasant, although if you sit up there during the daytime you are at the full scrutiny of the street. It has several comfy armchairs and a sofa, with tables to rest your drinks upon, and banana plants in pots which fight with your vision.

The Saint Helena flag flutters in the breeze and the full-sized (but accurately height-impaired) statue of Napoleon, with a little pot belly and a hand tucked into his waistcoat, stares down, with sad brown eyes, at the people below.

They tell 'lawyers' jokes' for a while, until Jack starts mouthing incomprehensibly around his pipe, and I understand that it is time for me to move away from their conversation. Time for them to talk work.

I walk to the far end of the balcony to join Napoleon, to chat with him, my glass in my hand.

"I expect you must find all of this rather tedious after the excitement of your campaigns," I say.

"What on earth are you doing?" Mark calls. But I have seen someone in the street, far below, drunkenly lurching towards us, and I recognise 'you-don't-know-my-mamma' Danny, the fisherman who was a client of Jack's and who sometimes volunteers himself into a cell without a fuss.

He is mumbling something, repeatedly and in a drunken fashion. I listen, trying to make sense of his slurred words.

"I see her," he is saying. "I see'd the little girl..." His voice is anxious, almost tremulous. I am touched by the tone of it, which betrays a kind heart beneath the criminal nature.

I look away from him as he disappears into a shop doorway, and notice something else – the erect form of a tall man who passed me during the day. I don't know who he is. He is wearing a suit. Briskly, he descends a flight of stone steps from one of the older buildings along the street, heading for his car. He looks up at the building once, a casual turn of the head. There is a young woman with tousled, long blonde hair looking down at him, but he does not wave back to her. The not waving back is deliberate, I think.

Chapter 17
A Set of Coasters

Angela Costner looked through the large windows at the redcurrants she had planted in the dry, dusty earth some while ago. She made a mental note to fix the hole made by the two wirebirds, who were now ignoring her as she rapped loudly on the kitchen window.

Angela and Dean loved their house in Half Tree Hollow, where long, lovely bungalows saw some of the most beautiful sunsets in the world.

There was only ever a cooling breeze, and they felt safe at the top of the volcanic layer cake above James Bay.

Angela wondered and worried about her family as she went about her work. This was something she did most mornings, in equal measure, both housework and worrying. Sometimes to drive the worries out of her head she put on country and western music and cleaned, cooked and ironed to it. It was something they had in common with the island people, a love of country music. She had often wondered why abused women, not herself, of course, devoured love songs. Ironic after what they'd been through.

Dean was going to work a little later this morning. She could hear his familiar footsteps in the bedroom as he searched for underpants and socks, the antique drawers of the dresser that she was very proud of sliding stiffly in and out as he shut them, each time with a grunt of impatience.

He had a meeting, so he'd told her yesterday evening, with some of the engineers building the new airport and he was not looking forward to it.

They had been in St Helena for four months. They hadn't seen their families in all that time. Before that, they'd lived on Ascension Island, where Dean had been involved in negotiations between the American army and the Brits about providing flights for the Saints who lived and worked there. It was all hush, hush, and consequently Dean rarely discussed it with her. "The less you know, the better," he'd said, like a spy.

Dean was busy most days, tied up with work and working long hours, whilst Angie, who had given up her long-term job in the library in Fort Myers to be with him, had become the model homebuilder and carer for the children.

Perhaps, she thought, loneliness was often the cause of worrying, but things had been getting so bad recently that she even worried about how much she was worrying. She didn't want to ask Dean to deal with anything. He was a good provider, firm but fair with the kids, but he worked such long hours.

Carrie, now twelve, had made the transition to life on Ascension reasonably well, chiefly because there, at least, she had other American friends in her class. Here, in Saint Helena, Carrie had to make friends all over again.

Carrie's teacher was lovely, and the island children were well disciplined and friendly. But the Saints were a tight-knit community, or perhaps, Angie had considered, it was her own shyness which meant that she found it difficult to stand outside the school gates and converse with the Saint mums.

Angie waited outside the school each day and watched the many tall, lithe young people of St Helena stride into the sunshine, followed by the small, blonde, skinny kid who was Angie's daughter.

Then there was the problem of Scott, Carrie's older brother, who was even more of a worry to her.

Scott seemed so quietly angry when he left the house each day with his school bag, speaking to no one and slamming the door shut, which was usually after Dean had left. He wouldn't dare do such a thing if Dean were present. He was slamming the door on her, on his mother, communicating something he hadn't the words to tell.

When Scott went out in the evenings, before Dean returned, he would never tell her where he was going, even after a full-scale battle. No longer quiet, his shouting reached manic proportions.

Then there was the time, recently, when he had returned with a whiff of cannabis on his clothing. He said he'd been playing football with Tyler and Pat, who Angie believed were nice boys. But Angie wasn't sure that Scott was to be believed.

Dean came into the kitchen for some toast. He smiled across at her, but his smile was distant. He was thinking of his work. She thought this affectionately and understood; it wasn't meant as a criticism. Angie was very proud of Dean, in every way, of the way he looked after them, his family. Proud of his generosity and of his good looks. He was square built, tall and broad of chest, with a light crew cut, through which you could still see his light brown hair.

"Could we meet Tammy and Charlie at the Chinese on Friday, if you're not too tired?" Angie asked him now. She was grateful for their few friends. Tammy was especially good fun, and she felt that she could trust her with some of these worries. It helped that Dean liked Charlie, too.

"Sure, great idea. Don't see why not. It'll have to be at seven thirty though; I won't be back before seven."

He drank the dregs of his black tea and brushed a crumb from his blue polo top.

Angie smiled at him. "Honey, shouldn't you have a suit on? I thought you had this big meeting; instead you look as if you have a round of golf!"

"Ah..." He glanced down at his own clothing. "But it's not formal, just..." he hesitated, important."

Then he crossed the kitchen in two strides to lift her off her feet in a hug, nuzzling her neck, and she was overcome with joy at it. As a rule, she was the one who kissed him goodbye.

"Will you be late again?" she asked his broad chest, hoping not, as he had been so late the previous evening.

"No, I'll be home earlier tonight," he assured her, kissing the top of her head. "Don't forget to get some coffee, will you? And I'm looking forward to seeing the finished coasters."

She watched as he picked up his car keys and left. It was a reference to her weaving class. They wove the flax which grew in abundance on the island, and had once been one of the main sources of living, into saleable souvenirs that could be sold in the tourist shop in Jamestown. Angie was getting quite good at it. This set was for their home. She had made four, and today she would make the final two.

She loved the way that Dean always encouraged her. After all, he might have been quite patronising about such a humble activity. But he never was. Here on the island he hadn't even suggested that she get a job.

In truth, since leaving her job in the home country, Angie felt that she had lost a bit of confidence. She was only just beginning to understand the island and its people, to feel a little bit more settled. Then there were the kids. Not working meant she could be around for them, keep an eye on them.

These things Angie thought about as she drove her car along the steeply winding road to Green Valley, where Penny lived.

Penny was older than Angie but someone who it was good to be friendly with. A contact with other expats. She was a little bossy, sometimes rather know-it-all in her efficient, English way, but to be friendly with her was one way to survive in this strange and remote place. Penny was married to the chief housing officer.

Her house was as old as Longwood, where Napoleon had lived, in a remote place below Alarm Forest. Angie adored such Saint Helenian names. There was Half Tree Hollow, Fairy Land, Lemon Valley, Blue Hill, Sandy Bay, all reminiscent of scenes from a film about pirates, with their craggy, intimidating rocks that stood like giant sentinels off the bay. Her favoured name was The Gates of Chaos, where two giant rocks stood like fortresses, the dark sea boiling between them in a giant cauldron. Not a place for swimming.

Right now, Angie cautiously traversed that bit of the road they called Frenchman's Leap, whilst listening to Cyndi Lauper and wondering about some of her friends back home.

When she first came here, she had thought that Frenchman's Leap must be named after a French pirate. The name of the valley was so romantic, after all, like the name of an old Errol Flynn movie. Then Miss Tessa had told her that in fact it was named after a Frenchman in the 1970s who was going too fast on a bend (with several female passengers, so it was said in a scandalised hiss) and careered over the ancient, low wall into the valley below. Incredibly, all his passengers survived.

Angie took no chances in this place. She gripped the wheel tightly and blasted the car horn loudly every time she reached a blind spot in the twisting road. It never helped her confidence to glimpse the valley below in which Jamestown lay, snug as a baby in a crib. One false move and the car might plummet toward the houses below.

She arrived at Penny's house at nine thirty, earlier than some of the others because she did not live so far away. She smiled to herself at that thought. On an island, eight miles by ten, with a population of four thousand people, no one was ever very far away. Angie had heard there were some very isolated cottages down near remote Sandy Bay, and that those people often had no car, so that their only communication was by bus or routine visits from social workers, especially in the case of the elderly.

Angie parked her car and wondered why the engine smelled very slightly of smoke.

But it was very hot, so maybe the heat had something to do with it. She knew that Dean had put water into the engine thingumabob recently, and the car had been serviced not long ago. Maybe the smell came from another car, or lay in her imagination, just something else to worry about. She dismissed the worry and fixed a positive smile upon Penny's house.

Penny's garden was beautifully tended. As she reached the gate, patting her red hair into some shape with her left hand, the two yellow Labradors came towards her, snuffling and wagging their tails.

Angie had met them before. She put her hand over the gate so that they could smell her just as a rather firm and British voice called out to them.

"Jasper, Tinker, come away and lie down. You silly dogs!"

The dogs turned instantly, the older one with less speed and a slightly superior objection on his face, like an old man who had been refused his pipe. The dogs left Angie alone and went to lie down on an old rug under the shade of a tree.

"Angela, so glad you're a bit early. Would you give me a hand? Could you carry that bundle of flax into the kitchen for me and set it on the dining room table? I've covered it with cloth."

The owner of the voice beamed at her from over the top of a stable door which was painted green. Penny was a handsome woman, in her mid-seventies now, with short, steely grey hair and piercing blue eyes.

"Sure," Angela replied. She went towards the pile of long, sharp-ended leaves and, juggling her handbag, lifted the bundle into her arms.

"Coffee or tea?" Penny asked her with brisk, bossy cheerfulness.

"Oh, coffee please, Penny."

Her kitchen was white, and an old but efficient space which, much as she loved her own kitchen, put Angie's in the shade. It had a large refectory table in the centre and high shelves stacked with plates. It was very beautiful and kind of clever, in a way Angie couldn't express.

The top part of the stable door remained open, to allow the tiniest of breezes inside and the oven's heat out. The lemon cake that had recently been made brought saliva to Angie's mouth.

"How is the family?" Penny asked as she made the coffee. She lifted her eyes to her guest's face as though she wanted the truth, the whole truth and nothing but the truth.

Angie had decided long ago that she would never confide such things to Penny.

"Fine, thank you. Dean is working very hard and the kids are doing well in their schools." It was kind of true.

"Have they got as far as the terminal yet?" Penny asked so briskly that for a moment Angie thought she was referring to her family still. She meant the new airport, of course.

"I think so; at least, they've had a meeting about what kind of shops there will be, so that's quite far on," Angie said, smiling and taking her mug of coffee from Penny.

"It's rather sad to think we will have a McDonald's and a Kentucky Fried Chicken on the island soon," Penny sighed.

Oh, I do hope so, it might cheer Scott up, Molly thought, wondering how long it had been since she'd eaten a cheeseburger and putting a hand to her rather plump waist. But she murmured, "Mmm... yes," in agreement.

"Halloo..." A head appeared over the top of the stable gate. It was Catherine, the wife of one of the magistrates. Molly smiled back. She liked Catherine, who always made her feel a little more comfortable in Penny's house, a little less American.

She was small, neat and in her fifties, with short, straight blonde hair and an expat tan. She worked hard for the islanders on a voluntary basis, working with a group of disabled people, and hearing children read in the primary school. She had applied gentle encouragement to Angie to give some of her time, too.

Catherine kissed Penny on the cheek and gave Angie a small hug.

"I'm glad you're here, Angie. Are you doing anything next Tuesday? Only one of those big yachts will be coming into the port and I need some volunteers to run the stalls, make some money for the different charities, only for the morning period," she added, apologetically.

"Sure." Angie nodded. "I'll come after the kids have gone to school, if that's alright with everyone."

"Would you like tea or coffee?" Penny asked her. "And there's lemon cake on the sideboard – help yourself; it's fresh out of the oven."

Angie thought about her own attempts at cake making, which were dismal.

Perhaps, she thought with some trepidation, that when it came at last to her turn to have everyone around, she could ask one of the island ladies to bake for her. Baking cakes was a skill handed down from a mother to her children in St Helena. Angie's own mother had hated mess too much to encourage baking, so she'd had to learn on her own.

The others arrived shortly after Catherine. Chloe, with her two pre-school boys who instantly picked up the flax for a sword fight and were turned out into the garden; Hannah, the doctor's wife, with her one-year-old chubby baby; Esme, married to one of the island's lay advocates, always so mousy and quiet that you had to get really close to her to hear her opinions; and Greta, from Brazil originally, who was the flax-weaving expert and part-time art teacher at the senior school.

They chatted with one another and crooned over Hannah's little baby until the kitchen became rather hot and claustrophobic and Penny's flushed and overheated face registered irritation. She signalled for them to move into the living room with its old but highly polished furniture, to start the business of weaving.

"Now," Greta called in her rolling, heavily accented tones, "do not forget to wash your hands after you have been weaving and before you help yourself to cake. Remember that the rats run in and out of the flax, so it is not very clean!"

Greta repeated her demonstration of the last week, cutting, trimming and softening the flax before the business of folding and weaving the green spiky leaves into whatever each woman was making. Some had made pots, others made flowers, but Angie was the only one to have made coasters, and she felt proud of their neat shapes.

They sat around the large dining room table to weave and to talk.

"Does anyone know how Cara's babies are, and what is happening now?"

It was a tactless question from Greta, perhaps, as Catherine was the only one of them who could possibly know and she would never discuss her husband's work.

"No," Chloe replied after a pause, "except that the babies are back on the island now with the parents who have been looking after them. Poor little mites. I can't understand why the mother has rejected them and why she won't tell anyone who the father is. She must be a very strange girl."

For Catherine's sake, nobody replied. The conversation was swiftly changed by Hannah, Catherine's good friend.

"Has there been any more talk of a free nursery in Jamestown?"

"A free nursery?" Penny sounded horrified. "Where is the funding coming from for that? And anyway, in most instances on the island, grandparents take care of the children if their parents work. What would be the point?"

Hannah shrugged her shoulders. "Well, I don't have my parents here, for a start, and surely that should be an option by now. I mean, in the UK, isn't it an option once a child reaches two?"

Penny made a small huffing noise. "I think, if you talk to some of the elders on the island, they don't necessarily want that change; they think things like child benefit and housing allowance will mean the younger parents will smoke and drink more," she said.

But Hannah was not afraid to argue with Penny as Angie was.

"The Saints are UK citizens, aren't they? We have those benefits; I mean, in a free society, shouldn't they have the option to choose? Young people in Britain drink and smoke, after all."

Penny opened her mouth to challenge this again, but Greta cut across in her decisive, Brazilian way. "We should do what they do in Cooba," she started. "In Cooba they give the ration books to parents, they limit the shops you can go to, so you have to purchase food with them, and clothes for the children; you do not get an option." She shrugged.

As an American, Angela wanted to object, point out that there must be poverty in Cuba. She didn't; she was as tongue-tied as quiet Esme.

The conversation changed then, to the subject of the new secondary school on the island. Angela listened whilst weaving her coasters, her tongue between her teeth in concentration, a childhood habit that had never been curbed.

She had become deft at the weaving now, had almost completed the fifth coaster when, to everyone's surprise, Esme, who hardly spoke at these gatherings, placed her weaving upon the table, drew her large bag from under her chair and produced a set of papers.

"Um, I have something to ask you all," she said.

The chattering and weaving stopped as everyone stared at Esme in open-mouthed astonishment.

"I have a petition," Esme continued, her small chin lifting with a defiant pride that Angie had never thought her capable of. "As you all know, I am in the early stages of pregnancy and I have thought hard about this, I mean from the point of view of everyone. I think we should have a paediatrician on the island, at the hospital, as there isn't one, and so I wondered whether you might add your names to this. I've collected quite a lot already, from the Saint ladies mostly."

Angela realised she was smiling at the girl, reassuringly and with new-found admiration, like a teacher who has taught a pupil confidence. But her smile wavered as she registered the uncomfortable admonishment of silence about her.

Penny stared hard over the top of her glasses, looking from one to the other of the company.

A dribble of saliva drooped from the open-mouthed baby Hannah held on her hip, landing with a splash upon the wooden floor.

"The thing is, dear," Penny said a little coldly, "my husband is a magistrate. I can't possibly sign it. It might create trouble for him, you see." Her voice held an overtone, suggesting great surprise and hurt that anyone should suggest such a thing.

But Esme was undeterred, turning to the kindly Catherine.

"I'm terribly sorry, Esme, but my reason would be the same," Catherine said quietly, her lower lip lifted towards her nose.

One by one, each woman declined, until it came to Angela, who had been sitting very quietly, studying her coaster, but who knew that she had to make the decision, one way or the other. She looked up at the girl's young, eager, imploring face and felt so sorry for her. In her mind, she saw Carrie as an older woman, hesitant, vulnerable. She knew why they were refusing, out of fear for their husbands' positions. All positions on the island were kept on short-term contracts, possibly so that the British Government would never be challenged. Changes would be slowly, if ever, effected. Angela wasn't aware of other reasons. Esme didn't understand this. She had been so courageous in producing her petition, so brave, after all.

Angela made up her mind in a rush. What harm could it do? Who the heck was going to find out?

"I'll sign it, Esme," she said swiftly, putting her hand out for the petition.

And the girl's relief at not being rejected yet again was so palpable that Angie knew she had made an ally forever. She took the papers from Esme, signing her own name with a shaky hand.

She hastened to finish the last coaster after that. Perhaps it was her imagination, but she felt Penny's surprised eyes upon her on several occasions as she moved about the dining room. She almost tingled with a kind of fear that she herself would be ejected from the island.

After this, it was a relief to realise the time, and to bid everyone goodbye. She received a grateful smile from Esme, and assured Catherine that she would help with the stalls.

As she stood at the kitchen sink to clean her hands, Penny joined her in the kitchen.

"It's so difficult being on this island sometimes, isn't it?" she said. "So hard for the young to understand the implications of their actions."

Angie smiled and nodded her agreement but said nothing about it, hastily thanking Penny for her hospitality. She felt a little nervous now, as if she had done something terribly wrong.

What if someone reported her? What if Dean lost his job? These questions bothered her, repeating themselves as she climbed into her car, the coasters inside her bag.

She frowned at her face in the mirror before starting the engine, pursing her lips. She was being ridiculous. Hardly the McCarthy era – not as though she was a traitor or a suspected communist. *It is done now*, she told herself, *put it out of your head*.

Easier than she would have thought. As she drove almost a mile away from the house, the smell of burning reached her small nose. Alarmingly noxious fumes billowed in through the open window. Angie's face puckered in distaste and concern.

There were no other cars on the road, nothing, so it had to be her car.

"Dammit," she muttered aloud. "Please don't do this to me."

Dean had had the car serviced recently, had topped up the water and oil and fuel. Perplexed, she slowed down but kept on driving, hoping that nothing would happen before she reached her own home. But in the driver's mirror she saw a plume of dirty grey smoke following the car.

As she reached the brow of the hill, the car began to judder – hardly noticeable at first, but then, as she had to hold the steering wheel more tightly, it became obvious that she would have to pull the car over to the side of the narrow road.

"Goddamned island," she swore under her breath. "Why do I have to live in the only place on earth where you can't use a mobile phone?"

But there was a low white bungalow a few yards along the road, with a track leading to it and a wide grass verge before that. She would have to pull over and park there; the car was juddering quite a bit now, as though the battery was about to give out on her.

She slowed, driving carefully over the road and onto the verge.

Maybe whoever lived at the house would let her use the house phone, then she could call Dean and ask for help.

She parked the car beneath overgrowing flax and woodland, got out, grabbing her handbag so that she could offer the householder some money if needed, and started to climb the sloping driveway. She wished she had more suitable shoes than the low heels she was wearing.

In the garden above, a shaggy, brown and white goat stared at her intently with evil eyes.

She didn't care for goats – they were sly, greedy things – but saw that it was tethered.

It watched her progress as she made her way to the front door.

Angie held her hand in a balled fist for a moment and hesitated before rapping it on the wood.

She waited. There was no reply. Cautiously, she went to the long window and peered inside. A neat little living room lay within, but there was no sign of life. She rapped on the door again, but there were no cars in the drive, no one inside, apparently.

And then she remembered. She recalled being close to this spot once before, shortly after they came to the island. They had climbed to the ridge above the house and admired the panoramic blue haze of the sea below.

There was a pathway above, stony, difficult to follow. Eventually it sloped down and down until it reached a lower path above a cove and ended up near the Jamestown harbour.

She made up her mind; she wasn't dressed for such a hike, but if she set out now it would save her more than half a mile of walking and she could get help and be back in time to fetch Carrie from school.

Lifting her handbag onto her shoulder, she started for the place marked by the ancient, rusting cannon which had once belonged to the East India Company.

The pathway was semi-overgrown, and the sun beat down upon her shoulders, turning her red hair to flame, though Dean wasn't there to admire it.

She swatted a fly from her arm and looked down at the never-ending vista of the sea below her at the place called Lemon Valley.

She had been daunted by the idea of walking so far, but after a little while she began to enjoy it, looking for the first time in ages at the flowers which grew at the very top, hearing the song of the crickets high above her. Dean would think her clever.

And even when the flowers stopped growing and all that remained was the dark brown, bare and arid rock, she still felt good, calmer now, assured that her plan would work.

Below her, the boats bobbed on the water, seeming minuscule, and gulls skimmed the warm sea breeze. It was a kind of freedom from worry she had forgotten recently.

Angie smiled to herself and remembered the walk with Dean and knew she must suggest to him that they do such a thing again.

The pathway began to descend to the sea; she rested a hand on the rocks to keep her balance, and yet it did not appear to be as stony as she remembered it and her feet felt quite secure.

She blew her fringe upward against the heat. She was halfway down the rock face and must be quite close to the little cove where she had swum with Dean. She remembered how excited she had felt when he had pointed at the heat-hazed horizon, saying, "Namibia is over there…"

There was a fork in the path. The one to the right led across the volcanic mountain to a valley, whilst the one to the left would take her to the cove and to Jamestown.

As she glanced down at the cove, she saw that a small dinghy was moored there, in the shallower water. It had a motor.

Then she heard a giggle, a woman's voice, soft and playful. There were people in the cove. Human faces at last.

She scrambled down to a place where she could rest for a moment, sitting on a sturdy rock to catch her breath and wipe her sweating cheeks with a tissue. She heard the giggle again. Curious now, Angie leaned out to get a better view of the cove and the people there.

She saw the rounded, plump bottom wriggling in its bikini. A young woman lying across a man. She had long, pale legs. The girl had removed the top part of her costume, presumably believing that she was safe from prying eyes in the secluded cove. The girl had long, thick, blonde tresses which swept the face of the man as he lay beneath her. A large man, like Dean, his hand stole around her bottom and slapped her buttock playfully.

Like Dean. There was something familiar in his movement that caused Angie's heart to lurch as though the blood had coagulated within her arteries. Something so familiar about the man, her heart appeared to have stopped beating.

And she saw the blue shirt, cast away on a rock. The blue Aertex shirt, which Angie had ironed, carefully folding it into the drawer.

She leapt up from the rock in a kind of terror and panic, quickly scrambling down towards the lower path, getting closer and closer to the couple regardless of the sweat pouring from her red face.

She stopped once more, leaning out even further over a sharp precipice, just in time to see the girl roll slowly into the crook of his arm. Her large, plump breast was squashed against his chest as he held her against him.

And she could see his face clearly then.

A large balloon appeared to be deflating in her stomach, emptying its pointless, toxic poison into her body.

"How could you?" she asked the flora in disbelief as she watched Dean caress the girl's breast.

Anyone present would have assumed the heat-dishevelled woman with the red hair had gone quite mad, as she expelled the scream of a wild animal in torture, hurling the bag down towards the lovers like a weapon.

The contents spun through the air above the two startled faces, the flaxen coasters floating after it – redundant, lightweight discs of green.

Chapter 18
Diary Thirteen

At breakfast the following morning, Helen's appearance is neat, her make-up subtle. One might not notice the turmoil within her small frame, but I have learned that a scarcely discernible frown, accompanied by a slight twist of the mouth, can mean trouble.

As I pour tea from the white teapot, Mark enters the dining room and wanders towards the breakfast table. Helen scarcely acknowledges him, but all becomes clear when she leans towards me slightly, mouthing in a whisper, "Does he behave like that at home?"

I wonder how he behaved in court yesterday to deserve this. I'm afraid I can't resist the reply, my sympathy for her an overriding factor.

"Oh yes, don't feel that you're alone. He has cross-examined the entire family over the years, especially me, and I'm not even allowed a lawyer in my defence... Having said that," I say, feeling obliged to be as fair as possible, "he has also accused me of speaking to him as though he were one of my primary school pupils. He once said to me, 'Please don't speak to me like that, I am a solicitor of the Crown Court.'"

We chortle quietly as Mark fills his bowl with cereal. I'm not being disloyal; this morning, Helen certainly needs a boost even though she is Mark's opponent, and at least I've made her laugh.

Across the week, Mark has become more and more frustrated. Frustrated with the lack of evidence in differing cases, frustrated with a lack of support for people in Saint Helena, frustrated also with the lethargy of some of the people who have come to the island to work, and indeed with some of the native people themselves.

This is our first Thursday here on the island. For the lawyers, each day revolves around their cases until about seven in the evening, when they walk a little wearily back up the Main Street hill. Sometimes it is later than this.

On the previous evening, I accompanied my new American friends from the ship to Mori's Bar, where we drank a Namibian beer overlooking the sea to the accompaniment of Wyclef's version of Pink Floyd's 'Wish You Were Here'.

"This island is too small," Julia complained. There again, she is American; Saint Helena probably has the dimensions of her back garden.

"Yeah, we've seen it all now…" her husband added, with a dismissive gesture of the hand.

I really didn't believe this could be true; but as I wandered a little disconsolately back along the street at a quarter to eight in the evening, I did wonder whether there were a significant number of expat partners with drink problems.

Living here can't be easy, neither for the Saints nor for the visitors; it is just so darned remote from the rest of the world.

I am feeling rather remote and insignificant myself as I look over to the courthouse through the dusk, the lights from within illuminating the street, to glimpse the judge through the open door of the robing room, hunched over his papers.

And past the cannons, beneath the single light, I am reminded of Atticus Finch in *To Kill a Mockingbird*, as I see Mark and Edward deep in discussion, whilst Edward holds the court telephone in his hand. Yet the sight is also reassuring somehow.

Other people have now moved into the hotel, some of them, like the engineers working on the airport, on a long-term basis.

Joshua is there, the foreman from Johannesburg in charge of the mostly Zimbabwean workforce. After his 'holiday' on the ship, he has quickly lost his good humour. He is weary again, and I suspect there are so many more issues to building an airport in such an isolated place than could be imagined.

There are two people from the Foreign Office staying here. I don't know what they are doing, though I suspect the lawyers do. Mark remarked that they had the innocent, eager expressions of sixth formers.

Once or twice, coming out onto the balcony to watch for Mark, I have come across Joshua, fast asleep at six thirty in the Blue Room, and still wearing his dusty construction gear, his heavy workman's boots lying on the lovely oriental carpet alongside his feet. I feel very sorry for him; he is weary and misses his missus.

We had a drink at the bar together. He told me that the sand around the fuel pipelines has cracked because the company used cheap materials; that they have the wrong tanks for fuel; that in one instance, the runway, narrower than recommended, has now to be widened because it is coming too close to the local houses.

"So what will happen about it?" I asked, feeling slightly alarmed at the sudden visions of fireballs dancing across Saint Helena before me.

He was sitting at the bar with his head resting on his knuckles, as though he hadn't the energy to straighten up.

"Those men, the ones you saw this morning? They are British engineers, come to inspect the work. They won't pass it, of course, so then there will be a lot of work to repair it."

I shook my head in sympathy. "So you have to start again?"

He nodded wearily. "Do you know what some of my guys said to me this morning?" He lifted a tired eyebrow. "I was accused of working them like slaves, for the first time in my life. I've never been accused of that before. My ancestors were slaves. So I've let them finish the work a little early. I've bought expensive tools that the company won't buy, with my own money, to help them get the work done faster. They've got a point. They get just over a pound an hour to work like this, to get the airport finished on time, and all because one of the royals has been booked in to open the damned airport."

I wondered whether you would find anyone in England prepared to work for that money.

"Ah well, Josh," I said, smiling at him, "nobody's been killed yet, have they, or injured?"

He rubbed his face then, as though to shut the question out and avoid my face, speaking through his fingers. "I couldn't possibly answer that," he said bleakly.

But perhaps it was all "Talk, talk," as the Saints described misinformation.

To lighten his weary load, I started speculating upon what the Foreign Office could be doing in the hotel. We drew the conclusion that they probably had more to do with the lawyers than anything else at present.

Shortly after this, Joshua and I started a little routine when we met in the hotel corridors, a reaction to secrecy and espionage and 'keeping a low profile', perhaps. When we saw each other after that conversation, we pretended to karate chop the air, like Cato in *The Pink Panther*. It's the kind of juvenile humour that Mark abhors, but I love.

But honestly, by now everyone is suggesting that we must be very careful. Aside from just being friendly, I'm worrying about what I have to be careful about. Perhaps they are really reminding one another... but it makes for paranoia.

On that Thursday morning, after breakfast, I leave the hotel and make my way to Justine and Nigel's apartment. I am greeted by almost everyone that I pass, not because, by now, everyone knows me, but because that's what happens in Jamestown.

Some people are just curious, like the old lady walking with her granddaughter who came to a standstill in the middle of the pavement and eyeballed me, whilst her small granddaughter stood before me, staring up at my face with her finger in her mouth.

There was no formal introduction, or any shyness on the old lady's part.

"Who you is?" she asks me. "I seen you with my friend. You walk up the street and then down again. Who you is?"

"I'm Stephanie." I smile from the old lady to the granddaughter. I'm tempted to ask her, *"Who you is?"* But instead I say, "I'm just here on holiday, ma'am."

She has a slight frown, as though she only half believes me.

"You a lawyer?"

"No. My husband is. I'm just enjoying the break."

She nods. "Where you going?"

"To see Justine Harris; we're kind of... related by marriage."

Mercifully, the old lady doesn't ask for my family tree. So I smile at the little girl and shake the old lady's hand, then afterwards think that it would have been polite of me to ask for her name, but we have now passed one another.

In the distance behind me, in the bay at the foot of the street, there is a massive ocean-going liner, ten times bigger than the RMS and about a tenth of the horizon. Emma told us to expect a lot of tourists in the town today; what she didn't say was that we should expect at least two thousand five hundred tourists.

From the courtyard in the centre of the town, I call up to Justine. Her door is open, and she calls back for me to come upstairs.

At the top of the staircase, Justine greets me with a welcome, maternal hug. I am taken by the hand to a beautiful, white-walled living room, which looks a little Spanish. It has white, gauze curtains and heavy, mahogany, antique furniture.

The windows are open to the noises of the street, of birdsong and voices in the market.

Justine's husband is an imposing figure, very likeable and obliging. He makes coffee for us and withdraws to a corner of the room to bury himself behind a local paper. There are seldom recent national papers to be seen in St Helena, unless you can get hold of one that is a few days old and has been delivered to you on the ship. Newspapers are devoured by hungry Saints eager for news.

Two women are sitting on the low settee, Sarah, who I met in The Standard, and the other an older lady called Jackie. Jackie has a sad little face, as though she is afraid of her own shadow.

They ask me about Mark and how his work is going; I tell them what I can, without referring to anyone or anything in any detail, which of course I can't. I am tempted to make something up, as my description of his work is a little boring, but I don't.

Jackie lives in Saint Helena and most of her family lives here, too, whilst Sarah has come to visit her father, Herman, for the first time in four years. She lives in the UK.

"We see the judge's wife sometimes, buying her vegetables from the market," Jackie says shyly. "Is she nice?"

"Oh yes, very nice, and very friendly," I assure her.

"What do you think of the island?" Sarah asks me.

"I love it, it's magical, so beautiful, although I've only seen a little of it yet. I think Mark and the others might have some free time at the weekend, so I'm hoping to see a bit more of it. I can't believe that the landscape changes so quickly and in such a short time. Do you have seasons here?"

"Not really," Justine says, laughing; "we get a little bit of rain sometimes, but it's sunny pretty much all the year round."

There is a knock at the door and a very tall, good-looking Saint with a walking stick appears. This is Sarah's father. I have seen them drinking tea together outside the Napoleon Hotel. He and Justine's husband join us then, regaling us with a few stories about their youth.

Herman talks about how much he misses his children, who all live in the UK, and what it feels like to have a place embedded so deeply in your heart, and a foot on the island when another foot is in your mother country.

And later, Jackie's small, harrowed face puckers a little and she asks, "Would your husband help me?" as though she has been waiting and wanting to ask the question all along.

"Help you?" I ask hesitantly.

The others fall quiet and listen, as though encouraging her to go on.

"It my grandson, you see. He always been a problem at school; his mamma don't know what to do 'bout him. Then one teacher say he have something called autism, something like that, but nothin' really done 'bout it, so he leave school, he don't go there now, he fifteen. But a few months ago, he got in trouble stealin' from a shop; he mixin' with some bad boys. He don't really understand what he doin', honest, ma'am…"

With the last few words, her voice has fallen to a whisper, and now there are tears in her eyes.

"Go on, Jackie," Justine encourages, putting a hand on the woman's knee and giving it a gentle squeeze.

"There weren't lawyers here at time, no one to deal with it for weeks. The police put him in the cells and he went crazy, injured hi'self. Out now; at home again. Miss Rachel say they shouldn't have done it 'cos Daniel, that's his name, was not yet fifteen. Just a kid still, in the cells with men; it wasn't right."

Justine goes to get a tissue for her. I wait whilst she blows her nose and composes herself. After a while she says, "Will your husband get him some help? His mamma can't cope on her own and Dan behave so strange sometime. But I don't want anyone know I complainin', don't want him in more trouble, see?"

For how long, I wonder, has there been a situation where police can be recruited at sixteen and young people locked up in an adult prison at fourteen? Wasn't that the plot for *The Lord of The Flies*? Sixteen-year-olds guarding fourteen-year-olds. I feel as though I've been catapulted back into the nineteenth century.

And why should people be as afraid as she clearly is? If she lived in Britain, she'd be shouting at everyone at the top of her voice for help by now.

"I don't know what he can do," I say with real sympathy. "I can't speak for Mark, I'm not a lawyer. I've been a teacher, I've taught autistic children, and they have very particular special needs. You've all been through a terrible time, that's clear. The only thing I can suggest is that first you go to Rachel, or Miss Tessa, make your complaint to her, and then perhaps she will talk to Mark."

I don't know what else to say, I can't interfere; I am a visitor and my being here will change nothing.

One day, now that the airport has arrived, Saint Helena will be a tourist destination, but there is still a lot to be done.

As I turn the corner from the market, I am woken from my thoughts by the loud chatter and bustle of a thousand loud, strange voices speaking in French, in German, in Italian as well as English, drowning out the lovely birdsong. No wonder the Cornish call tourists 'emmets', I think, watching them as they swarm like ants upon Jamestown. They pester the local children and mild-mannered old men for photographs; the teenage tourists sit on the Napoleon's stone steps, heedless of people trying to get in and out of the place.

Tourists swarm into the little shops and, in some cases, they demand that the shopkeepers take their euros instead of the Saint Helena currency. There are queues stretching back for almost ten metres.

At least they bring money to the town, I think, then change my mind as I watch a large man drop his crisp packet in the Castle Gardens and another failing to say either please or thank you at the coffee shop, easy words to acquire.

The tourists hunt for taxis to take them to Longwood to see Napoleon's empty tomb. There are not enough taxis in a population of four thousand, invaded all of a sudden by another two and a half thousand. The local radio station puts out an emergency call for drivers with clean licences who may be available as temporary taxis, after there is a dramatic punch-up in Main Street between a Frenchman and an Italian.

They push their way up the hotel's private staircase, so they can use Emma's bathrooms. She is forced to hang chains across the passageways to bar their entrance so that guests are forced climb across them.

Some tourists become upset because they can't purchase Silk Cut and because there won't be any mobile coverage until the airport is built. They ask to buy into the internet at the hotel.

Down at the courts, Helen is asked by a Frenchwoman whether she can use the court internet system. Helen declines. The girl says, "If I commit a crime, will you let me?"

"No," is Helen's short reply, "because then you'll be a criminal."

At Longwood House, the rabbits scuttle terrified into the bushes as they are outnumbered by tourists, whilst Jonathan the tortoise draws his head into his shell, refusing to emerge until the place has grown quiet and is habitable again.

It is all rather too much for the tiny island, but perhaps it is a learning curve for when the airport arrives and the real business of tourism begins.

And then, just as suddenly as they arrived, so they leave, and the place is quiet once more. But they leave knowing absolutely nothing about the true beauty of the place. Knowing nothing of the soft, rolling hills in the lush green landscape, nothing of the pretty, pointed peaks that tower above the sea, nothing of the savage beauty of the cliffs, of Lemon Valley or Egg Island. They know nothing of the sudden jewelled colours of the rainforest towards Sandy Bay, nothing of the panoramic dizziness that takes your breath away at the very peak of High Knoll Fort.

They leave, having spent seven hours, mostly in Jamestown, knowing nothing of the real island.

***

Emma had slipped a note beneath the door of our room. It was from Mark.

"It's Oliver's birthday, so we are all going down to Mori's Bar at seven thirty. I'll come back and get changed first."

Oliver was a young lawyer, not yet qualified. I didn't really know him, but everyone said he was very nice.

I was happy and excited at the prospect. Mori's Bar mightn't be the most glamorous place, but it would be fun; a time for Mark and the lawyers to relax, and for Mark and I to be together; and Rachel had told me that on Thursday evenings there was usually a rather good band, made up of local talent.

Music is a big thing on the island. The school's inspector, whom I met on the ship, told me that the standard of music in the schools in St Helena is higher than the standard reached anywhere in the world.

I had a nap, woke hungry and ate all the biscuits the ladies had left in the room for us. I changed into a black dress which was slightly too tight and for which I had to contort myself like an overweight gymnast to do up the zip.

We could hear the band loud and clear as we trotted down Main Street towards Mori's. It was obvious that they were going to be fantastic from their rendition of 'Mustang Sally', and I liked to dance, as I've said before. Oh yes, I do like to dance.

When we arrived at about seven thirty, the party was in full swing. They were mostly local people, with some expats and people from the court, including the court clerks and the lay advocates. They spilled out from Mori's Bar, the bar on the seafront which is open to the stars, with pockets of people crowding into the mule yard, so-called because centuries ago it was where they tied up the patient mules. Now, the partygoers spilled onto the grass beneath the trees which were festooned with fairy lights. A pretty summer scene in November.

SEE YOU AGAIN, ONE TIME IN SAINT HELENA

There were about eight people in the band, not including the female vocalist, whose dynamic, soulful voice might have filled the Albert Hall.

Before long, as I stood in a little group with Helen and some of the lawyers, I found my mind drifting away from their conversation, whilst my foot jigged up and down to the band and my shoulders started to move to the music with a life of their own, just like Baloo, *The Jungle Book* bear.

Gradually, tentatively, heeding the impulse within rather than anything else, I edged away from the group and towards the stage where there were several other dancers enjoying the vibes.

I looked about me for Mark, who had left my elbow shortly after arriving. I'm not a shrinking violet, so his absence didn't really bother me, although I had been looking forward to us being together. When I saw him in conversation with an attractive, skinny redhead in a red dress, someone I had never seen before, and surrounded by the lovely blonde lawyers who had also been joined by Edward and Phil, I suppose I changed my mind about the dancing. Why did Mark only appear to get into conversation with lovely young women, nowadays? Anyway, he would hardly notice me if I let myself go a little.

I mean, I really wasn't going to join Mark at that point; how desperate would that have made me look?

So, when I saw Sam and Cheryl and Zena from the ship, now on onshore leave, I sidled over to them. A positive move, as it turned out. Sam bought me my second large glass of wine that evening, and I could see that Cheryl and Zena were getting close to taking the stage by storm, unable to contain their stifled jigging about any more than I could.

We began to chat about this and that, shouting a little over the music. At one point, I remarked to Sam, stretching up a little to speak into his ear, "I bet you'll be sorry to see the ship go."

"Oh, we will. The RMS has seen some great times and we've had a lot of fun; 'course, you can't get away with the same kinds of things we used to, parties and such." He grinned.

"Parties for the passengers?" I asked. I was drinking rather too quickly. In my peripheral vision, I noticed the lovely redhead reaching up to speak into Mark's ear.

"No, parties for the crew when the passengers were on shore," Sam said. "Once, we organised our own version of 'Miss World', only it was a competition for the woman with the biggest cleavage!" He grinned. "We held it on ship, but it was organised by the Saint Helena radio station, see? That was a great party; the disco went on all evening."

He paused, his eyes diverted momentarily by Cheryl's own deep cleavage.

"Yes, that was a great party, at least it was until the attorney general stopped it. He wasn't very happy about it being broadcast on the local radio, the spoilsport."

So very Benny Hill, so very '70s; so very sexist, I thought. Which makes me similarly a spoilsport, I suppose.

By now, Cheryl, Zena and I were so close to dancing, there was little point in not being on the wooden stage, next to the band.

All would have been well if I hadn't followed them to the place where the dance floor was temporarily being used by three little girls doing handstands.

Cheryl smiled at me and took my hand, encouragingly.

They were far better dancers than me, but I didn't mind that. It's good to lose yourself. Perhaps, had Mark not been surrounded by women, I would not have rolled my bottom with such abandon – who knows? Perhaps Catherine would not have stared at me with such disapproval.

Perhaps a lot of things, but it was too late.

The young, thin disabled lad, balancing upon a crutch, appeared from nowhere, standing right before me, demanding that he should be my partner. I smiled at him and obliged. He was great fun and we danced well together despite his disability and my two left feet, danced, indeed, until sweat poured down my face.

My second dance partner had been unnoticed by me until the moment he came forward, from the rear of the stage where the musicians were performing, a broad grin on his face. Fleetingly, I registered a tall man with grey hair and a neat, triangular beard. To my surprise, he took my fingers in his hand as though we had known each other for a long time – impetuosity of the moment, perhaps. Surprised by it, I let my hand rest in his and carried on dancing, but I didn't really look at him, although I remember wishing that Mark would come and dance with me as he used to.

When I did look up at him at last, realising that he was quite a good-looking man, I grew aware suddenly of my dishevelled appearance and messy hair in a way I had not been all evening. He carried on dancing, pulling me with him for a while until I became anxious about Mark, feeling a rush of guilt, then ridiculously drawing my hand away from his and fleeing the scene like Cinderella at midnight without a word to him.

It was Edward's remark, "I wish my wife would dance like that," which, according to Helen, drew Mark's attention to what I was doing.

When I looked for him again, after our own group performance had brought several others to the dance floor, he was standing beneath the trees, illuminated by the fairy lights.

There wasn't a lovely blonde in sight, and his shoulders had collapsed in anger and disappointment, whilst contained fury was etched upon his face as if drawn in charcoal. His sharp eyes stared towards me in moody reproach.

I decided I'd better beat a hasty retreat, so I thanked Cheryl and Zena then, leaving the dance floor for the place where Mark had been standing. But when I reached the spot beneath the trees, he had gone. I was just in time to see his tall figure marching away from the party, striding up Main Street towards the hotel, his fists balled in anger.

Chapter 19
Diary Fourteen

And so we had a row that evening, worthy of Elizabeth Taylor and Richard Burton, although Mark, at least, wasn't tipsy.

"What on earth are you playing at?" he demanded as I caught up with him finally as he reached our room.

He closed the bedroom door a little harder than he needed to and began pacing up and down, his fists clenched in hard, angry balls upon his hips.

"What do you mean? I was only dancing," I said.

I knew I was in the wrong, but not quite *how* I was in the wrong. I had been annoyed, about the earring; about the lovely blondes and the redhead; about being ignored.

He faced me across the bed. "I'm appalled at the way you behaved," he said.

"The way I behaved?! That's a bit priggish in the circumstances, isn't it?"

"What circumstances?" he demanded, raising his voice now, for the Foreign Office people, for Joshua, for the blue-rinsed lady next door who still hadn't returned my hairdryer.

So I told him all of it, with equal force.

"You are being ridiculous. I told you, I don't know anything about the earring; and as for those people, they are work colleagues, I can't ignore them!"

"Ignore them, ha!" I retorted. Edward and Phil were made of the same stuff, I thought. But no, that wasn't quite the truth, because Mark's male menopause was completely out of control so far as I was concerned; at least Edward and Phil talked to ordinary, non-attractive people.

He glared at me. No one can do 'contempt' quite like Mark.

"Wiggling your bottom like that…"

Then he sat down on the edge of the bed and stared at the wall, his mouth pursed in anger, his jaw resolute.

"I wasn't wiggling my bottom, I was dancing!"

That wasn't true. I had been wiggling my bottom, perhaps in an effort to make him notice me, and it had worked, but not in the way I had hoped.

"In front of all those people, the attorney general, the lay advocates, the lawyers, for Christ's sake… Idiot woman!"

"If you are going to start calling me names, I can think of a few for you," I retorted, the drink making me bold. "Vain, conceited, self-centred, and often just plain rude. You make me feel that I should be grateful for everything you offer me, not as though you actually want me here."

"Keep your voice down!" he warned.

"I'm not doing the shouting, you are!" I shouted.

He got up then, his back turned against me, to breathe in the warm air from the open window.

"Look, this trip is very important to me, that's all," he said, his voice a little more conciliatory.

"Don't you think I know that? You don't have to ignore me; can't you try being friendly with some ugly people, just sometimes?"

I was talking gobbledygook now. I was tired. We took it in turns to use the small bathroom and went to bed with our backs turned to each other, without saying goodnight.

I was angry, and I suppose I should have been upset, but as I lay there my lips twisted into a self-satisfied smile. I allowed myself to think of the guy with the short grey beard who had pulled me onto the dance floor, and for the first time in years I felt younger and attractive again. As Mark fell into a restless sleep I thought, *I am an idiot*, and stifled a self-deprecating, wine-fuelled giggle.

At breakfast the next morning, we were eventually forced into conversation by the presence of the others, but Helen, quick to heed the stony atmosphere between us, frowned at me over a fork full of sausage and mouthed, "Are you alright?"

I nodded, without explanation. It was Jack who grinned and said tactlessly, "Great dancing; I've never seen the headteacher of Saint Matthew Secondary School having so much fun, although he's an enthusiastic chap."

"Headteacher?" I repeated, as innocently as I could.

"Yes. Music teacher, too, plays the saxophone. Most of the band are students at his school."

Mark got up from the table, making his way to the breakfast bar. I thought it best to make no comment, so I smiled benignly at Jack and followed Mark, mouth dry, in search of orange juice. When I returned, Jack reminded us that the ship carrying Janine would arrive later this afternoon.

After the previous evening, I really didn't want to include Janine in our plans, on our first day off. There was a trip to Longwood, Napoleon's home, or prison. This viewpoint depended upon your nationality. It was planned for tomorrow. Then there was a boat trip arranged for later on in the day.

We had managed to arrange a visit independently of the two rival tour groups, one French, one English. To avoid a second Napoleonic war, presumably, Emma kept the two groups staying at the hotel as far away from each other as possible. Their rooms were on different landings and they ate breakfast at two large trestle tables, at some distance from each other, whilst Lizzie and the other women whizzed between them.

The coordinator of the English tour group was the gruff and impatient lady who had shared a cabin with Helen on the way over. The woman, who we had been told had a heart of gold, also snored, and spat ferociously, albeit unintentionally, when she spoke.

Her vice was that she seemed to expect everyone to have the highest standard of English, no matter what their mother tongue. We heard her loudly berating a small Spanish woman for mispronunciation one morning. She knew everything about the history and geography of Saint Helena; even the locals declined to challenge her.

But Didi, whose real name was Didier, the French tour guide, did argue with her quite a lot, both loudly and passionately, and especially when he had finished work for the day and was sitting at the bar with a few glasses of wine inside him.

"Ah, you silly English woman," we heard him hissing at her one evening, "Napoleon Bonaparte was one of ze greatest generals in the history of ze world, even your own nation believe zis!"

If duelling were still legal, they would certainly have duelled. These two tour guides hated one another, cast each other damning looks and avoided one another as much as it was humanly possible, other than to be loudly disparaging.

"Really?! Zat is preposterous! Where is she getting her information from!"

Immediately after their breakfasts, the poor tourists in their custody would be whipped into a feverish frenzy that left them covered in toothpaste stains and still brushing their hair as the eager tour guides herded them to their waiting vehicles, as though Longwood or High Knoll might have disappeared overnight.

At four o'clock, Mark came up to the bedroom. He rested his chin on my head as I sat at the dressing table, putting his arms lightly about my shoulders.

"Come on," he said, "this is our first day off, let's not spoil it."

I nodded, twisting around to find his lips, glad of his forgiveness.

Then we all walked down to meet Janine from the ship that had arrived from Ascension Island.

At the harbour once again, there were crowds of people greeting family and friends.

"There she is." Edward smiled, waving his hand. I strained my neck up to catch a glimpse. They all knew her well, or so it seemed. I should have realised they would. Phil had said that she was quite well known as a divorce lawyer as well as a family lawyer and that she had 'been in the papers'. But if I had hoped she would be vaguely unattractive, I was going to be disappointed.

More resembling Holly Golightly, she was a tiny size ten in a white sundress with a black motif of flowers and a broad-brimmed sun hat; this she held deftly against a small breeze with her left hand. She wore strappy black sandals with a modest heel on her shapely feet. She had a light tan and her breasts were too large for her figure though corseted neatly within the dress. As she approached us, I noted the dimpled curve of her plump, raspberry lips, which seemed to smile, especially for Mark.

I felt Mark reach for my fingers and knew, without looking, and with a long, cynical sigh, that he would have eyes for none but her whilst she was in our company. Yet again, the idea that he had me confused with his mother popped into my head, that he sought my permission to flirt.

When she reached us, her eyes lifted to my own. The smile remained. She greeted all, male or female, with a kiss upon the cheek. Acknowledging Mark last of all, who released the fingers of my hand, she reached out with dainty fingers, gently touching his elbow.

I had an urge to karate chop her, Miss Piggy style. Beside her, I was ungainly.

Instead, I held my own hand out towards her as Mark introduced us. What can I say to excuse myself for behaving like a petulant child? Nothing, other than the discovery of the earring, and the fact that Mark had spent so long away from me before coming here, and the subtle ways in which he had changed, as though he were suddenly aware, through someone else, of how attractive he was.

Once, he had made me feel powerful. Now, he made me feel unimportant in little ways that I naturally resented.

And then, of course, there had been the less than reassuring incident on Table Mountain, when it had struck me that he might have been wanting me out of the way. I simply didn't want to think about that. It was nonsense, of course, merely a low self-esteem.

As we walked back to the hotel, Janine held court, telling us about her journey, about the travellers she had met. She had a gentle, placid way about her. I suppose that I wished she had been sharper of voice, but she had a voice like honey coating the throat. Certainly, it wasn't Mark alone who hung upon her every word.

I didn't want to be in her company, and Mark stared after me as though surprised, as we reached the hotel courtyard to order coffee, when I asked for one of his cigarettes and wandered away to smoke it. *You can't be surprised, Mark*, I thought. *I am now, officially, your mother, no longer your wife.*

I passed Valerie who greeted me with "Hello, sweetie"; and Gladys, who stared at me in her strange, cross-eyed, permanently startled way. Across the week, I had learned to translate Gladys's peculiar crooked expressions, and it was a smile rather than practice for a gurning competition.

She was carrying a tray of cups and had been intent on muttering a complaint to Valerie before they bumped into me.

Gladys was brave enough to talk to me now.

"Hello, baby, how are you today?"

It's an odd, though lovely feeling to be called 'baby' by another woman when you are in your fifties.

"I like your top," I said, for something to say and because it was apparent that the blouse was new.

"Thanks, sweetie, I not know you smoke."

"I used to, but I gave it up," I said, taking a puff of the cigarette and brooding upon the subject of Janine. She cast me a quizzical look which twisted her mouth into greater peculiarity.

"My friend Bingo say you swim in the pool."

Gladys clearly wanted to talk. Valerie frowned at her because there was much work to be done, disappearing through the kitchen doors to get on with it herself with an air of resignation to the tasks ahead.

"Yes. It's a lovely pool, and very quiet when the schoolchildren aren't using it."

She pressed her lips into a crooked button grin.

"I swim. Yes, ma'am, I swim. Sister Elsie taught me when I little, years back. Threw me into the sea at Lemon Valley, then jump in with me, hold me under my belly; that how she taught me after I almost drown first..."

Valerie stuck her head out of the kitchen door and called after her then, and she went off, muttering to herself, "Yes, ma'am, I swim, I can swim," and she tripped over one of the scabby, dusty cats that were half feral, juggling the tray before her with the skill of a circus acrobat. She swore at the cat, none too quietly.

I sat at one of the little white tables to finish my cigarette. Woebegone at the Napoleon, I mused, hearing Mark's loud, exuberant laughter in the distance.

Then I noticed a young man seated upon the steps nearby. I had noticed him before. He must have been in his very early twenties; he was heavily built; hench, they call it nowadays. He was the young man who did all the heavy lifting, and he very much reminded me of our son, Henry, who was a similar age and build.

SEE YOU AGAIN, ONE TIME IN SAINT HELENA

The young man was good-looking, had a kind face and, quite often, a rather careworn expression. Now he nodded a greeting at me. "Morning, ma'am."

In a place where everyone was curious about 'new' people, understandable when you know everyone and desperately need other company, this young man had never spoken to me before.

I said hello with a smile I didn't genuinely feel, but I liked this young man with the small troubled frown that seemed a permanent fixture upon his face.

Brooding over Mark's behaviour had made me disregard other people's difficulties, some considerably greater than my own.

"You been stayin' here, ma'am?"

"Yes, it's a lovely hotel. I'm very lucky. My husband is working at the court but I'm just here on a holiday." This had become a standard introduction now.

"You like it here?"

"Oh yes, it's beautiful."

He grunted good-humouredly. "I like to see the UK," he said.

"Perhaps you will, one day... What's your name?"

"Nemuel; people call me Nem. I never even been to Ascension. Carrie, my partner, she think we get beaten up if we go to UK." He gave a grim chuckle.

My mouth fell open in horror. "Why? Why would she think that?"

Nemuel stubbed his cigarette out on one of the stone steps, picking it up to flick it into some nearby bushes, then got up and came over to me, holding out his dark brown, muscular bare arm to let it lie beside the paler skin of my arm.

"You white, I black; you a better colour than me," he said.

The comment took my breath away, until I realised he didn't mean this literally; it wasn't what he believed, but what he thought other people might believe.

"They attacks right now, in Johannesburg, don't they?"

"Ah…" I understood. "Yes, maybe that's true. But such things aren't allowed in England, Nemuel." I stared directly at him, imploring him to believe me, wondering momentarily whether it was a method used by mothers here, on occasion, to ensure they didn't lose their children and grandchildren forever. But there had been xenophobic attacks against Zimbabweans in South Africa, so he had a right to be afraid, and this was a far more likely reason.

"There are racist people still, yes of course there are, but you can't beat someone up in the UK for their colour, or for any other reason… not without being arrested! Most of our younger son's friends are black. They don't walk around thinking they are going to get beaten up, not nowadays… although admittedly they might have, once upon a time."

They just worry about being deported to impossible situations in impossible countries, I thought. Maybe they do worry about these things – truthfully, what do I know?

He seemed a little more convinced. "But it expensive to get to UK…"

"Yes, that's true. But perhaps after the airport has been up and running for a while, the price of travel will come down, hopefully."

"Think I maybe afford fo' Carrie and our baby go too?" He smiled.

"It's possible... You just have to save for a while."

Knowing how much the average person was paid there, it would probably take a long while, and there were few benefits or handouts as there were in the UK, which seemed very wrong, as the people of Saint Helena were UK citizens.

I bid Nemuel goodbye, wandering back to where Mark had been sitting, but only Helen was left of the party, a laptop before her. As I approached, she looked up with a friendly but almost concerned smile.

"Mark says he won't be long, he's just gone to the court with Janine to show her where her files can be stored."

I nodded. But my own smile was a bit flat.

"Are you alright?" she asked, for the second time that day.

"Fine, just getting over a bit of a headache," I said, longing to talk woman to woman. But I couldn't, so I squeezed her shoulder and left her in peace to get on with her work.

I decided to walk down to the sea to rid myself of tension. As I walked, I imagined the sailors and soldiers of long ago, unloading cargo, spending their earnings in the public houses; ghosts, striding toward me along the main street.

The sea at the foot of the hill was calm and smooth, sapphire blue and shining. Loud pop music resounded from the bar where I had danced the evening before, waking me from imaginings about an ancient Saint Helena.

There were figures in the distance, bent over the iron rails that ran the length of the harbour, painting them with a fresh coat of white paint. As I drew closer, I saw half a dozen youngsters set to the task, intent on their work but chatting to one another.

Then I saw him, my saxophone-playing headteacher.

An overwhelming urge to turn and run away. I was behaving like a teenager. Too old for such stuff. Anyway, too late, because he turned away from a lad he was talking to and saw me. His face broke into a smile. "Hey," he greeted me. "Hello. It's the dancer!"

I think I blushed a bit, but kept my stride and walked towards him.

"Ned Sheldon, nice to see you again." He stuck out a hand, the brown fingers smeared with white paint. "It's okay, it's dried paint, from yesterday," he assured me.

"Stephanie." I smiled, shaking his hand. "What's going on here?" It was a bit of a stupid question, but I couldn't think of anything else to say.

"These guys have kindly volunteered, with a bit of bribery, to repaint the harbour rails. In preparation for lots of things: the Remembrance Day service next weekend; the possibility of a royal visitor arriving to open the airport."

"Are they from your school?" I asked it without thinking. He would know now that someone had told me about him, might even think I was interested in him. I felt a wave of gratitude when he skipped over the question.

"Oh yes, six of the best and all musicians. They're a great bunch." He turned to them thoughtfully, stroking the short, grey beard. "Matter of fact, we've been up and at it since seven this morning, so I was just about to take a break. Fancy a coffee and a sandwich?"

The question kind of took me by surprise, but I had nothing urgent to do. Had he been an old gent I would have said yes, so why not say yes to a younger gent?

"How long are you here for?" he asked as we walked towards the coffee shop.

"Just a couple of weeks, although there's a lot of stuff for Mark to fit in during his time here," I added.

"He's your husband, right? The lawyer."

"Yes..."

"He appears to be quite popular, although I think he will have made a few enemies too. He's not slow with criticism, is he?" He grinned.

I smiled. "No. That much is true. I'm sure some of those criticisms are justified, though."

"Well, as someone who has his own enemies here, I sympathise. It's not easy to change things."

We had arrived at the little cabin where two ladies made sandwiches to order. He insisted upon paying for me, so, rather fancying the crab sandwich, I had cheese and tomato instead, which was a pound cheaper. I listened as he chatted with the two women as they were busy in the kitchen. From the conversation, he had taught the young girl, and the older woman had a son at his school.

There were quite a few customers seated at the wooden tables on the headland. We found a wooden table to ourselves and sat opposite one another.

I asked him about his school and started to feel relaxed at last; I was a teacher and so was he; the conversation came more naturally than it did with the lawyers, after all. It was only when my mind turned to his eyes, thinking them the hazel of a willow tree flecked with moss, that I had to shake myself out of a ridiculous kind of flirtation. Why was I here? Because I wanted to be? Or was it incidental or contrived to annoy Mark in some way, to make him notice me?

And yet I liked Ned, and I was curious about him; he didn't make me feel less clever, less important.

He asked me about my family, so I told him about the children and what was happening to my mother. Ned chewed his thumbnail, gazing at me.

"That's how I lost Carrie, Caroline, my wife, although she was in her late forties. She had pancreatic cancer; she died ten years ago." He realised what he had said, putting his hand quickly over mine. "I'm sure your mother will be fine; with Carrie, they didn't diagnose it early enough."

I nodded, leaving my hand beneath his. "I'm sorry," I said. "Did… do you have children?"

"Two grown-up daughters, both doing their own thing. Joanne is married, has a little girl. They live in Wantage, which is where I used to live. And Anna is an actress, lives in America. She's been in a couple of good films recently, and a TV sitcom." He smiled. "They come here to visit me once a year, and I alternate visits to the States or the UK to visit them at Christmas or in the Easter holiday…"

A sudden shout from the pool entrance made us both turn our heads. Two lads were running across the road, or rather a larger boy, laughing, shouting at a smaller, skinnier lad, then catching up with him, was beating him about the head with bare fists. Teachers find it hard to turn a blind eye. Ned rose from the table and strode across to them whilst I watched.

He called out to the small one, who wheeled around at the sound of his name, and I recognised David, Rachel's boy, who I had childminded with his sister. I watched as Ned stood before him, talking to him, perhaps checking that he was alright. I saw David shrug his small shoulders, and thought of David and Goliath. Ned patted his shoulder and the boy walked away, his shoulders back, maintaining his cool after the attack. Then Ned turned to the other boy and spoke to him, whilst he scowled back, angry, defensive.

When he returned to me, Ned smiled and shook his head.

"Everything alright?" I asked.

"The Jessop boy is a bit of a troublemaker, had to have his parents in to talk to them before. Trouble is that Alan Jessop, the boy's dad, is a bit of a bully himself. Thinks his son can do no wrong; a chip off the old block, in fact." He sat down to finish his coffee.

"I know David. He's Rachel's son, isn't he?"

Ned nodded. "That's right."

"Poor kid told me he'd lost his dad in a boating accident," I remarked.

"Yes. Terrible for them all." He shook his head, frowning. "Instinct is to blame that incident on Ryan Jessop, but..." he hesitated.

"But what?" I asked, feeling that David was the certain victim.

"But Alan sold the boat to David's father, and intuition tells me that David is blaming Jessop for his father's death. I've observed the two boys together and I think David might be saying underhand things to Ryan, asking for it, if you like."

"I've heard the name Jessop on several occasions," I said.

"He's the landlord of The Jolly Sailor. The kind of person people either like or hate, there's little in the middle. A bit of a bully, but respected, and with some influential friends within the police force and the fishing community. Old Saint family, fought in the Falklands

War. He's a fireman in his spare time and a diver, too, so he has friends all over the place. He's not the kind of person you mess with."

"Have you ever messed with him?" I asked.

"On occasion, oh yes." Ned smiled. "You can't run a school without a bit of mess."

Chapter 20
Diary Fifteen

I missed Ned's company when he left. He had to return to supervising the young people, of course. I wandered back to the hotel, passing the court whilst wondering about Mark and Janine. I decided to return to my writing, my murder mystery set in Saint Helena, and became engrossed in the story for the rest of the day, sitting at the dressing table as Mark had left his court papers all over the desk and I was afraid of disturbing them. Occasionally I would yawn and stretch and think of Ned, then feel half guilty; after all, I should have been thinking of Mark. But thinking about Mark and Janine and earrings upset the mood. This was all luxury compared with teaching or caring for a busy family, and I found myself enjoying the solitude. I found myself engaged in my creation until, in the wide street, the light began to fade and the shops closed.

I rose from my chair and scanned the street beyond the window for Mark or any company. A small, graceful figure was making her way down the sloping pavement opposite the hotel, a slight ripple in the muscles of her thighs beneath the shorts as her legs took the weight of the day. It was Thadie. She looked up, saw me and waved.

"Wait!" I called out to her through the open window, then grabbed my bag and my keys and raced for the bedroom door.

At the front entrance, I descended the stone steps to meet with her as she started out towards me.

"Hey, how are you?" I greeted her.

"Good thanks, hot and thirsty, but we're making progress with the protected breeding ground."

"So the turtles will be happy…" I said, for want of anything more knowledgeable to say.

"Yes, much happier." She smiled.

I hesitated. "Would you care for a drink?"

"Love one." She checked her pockets. "But I don't have any cash on me…"

"No worries, I do. Shall I follow you back to The Jolly Sailor?"

We chatted as we strolled along the street between parked cars, Thadie talking about the green turtles attempting to nest at Sandy Bay, where a large part of the beach had been closed to the public. She told me about the female turtles who swim an incredible one thousand, two hundred and thirty-nine nautical miles from Brazil, just to lay their eggs on the Saint Helena beach. It was good to hear her enthusiasm. Here, at least, there was no need for secrecy.

The Jolly Sailor looked nice enough. A couple sitting outside, above the panorama of the sea, greeted us with a nod. The interior, as I followed Thadie inside, was a film set depicting an '80s bar. Beyond it, it was clear that the inn was much older than that.

Six men and one woman sat at a curved bar of polished wood. Behind the bar, the short, rather paunchy landlord smiled broadly and nodded in Thadie's direction as he poured beer from the tap.

"Evenin', missy," he greeted. "Care for a drink before dinner?" This, then, was Alan Jessop, whom Ned had called a bully.

When he had handed over the change for the two green beers, he scrutinised me, one eye closed as if in thought. "You been in The Standard," he said. I took it as a statement rather than an accusation, or perhaps he was offended because I'd visited that particular pub first. I didn't ask how he knew that, just took it that nothing, no matter how trivial, was missed in Saint Helena.

"I have."

"You related to Justine, right?"

"I am," I answered, keeping conversation short but sweet.

"You like her? She a dragon lady."

I raised my eyebrows slightly. I have to say, I'd never thought of Justine as a dragon lady; perhaps Alan Jessop had fallen foul of her. Thadie smiled politely and turned away from him.

We carried our green beers through to the quieter back room.

"So, tell me about your family," Thadie asked as we sat down. "Do you have children?"

"Two, though my figure would suggest I'd had more." I smiled, patting my stomach.

"Nonsense!" She laughed.

"Ginnie is thirty, she was my wild child, but she's married to an optician now, with two children, so I think her wild days are done. Henry has only just left school. He can be a bit on the wild side, too. Stole a motorbike a couple of years ago and drove it to Oxford with a friend riding pillion. The police were rather nice actually; he returned it, you see."

I pursed my lips in thought. "Only, recently, he's had a few battles with Mark, who wants him to go to university; we both want that, but Henry's not interested. He wants to be a rapper. Actually, his music is good," I added, with pride. "My aunt says they'll all be alright by the time they're forty. I bloody well hope so!"

She laughed, an infectious sound.

I regarded her. "But what about you? Boyfriend, husband?"

"I'm married to my cause." She smiled.

"Which is presently the turtles?"

"Amongst other things, yes."

"Parents? Brothers and sisters?"

She nodded. "The best parents. I was fostered when I was a baby, then adopted by them. They gave me a lot of love and support in life and treated me just the same way as they treated their own children. No complaints there. I think they were the ones who encouraged me into marine biology. He was a teacher, fascinated by all living things, especially the animal world."

I wanted to ask Thadie if she knew anything about her birth parents, but I didn't. It might have been a little intrusive and, although friendly, she seemed the kind of person who liked her personal space.

"What's the landlord like?" I asked at length.

"Alan? Seems alright, no complaints about the place. My room is comfortable, his wife is a good cook. Some of his comments are a bit sexist…"

"Such as?" I asked.

"That women don't make good divers." She shrugged. "I told him that was nonsense; women tend to have a better sense of orientation, they are calmer, less likely to look for danger or excitement. I told him that the navy now has female mine-clearance divers – that shut him up!"

Suddenly, her mouth fell open. Excitedly, she grabbed my arm. "I've had a fantastic idea!"

I stared back at her in some trepidation. *Please God, don't ask me to go diving with you*, I thought. The idea of diving consumed me with terror.

But, "How would you like to come with me to see the turtles hatching from their eggs?" she asked. "The only thing is that it'll be very early; you'd have to meet me in the town car park at four thirty in the morning."

"What, tomorrow you mean?"

I liked the idea, though the four thirty came as a shock. Thadie was being very generous; when else would I get to witness something as remarkable as that?

"I'd love to," I said in an instant, "if I'm not going to get in the way, of course. Do I need anything? A torch, for example?"

She shook her small head. "No, just a warm sweater. An ordinary torch will disturb the turtles; I'll lend you an infrared. Other than that, you just have to be quiet and still."

She smiled, and I began to feel excited about it.

I took another swig of beer. "Do they lay many eggs?" I asked her.

"They can lay up to one hundred and twenty in the nesting season... not all at once." She giggled.

"Are there a lot of predators, then?"

She nodded. "Tiger sharks, killer whales, fish; then there are the nasty frigate birds who hover above the babies as they struggle towards the sea."

"Talking turtles again?" I looked behind me; the landlord had entered the bar.

"Certainly. Care to join in, Alan?" Her voice was pleasant as always, but I discerned a crispness to its tone.

"No thanks. There's an Aston Villa game on; just about to turn on the TV for my regulars. Would you care for another drink, ladies, before I do?"

We shook our heads. "Stoopid creatures, mamma turtles, swimmin' thousands of miles to protect their young. S'pose they can't understand that they could lay their eggs in their own back yard..." He picked up our empty bottles with a slight clink of glass.

Thadie's smile was sweet as it was wide. "Maybe it's to escape the daddies," she said softly.

Alan's olive cheeks coloured up then, his own head disappearing into his neck, much like a turtle. I knew little about either of them, but it occurred to me that Thadie could also be a dragon woman.

The sky was still blue black when the alarm on my phone rang in my ear. Mark grumbled through his sleep then went back to snoring. Edging myself as silently as possible from the bed, I pulled on a pair of jeans and a sweater over the underwear I had worn through the night. I grabbed a handful of biscuits left in a dish by the cleaning ladies, crossing the creaking, carpeted floor and carrying my sneakers.

The tall houses of the Jamestown street were masked in purple shadow. A rather beaten-up Land Rover had parked on the double yellow lines opposite the hotel. As I appeared in the street, Thadie stepped out from it.

"I wondered how we would get there," I whispered, clambering into the passenger's seat.

"It was dropped off to me last night, for my own use. Nice, isn't it? Apart from the smell of tobacco and the chewing gum still stuck to the dashboard." She grinned.

I clicked on my seatbelt, offering her a biscuit or two, and she started the engine.

"You can still see the stars," I remarked.

"Yes, but not for long, not when the airport is finished. So enjoy it whilst you can."

A small puff of environmentally unfriendly, blackish smoke emitted from the exhaust and the Land Rover chugged its way up the hill and out of the town. The engine groaned like an ancient, overworked animal, but it didn't appear to bother Thadie.

At the top of the rise, a fisherman making his way down to the wharf threw up his hand to us in the usual friendly greeting of the Saints. Once out of the town the spikes of flax at the edge of the road and in the fields beyond seemed as dense and dark as hemlock. Through the open window, I heard the lonely cry of a solitary seagull.

Thadie drove with a rash surety that nothing would be an obstacle to the journey, once slamming on the brakes as a young goat trotted across the road. I gasped, then spluttered, silently holding my breath as I prayed for a safe journey. I did my best to concentrate on the landscape as moment by moment the stars faded and the dark sky turned mink-grey.

We passed several little houses and hamlets until we arrived at a dusty, rocky track at the top of a craggy ridge. Thadie ground to a halt and yanked on the brakes whilst I stared down at the bay below us, relieved that she wasn't about to attempt the ride to the beach below as the road looked steep and dangerous.

I placed my hand across my heart, muttering, "Oh, thank God for that!"

"What? I'm quite a good driver, I'll have you know." She grinned at me.

"Thank God you're not going to drive down to the beach, I meant," I explained.

"I would, but we'd disturb the mamma turtles." She reached into the small haversack resting at my feet for a headband, attached to which was a contraption like a miner's torch. "You turn it on like so," she demonstrated. "Now you'll be able to watch the little ones hatching without disturbing them."

We left the vehicle unlocked. Thadie lifted the binoculars from her neck. "We'll have to share these," she said, her voice dipping to a half whisper.

I was glad of my sweater as we walked together down the track. The wool was a barrier against the wind rising from the waves below.

On either side of us, the harsh black rocks cradled the beach, majestic but intimidating. The sea was a strip of pewter-grey, the golden ribbon of the rising sun reflected upon its surface. I could see nothing of the turtles yet, but when our feet met with sand Thadie touched my arm, beckoning to me to stoop down beside her so that we both lay across a low, smooth boulder.

From this distance, the journey of the patient turtles was clear to see, the sand pitted with tracks where the scaly, webbed claws had dug at the hot, dry sand. For the first time I saw one of them as a halo of dust flew into the air. Lumbering, cumbersome, but even more impressive to hear than it was to see. The gentle, resolute sigh as a mother paused to rest amidst the others, so much more dignified than the sounds I had made in giving birth! A gentle sigh, every now and then, heard above the rushing of waves on the shore. She would lift her bulk from the sand and stagger forward once more, having buried her clutch of eggs in the pit she had dug.

As the sky became paler in colour and the first morning colours arrived, Thadie whispered, "Can you see the hatchlings?"

My eyes strained behind the binoculars. I shook my head. "Not yet," I said. She handed me the night-vision binoculars.

"Try these. Come then, we'll go closer. Watch where you put your feet."

So, we picked our way carefully over the beach until we reached the nesting mounds. I stifled a cry of excitement and surprise, covering my mouth with a hand. There must have been hundreds of them, tiny black turtles, no larger than a small crab, that you could hold in the palm of your hand, drawn towards the smell of the surf in the first moments of their adventure on the planet. Sometimes they followed in the powerful tracks made by their mothers.

We stepped carefully around them, following their tiny trails, until Thadie pointed skyward. Three enormous black birds with broad, streamlined wings were hovering above us, watching the progress of the tiny turtles.

"Frigate birds!" Thadie groaned in disgust.

As we watched, one of them swooped suddenly, close by us, landing upon one of the hatchlings and lifting it deftly in its beak. With sudden, ferocious energy, Thadie tore away from my side, leaping at the bird so that her small head was dancing below the dangling feet. Her sudden attack surprised the bird, and it dropped the small turtle, whilst Thadie hovered below like a rounders player trying to catch a ball.

Catch it she did, whilst I laughed and clapped in applause. The tiny turtle lay cradled in her hands, a little surprised but none the worse for wear, and we strolled to the sea together, saving it the journey, and watched it floating, bobbing on the first waves that lapped the shore as it acclimatised to the waves in some surprise.

As we drove back towards the town, my body and mind felt clean again. I had seen something wonderful and had enjoyed being with Thadie, feeling some of her passion for the natural world. I also had a healthy, energising hunger for breakfast.

It was as we reached the isolated spot of roadside curving to Frenchman's Leap that Thadie asked, "What the hell is that?"

I looked at her, then through the far right of the window through which she was staring. A patch of sky had changed colour. The early morning bright blues and golds were misted and dirty smoke smudged as waves of heat rippled the air. Through her open window, the smoke reached our nostrils.

"No one would have a bonfire there, not at this time of the day. It's the Boer museum, Sussex House..." She left off.

I grabbed the torn material of the seat with my nails as she fearlessly swerved the vehicle off the road, ploughing through the flax and bushes either side of a tiny path unfit for vehicles. Stupidly I thought of a photograph in the town museum, of General Piet Cronje, the leader of the Boers, surrounded by a raggle-taggle group of his men, imprisoned here. Then I thought, *We are going to die.*

I wanted to put my hands in front of my face as we bounced dangerously out of our seats and the oncoming branches threatened to smash the windows, scraping the glass and the sides of the Land Rover in complaint.

At last we broke through, arriving at a well-preserved cottage with carefully tended lawns. Instantly we saw the low annexed roof at the side of it ablaze. The heat swell, fierce and intense, orange flames licking at the slate roof, shimmering the air.

I put my hand inside my pocket to call Mark, the fire brigade, anyone, before realising that mobile phones didn't work in Saint Helena.

"We'll never put that out on our own, but I know where the fire station is," Thadie muttered.

I nodded, bracing myself again for another bumpy ride. To my relief, she followed the track running past the house this time, joining the main road and racing down the quiet hill. At the bridge, a figure turned at the sound of our coming, flattening himself against a cottage wall. Seeing us, he raised a hand and waved. I waved back.

I recognised him but couldn't think from where.

"Sanele," Thadie murmured. "Probably going for an early morning walk. He's staying at The Jolly Sailor. Quite early for him…"

Chapter 21
Diary Sixteen

Mark had breakfasted and disappeared to the courts; so had Helen and the others. So, in a most unladylike way, scoffing large mouthfuls of egg, bacon and toast, I told Gladys about the fire, about Thadie and I speeding to the fire station to raise the alarm. She didn't appear to be mortified by the destruction of the Boer museum; her usual, slightly lopsided expression remained the same.

"Ma near burned down our house when I was a babby," she said. "Used to hang our nappies in the pantry to dry, but her went into it one night with a lighted candle…"

"Gladys!" Emma called, somewhat snappily from the dining room door, and Gladys jumped to it, scuttling out of the room with breakfast plates, muttering to herself in the way she had. "Yes, ma'am. Nappies catched fire…"

I smiled at her, feeling guilty. Gladys loved to talk and I liked her a lot, but I shouldn't have been talking to her, getting her into trouble.

I wandered out of the room. I should have been tired after the early start and eventful morning, but I wasn't. Today we were going to visit Longwood, so long as no one had tried to burn it down. What was I saying? Of course it must have been an accident, but I had to agree with Thadie, it was all a little strange.

Longwood is a pleasant estate with small bungalows and gardens; this was obviously not the case during Napoleon's time. I don't think they had bungalows then, or primary schools, or cafés, so it was probably an open vista.

Many of the local families own a goat, and the shaggy goats bleat at the children who ride their bikes in and out of the trees on this sunny Sunday morning.

Longwood House is a modest building by country house standards, certainly rather humble for an emperor.

Mark drove us to Longwood in Tessa's car, with Jack's bulky figure in the front passenger seat. Helen sat between Janine and I in the back, as though some female intuition told her we might be quarrelling children, that a diplomatic incident could occur at any given time. Perhaps she was right. I tried hard to be polite, even friendly, towards Janine, but I resented her all the same.

It was hot. We sweated in the rear of the car. Jack brought up the subject of the fire. "Dreadful thing to happen; the museum relies on charity. It will cost hundreds of thousands to repair the damage; some of those artefacts can never be replaced... Angus was crying this morning. Never seen him cry. It was awful."

"Who is Angus?" I asked.

"The curator. The Boer museum is his life's work. Not like he's a young man. Now he has to start over again to find funding."

"Was it an accident, or arson?" Helen's criminal experience kicked in.

"Can't see how an accident like that could have occurred. Guess the police will investigate it."

When we got out, Mark took the fingers of my hand and squeezed them again.

I wanted it to be fun, and it would have been had Janine not been there.

Little Grace was the tour guide. She met us at the open front gate of the house.

'Little Grace' because she was height-impaired, only as tall, in fact, as our nine-year-old granddaughter. But she compensated for this with supreme and unique authority, and although she was very welcoming she had a rehearsed routine and didn't take kindly to any interruption, although in fairness she made it clear that she would welcome questions at the end of the tour. Little Grace was the name that some of the islanders had given her, with affection rather than anything else, and they had each made it clear that she was a supreme authority upon the subject of Napoleon Bonaparte.

We followed her along the garden path, past the sign which read 'Maison de Napoleon' and between the flower beds, which Grace said were put down in Napoleon's day.

There were small buff brown rabbits bounding uninhibitedly and fearlessly through the foliage. Little Grace assured us that they were a pest and that she had often thought about getting "one for the pot".

Longwood had a red roof and white exterior walls, the French flag hanging rather limply in the heat outside the front entrance.

I'm not sure at what point my irritability began. Our visit would have been more enjoyable if it hadn't been for my self-imposed task of guarding him from Janine. Mark gestured for the women to walk ahead of him, which is how it should be, except that my neurosis insisted that Mark's eyes would be upon Janine's curvaceous bum, and so I dropped behind at every opportunity, simply to thwart his plan.

He stared at me, as well he might, looking more fearful and suspicious than I had ever seen him look before, as I appeared to dodge from spot to spot like a child running from its shadow. Only, I suppose I didn't think it odd at the time; only afterwards did I realise how crazily I had behaved.

Inside the green-walled billiard room, which Little Grace assured us had never been used by Napoleon for billiards but was where he had stored his vast collection of maps, Janine stared at me in a way I shouldn't be encouraging, clearly thinking I was deranged. I could hear my daughter's voice from thousands of miles away, stating: "That's not very cool, is it, Mum?"

In the end I had to desist from the idiocy of trying to observe them together. I couldn't help wondering whether Janine was the owner of the earring. It was apparent from the brief conversations between them that they had worked often together, knew each other very well. And yet, I had never heard anything about her before this trip to the island.

By the time we had reached the red-walled drawing room, I was breathing steadily once more. Gradually, Mark relaxed too, clearly relieved.

So, I half listened to our tour guide whilst admiring the busts of Napoleon and that notorious slapper, Josephine.

It was then that Janine sidled up to me, saying in a whisper so that she wouldn't upset the tour guide, "I'm not very keen on Napoleon, but I rather admire her."

She was probably trying to be polite, as Mark had mentioned my degree in history. In truth, she could not have said anything more likely to annoy me, unless perhaps, *"Do you mind awfully if I go to bed with your husband?"*

"Who?" I asked her, my voice as sharp as a hussar's rapier. "Josephine? The woman who became the second wife of her brother-in-law and cheated on Napoleon at every possible opportunity?"

There was a sudden, even greater chill in the very chilly room. My voice was a tad too loud.

Little Grace was left speechless at my lack of respect, her flow having been interrupted, and she stared at me open-mouthed. A tiny dent appeared in Janine's dimple.

"Ah, but she came from a very poor background," Janine said, levelling her brown eyes with the perfectly plucked eyebrows at me, before strolling, elegant and composed in a way I was not, through to Napoleon's chandeliered bed chamber.

"So, like Becky Sharp, then?" I muttered to myself, catching Helen's expression of discomfort.

Mark had turned away from all of this by now, no doubt embarrassed. But then I stopped feeling sorry for him, as the shameless hussy – Janine, not Josephine – placed her arm through his and he half turned to me, red-cheeked as a guilty schoolboy, and making no attempt to extract himself until we reached the famous bathroom where Napoleon wrote his diaries on a table across his bath.

My comment about the empress appeared to have brought out the temptress in Janine. I should have bitten my tongue, I suppose.

As we stared down at the bath with the large writing plank balanced upon it, whilst listening to Grace's spiel about this being Napoleon's favourite place, the place where he ate and read and recorded his memoirs whilst having a darned good soak, Mark moved away from Janine and hastened to my side once more, and I wondered for a moment whether my moral support was necessary in the flirting process, or whether he was seeking my permission for something else.

We drove back to Jamestown to have lunch before our boat trip, eating sandwiches at the little coffee shop overlooking the calm blue sea. I felt in need of a bit of calm blue sea by this time, feeling grateful that none of the others had made reference to my behaviour. I listened to their conversation and was polite but cool towards Janine.

"What do you make of Amelia?" Helen asked Jack.

I wasn't sure who Amelia was, until I remembered someone referring to her as a lawyer tipped to be the next governor.

"She scares the pants off me," Jack winced. "You know, she whips off her skirt to change into her court clothes without the least inhibition? Right in front of you, for God's sake, just like a Tom Sharpe character... so you can actually see her suspenders. The woman has no restraint... and that booming voice of hers? She terrifies the younger lawyers; she terrifies me," he admitted.

"Does everyone have their swimming things for the boat?" Mark asked. Everyone had, except for me, the one with the least to think about, the one who wasn't a lawyer.

"I've got mine," Janine said.

Yes, she struck me as being highly organised in every way. She had probably unpacked by now. She was probably wearing the skimpy thing beneath her clothes.

"Don't look now, but the Giles couple have just passed us; they're sitting at the table nearest to the coffee shop," Jack said. "They make a very handsome couple, don't they?"

I tilted my head slightly, but had no idea, again, who Jack meant by "the Giles couple", until a handsome, middle-aged man reached a hand lovingly across the table to his partner, a man about ten years younger.

Of course; the same-sex couple who wanted to adopt Cara's other little girl.

Mark had acted for gay couples before, in cases of adoption. But this time I knew he felt very strongly that the children should remain together, if at all possible, and be adopted by a native of Saint Helena, gay or otherwise.

"Are you going to get your costume, then?" Mark asked me, a little over brightly, anxious not to be late for the boat.

I nodded. "Yes, I'd better. I won't be many minutes."

I rose from the table, walking away from them after a smile from Helen, then quickening my pace past the Castle Gardens with the ornate fountain, past the massive trees with the knotted trunks, running along the street when I thought I was safely out of sight.

I thought about Janine, posing on the side of the boat in a sexy bikini whilst I covered up my birth surplus with an all-in-one. Janine was a career woman; she didn't have children, so she wouldn't have stretch marks. I spat inside my head.

SEE YOU AGAIN, ONE TIME IN SAINT HELENA

Through the open door of the library I could see a group of pre-school children intent upon a story the librarian was reading to them. They were incredibly well behaved, sitting very still with their legs crossed as though magicked; not one of them was picking their nose.

The hotel courtyard was buzzing with noisy conversation as I mounted the staircase to our room. The door was propped open. All the surrounding doors were propped open. A radio stood upon the top staircase, the Saints' radio, which was mostly country and western music interrupted by local recipes.

None of the cleaning ladies appeared to be in any of the rooms. Gone to collect fresh laundry and cups, I thought, whilst pausing on the landing to stare into a large front room filled with sunlight.

It was hers. It was Janine's room. Her cases stood at the foot of the double bed.

I recognised the floppy sun hat on the chaise longue. My mischievous heart palpitated as I spotted a jewellery box on the dressing table, and I raced across the room towards it on tiptoe, blind to the risk I was taking and with one thought only inside my head.

The box was a small, chest-shaped thing, covered in material. I took a look over my shoulder into the corridor. I felt my heart might explode, it was beating so fast as I lifted the lid and stirred the assortment of necklaces and bracelets and earrings with my forefinger.

Within a few seconds, I saw it caught upon a brooch. The matching earring!

Triumph and indignation soared through my body with the pain and pleasure of a sneeze. And still I couldn't quite believe it was there, couldn't quite believe, or didn't want to believe. Not sure which. I thought, Maybe there's another in the box; perhaps it is only a similar item of jewellery. But my fingers didn't find the other earring, didn't find it because I had it all along, wrapped in a tissue in my washbag. Janine was guilty as charged. Bitch.

The probability of a different woman with the same distinctive earring was highly improbable. Yes, it was.

As I held it to the light, troubled yet triumphant in the same breath, a muffled noise behind me caused my heart to leap out of my mouth, and suddenly I was rigid with embarrassment and shame, a child caught out. But it wasn't Janine who stood there with a smile dancing in her eyes but a mouth pursed like a button.

It was Tessa, leaning on the door jamb, one hand upon her hip.

"I think you have the wrong room," she said with a frown.

I clenched the earring tightly in my fist.

"Oh God, I know what this must look like... You must think I'm a petty burglar," I spluttered, shaking my head. Then I said nothing for a moment and chewed my lip.

"I came looking for Janine before she goes on the boat," Tessa said, but now her lips were twisted in curiosity whilst the frown had deepened. "This is her room, right? Has she asked you to fetch something for her?"

My shoulders and chest collapsed then, because I was going to have to tell her what I was doing there. I would have to confide in her, otherwise Tessa would believe that I was just a thief, or a total lunatic. I was a lunatic.

"Come with me, I can explain," I said meekly. Protest was pointless.

She followed me, watching me as I walked towards our room.

They would all be waiting for me. Well, Mark would have to be annoyed; they would simply have to wait, or I would have to miss the boat trip, one or the other. This was his fault, anyway, I told myself.

This was a conversation I couldn't escape if I wanted to salvage a morsel of Tessa's friendship and respect, and I did.

We sat upon the bed and she regarded me with her small head upon one side, in a friendly and half amused way. Through the open window above the Jamestown street, a gospel band, collecting money for their church, sang soulfully, 'One Day at a Time, Sweet Jesus', to the accompaniment of a Jew's harp.

I think I hoped that she had never formed the opinion up until that point that I was a kleptomaniac. I knew that she had a full and interesting life behind her; perhaps more peculiar things had occurred in it than this.

So, I told her about the unhappiness caused by finding the earring and where it had been found, hooked into Mark's shirt. I told her something of Mark's recent behaviour, too. I tried to be subtle, not telling her that the thought had occurred to me that he wanted me well and truly out of the way, that he might have liked it had I toppled from Table Mountain. Then I fetched the washbag, pulling out the other of the pair to dangle before her.

Her dark eyebrows dipped in a concerned frown before she reached out and laid her fingers across mine.

"So, you were looking to see whether the other in the pair was on Janine's dressing table?"

I nodded, holding both the earrings in the palm of my hand.

"And it was. The only one there. I looked very carefully. Women keep things like that, don't they? In case the other turns up."

She nodded slowly, thrusting her lips forward in thought.

"I found it in the laundry basket when he came home from London. It had got caught in his collar. Why would that have happened?" I was aware that my voice was limp with a kind of emotional fatigue. Maybe it was just the heat getting to me, or the guilt.

"It doesn't necessarily mean they are having an affair," she said. But she didn't sound very convinced. "They might have been dancing together at some legal function."

"How did it get caught on his collar? They must have been pretty close, surely? She must have had her head resting upon his shoulder, anyway." I stared at her in exasperation and sadness. "Mark doesn't like dancing. He used to, but he never does now," I finished dully.

And just as I stopped speaking, Mark appeared at the door. Presumably he was about to give me a small lecture on my time-keeping, before he saw that Tessa was with me.

"Hello, Mark," Tessa trilled. "My fault, I'm afraid. I came to ask whether you would like to come over for dinner again, and we got chatting."

I felt such relief that I could have hugged her.

"You'd better go." She smiled at me, then said in a conspiratorial whisper, "I think you must come over for a pyjama party... We'll talk some more."

I looked up then, noting Mark's perplexed expression. Presumably he was wondering why her invitation hadn't come through him, as she had spent long hours with Mark in the courthouse.

We rose from the bed and I planted a peck of a kiss upon her cheek in gratitude, then left her talking to Mark whilst I escaped to forage about in my case for my costume.

In an instant, the leaden feeling inside of me had lifted.

Tessa believed me, and I didn't think she thought me a kleptomaniac anymore. I had an ally.

"Well," Mark muttered a little irritably from the door, "are you coming? The boat won't wait forever."

Chapter 22
Diary Seventeen

I hadn't realised that so many people were going on the boat trip, which was a rescue boat from the Moray Firth in a previous life.

There were three crew with Declan, who was the captain and owner of the boat. Declan is a remarkable chap. It was the first time I had met him, but the others all knew him because he was married to Isla, one of the magistrates.

Declan, it seems, does a bit of everything. He takes people diving, he is a fisherman and, on top of this, a part-time policeman and fireman too.

Declan is large and a bit of an action man. The kind of person who dives into the icy sea to release a ship's moorings rather than going out in a dinghy. The kind of person who, on one memorable occasion, ran helter-skelter from the police station to wrestle down a man who was going through a particularly horrible time in his life and was threatening to shoot everyone in the courthouse, including Tessa and Isla.

Declan is the kind of man you need on your side in a crisis. Not only is he the friend of authority but the friend of past criminals too. I realised with some considerable surprise that 'you-don't-know-my-mamma'

Danny was one of his three crewmen, now helping people in the kindest and most well-mannered way onto the *Puffin*, with a roguish, but slightly deadened by alcohol, red eye.

He held my hand as I leapt from the jetty onto the deck of the *Puffin*, where a gallant Phil irritated the hell out of me once again, by saying, "Come on, princess." I don't believe that any woman over the age of fifty wants to be called 'princess'; it's reminiscent of Bette Davis in *What Ever Happened to Baby Jane*, just a mocking, passive aggression.

I narrowed my eyes at him and he winced, then didn't say a word to me all morning.

I was only grateful that Janine hadn't heard. So humiliating, for she had already come aboard and was seated next to Helen at the bow, talking legal shop.

Rachel and her children were there too; I could hear her shouting at them not to bother the crew and to climb down from the rails, as they hurtled excitedly in orange life jackets from bow to stern.

The other young woman accompanying us was a small, quietly spoken Saint called Shayla, dressed in the blue polo shirt and trousers of the island's environmental group.

Where there are men, there is always beer, and Mark, Jack, Edward and Phil had brought quite a lot of it in a large ice bag, along with a token bottle of wine for the women.

As I settled myself next to Rachel opposite Helen and Janine, I noticed for the first time the young man seated on the other side of her.

"Meet Sanele." Rachel smiled.

The young man held out his hand to me and I shook it, noticing his tee shirt for the first time.

"Ha! Che Guevara," I said, musing over the motif on the front. "Our son is a big fan." (Despite all attempts to explain to him that his hero was also well known for his brutality and ruthlessness.)

Sanele thumped his fist into the air in an enthusiastic salute, startling both of us and frightening Shayla into the bargain.

"This island needs a revolution," he said sombrely, as an introduction.

Rachel nodded wisely.

"Sanele, I think many people might agree with you," she remarked. "But the Saints don't even grow their own vegetables to combat the dramatic rise in cancer amongst the islanders, let alone find the energy for a revolution."

"I have been here long enough," Sanele argued with the passion of youth, "long enough to have seen that your government neglects these good, loyal people."

I nodded. "I don't think any of the lawyers would disagree with that, though they might disagree a little more quietly."

Then I realised it was the young man who was staying at The Jolly Sailor with Thadie.

"Sanele is our interpreter," Rachel explained, tying up her blonde hair as a caution against the wind as the *Puffin* began to move away from the jetty. "He has come to work with us on the case of some men from Zimbabwe who are working at the airport."

"Ah, I see. What language do you speak, Sanele?" I asked, at the same time as watching the children leaping from the jetty into the clear blue-green water where a turtle bobbed.

I smiled at him. He wore a very large and expensive pair of sunglasses, which almost dwarfed the fine features of his face.

"Zulu, Afrikaans, Xhosa, Ndebele, English and a little French..."

"That's very impressive. I only speak a little French. You must have a flair for languages and a very good teacher."

"My father is a teacher," he said, "in Johannesburg."

I nodded. His parents must be very proud of him, I thought. Henry had hated French and, despite the stalwart efforts of his French teacher, had refused to take the subject seriously.

Rachel suddenly shrieked to her daughter to move slowly or she would fall in the briny, as little Deborah scanned the waves excitedly for dolphins. My admiration for Rachel and for her children was great; if I had lost my husband in a boating accident, I would be less inclined to venture out on the sea.

The boat had been moving slowly in and out of other sea vessels, but Declan's prized possession (apart from his children and a collection of antique machetes, so he told me later) was now picking up speed.

One of the crew had made and brought a large pan of *plo*, a delicious and filling Saint Helena recipe; my stomach gurgled with the smell of it. I'd only recently eaten; I couldn't possibly be hungry. Must be the sea air, I excused myself, gazing enviously at Janine's wasp-like waist as she reclined against the seat in tiny shorts and a bikini top.

The boat bumped uncomfortably over a wave and she leapt into the air, giggling and attracting Mark's attention as he stood against the rail with Jack.

It wouldn't catch his attention if I fell headlong into the water, I thought, with a sudden and now familiar rush of bitterness.

The sun was very hot despite the sea breeze. After a while, sun creams and bottles of water emerged from various backpacks, whilst tee shirts were removed and sun cream applied.

Mark donned his expensive shades, presumably so he could admire Janine's Sophia Loren breasts in the skimpy bikini without it being too obvious. Edward, who had grown up in Kenya, looked endearingly British in pink floral shorts and a broad hat knotted beneath the chin in public schoolboy fashion.

"Hello," I called over to Shyla, whose name suited her because she had smiled at everyone and listened to them until that point but had said hardly a word. Then again, no one had yet drawn her into conversation. Had she been one of the lovely blondes, I mused, the men would have been all over her. But she was rather plain, with a fine and intelligent face.

"Have you worked for the group for long?" I called to her, carefully crossing the perils of the deck to reach her side. She couldn't have; she looked as young as Sanele.

She moved along and I squeezed myself beside her, staring out at the pale pastel sea, its surface glinting with bright white daytime stars.

She was the eldest of three children, she told me. She had wanted to go to university in the UK but her parents couldn't afford that.

It was very rare for a young Saint to go away to university. There was no university on the island, not even a department of a university.

Everyone I had spoken to felt that it would make so much difference to the aspirations of the young people there if there were. What could they aspire to, unless they could afford to go away?

Careers in Saint Helena were limited; you could train as a lawyer, for example, but you would have to go to the UK to complete your legal training, so you would have to have money. It's the same with teachers and other professions.

In Britain, Shayla might aspire to be anything she wanted, but not here. However, she seemed to be one of the few young people to be truly contented. She was clearly happy in her job and felt that she had career prospects. I asked her whether she had met Thadie and she replied that she had, and liked her, believing she would make a big difference to the aid the environmental groups would receive. I made a mental note to tell Thadie this.

It was as we came close to Egg Island, a massive outcrop of rock turned white by guano as if draped in an old lady's lacy shawl, and as I was listening to Shayla talking about the fairy terns and the work her group did to protect the interest of the seabirds, that Helen and Janine joined us to ask their own questions.

By the time we had reached Lemon Valley to swim, Shayla had come out of herself a little and was proving to be a very knowledgeable guide.

In Lemon Valley the pastels and the bright stars vanished and the water broke into curved tessellations of dark blues and greens beneath the massive shadow of the undulating rocks, rising from the sea like giant slabs of coffee cake with volcanic veins of soft brown fudge.

Everyone helped where they could as Declan and his crew moored the boat and set down the ladder for us to swim.

In the distance there was a natural picnic area beneath the rocks, in a natural crevice like a wormhole, big enough for a large man to stand beneath.

Picnic tables had been erected there and, as it was Sunday, various families were holding picnics or barbeques whilst a few people swam close by.

Another small boat was moored there, trailing an inflatable Loch Ness Monster straddled by shrieking children.

David, Rachel's son, had recognised some schoolfriends, and he and his sister were amongst the first to descend the ladder, plunging excitedly into the sea.

"Is it warm?" Rachel called down. We could see by their chattering teeth that it was not.

Mark was standing before me, his face as excited as one of the children's.

"Coming in?" he asked. I smiled at his broad, muscular chest and then looked up at his face, wondering for a moment whether it had 'gone that far'. The thought came upon me in a sudden intrusion, confusing me. Had Janine seen him naked?

I smiled at him. "Yes, of course…"

Declan stretched out his large hand, pointing towards the far horizon.

"Namibia is the nearest point of land," he said, in answer to one of Edward's questions. He drew a canvas bag from beneath one of the seats. "There are plenty of snorkels and masks inside the bag. You may want to have a look at the wreck of a fishing boat, not anything like as big as the RFA *Darkdale*, of course, but worth seeing. I took a great photograph of a conger eel at that very same spot."

I thought of the film *The Deep* and resolved not to go anywhere near the wreck; conger eels are not my thing, or sharks. I'm not a diver. I love swimming in safe little Cornish coves where you can see everything beneath the water, and I like belly boarding. I have handled pet rats and nurtured tarantulas in a classroom, even stroked snakes, but I don't trust what I can't see and I'm not keen on swimming under the surface of sea water for any length of time.

Mark could do it; he'd once been a member of a diving club, years ago, and I felt very certain that the well-endowed Janine, standing there like a brunette Ursula Andress, was a diver.

I was going to lose out, I thought heavily, as Helen and Janine cavorted happily as mermaids beneath the surface, but nothing would persuade me to dive.

Mark smiled down at me as I descended the ladder after Jack and Phil. The water was freezing at first, despite the sunshine, certainly not the sea of the Mediterranean.

I shivered a little with the shock of it against my legs, deciding that to drop straight in was the only way to tackle it. I gave a small shriek as the chill waters attacked my body thermometer, wincing up at Mark's laughing face and Edward's gorgeous pink shorts as he followed me into the sea.

I swam about in circles for a bit like a Labrador with a stick in its mouth, until I had warmed up and felt comfortable with the temperature. Helen joined me. "It's a bit parky!" she said, laughing. Then, after a little while, the sea felt wonderfully soothing on hot skin.

"Shayla said that you often find turtles swimming in this cove."

I nodded enthusiastically but wasn't genuinely convinced that I wanted to encounter one, no matter how harmless and jolly friendly they may be.

Shayla and Sanele stayed on the boat with the fishermen. I'm not sure that Sanele could swim. At times, when the boat ride had been a little bumpy, he had looked rather anxious.

Mark and Janine struck out confidently across the water as predicted, followed by Phil, all of them clutching snorkels and masks. Janine and Mark were chatting with one another. I imagined a hideously ugly kraken dragging Janine beneath the waves.

"It's here!" Phil called to them. "You can see it quite clearly, even without masks."

I watched them making their dives and then swam through the water after Jack, who was heading towards the rocks and the little spiny creatures we had been shown a film about on the RMS by one of Shayla's colleagues.

But I didn't want to spend too much time with the spiny creatures and my body had cooled down a lot, so I swam back to the boat after a shortish while, where Declan threw down a hand to help me up the ladder.

"Shayla has just spotted some dolphins," he said. "When the others get out, we'll go and look for them."

I watched Mark swimming as I towelled my hair dry. Perhaps, I thought distractedly, I should have changed careers, become a lawyer instead of a teacher. I had a friend who had done that, just so that she could keep an eye on her husband's daily contacts.

Before the earring, such a thing had never occurred to me. Obsession was a new pastime.

When the others were back on the boat, we set off again. For a while the dolphins seemed to be hiding from us. You know that experience? When you think that someone must have been exaggerating when they said, "You'll see lots of dolphins!"

But then Helen cried joyfully, "Look, oh look!"

And I looked and could hardly believe what I saw. So many of them, leaping and cavorting over the waves in the sunshine. Suddenly, appearing from nowhere, creating such joy inside me that I forgot my angst and inhibitions and was laughing out loud. Perhaps all sadness could be reduced by dolphins, the most joyful celebration of life. Perhaps, I thought, anyone with worries, or any kind of mental health problem could be helped by a dolphin experience. But that didn't explain the confused personality that was 'you-don't-know-my-mamma' Danny, now working on the boat. He must see a lot of dolphins in his line of work.

They arced, dived; chased our boat relentlessly, their grey-blue silhouettes catching the sunlight in beads of seawater. They were streamlined, perfectly shaped for their environment. The most confident creatures on earth.

"What on earth is that one doing?" I asked of Jack, as one of the dolphins appeared to slam itself on the crest of a wave.

"Killing tuna, to eat it," he explained. "Look at their dorsal fins; each fin is like a fingerprint, each one unique to that dolphin." He stretched his finger towards the creature and I saw what he meant. The dolphin killing a tuna had an old tear in its fin.

"See the scars? Brave creatures, dolphins, brave and loyal to the pod; they'll protect each other against sharks, or even a killer whale."

I thought of my mother and father then; I wanted them to see these magical creatures; they gave me such a feeling of hope, the charm would work on them, too – take the cancer away.

Mark came over to me, putting his arm around me and giving my shoulder a small squeeze.

He had been photographing them with the camera I had bought him. I think he would have kissed me if Janine had not been there. I felt it very strongly at the time, and yet I couldn't say if it were true.

We were heading out towards Manatee Bay and Sperry Island. The closer we came to them, the colder the wind; the sea which had been so calm had grown rough and unpredictable within a few minutes.

The waves tossed the boat and the pirate crew laughed out loud at the shrieks as we were thrown about like a toy boat in a Jacuzzi. I gripped Shayla's arm, but in truth I was excited. Declan grinned out at us from the cabin; it was all part of the fun and more thrilling than a ride at a Disney theme park.

We seemed so very far away from the land now, I thought, as I donned a sweatshirt and stared towards the looming shape of the needlepoint dark rock. It was high and narrow, shaped like a thick spear, which could be why it was called Sperry Island, perhaps. I would ask Tessa; she would know, I thought.

When disreputable Danny smiled at me, his gaping mouth flashing a silver filling, I smiled back at him with glee as the boat roared over the large waves, so dangerously close to the rock. The fishermen knew what they were doing; they were trying to provide the thrill of a fairground ride. I had not had so much fun in years.

But poor Sanele was not enjoying the ride at all. His thin form was hunched in the corner of the boat as he held on to the wooden seating with clenched fists, trying to smile but looking desperately sick. I crawled across the floor to reach him, almost thrown off balance at the same time that Rachel yelled, "Sit still!" at the children and the hull met with a great wall of a wave.

I placed an arm about his shoulder and patted it in sympathy, but he turned away, leaning over the side, and was sick as a dog, his vomit splattering the side of the fishing boat.

Chapter 23

Diary Eighteen

Two days after the boat trip, I was seated with Helen and Janine at the bar of the Napoleon, drinking gin and tonic after another long, hot day in court. They had been in court; I was simply enjoying the drink. I had been acquainting myself with Saint Helena and writing my murder mystery, in which there was no obvious murderer, as yet. Oh yes, and swimming, and occasionally fretting about where Mark and Janine were during the day.

Janine came everywhere with us now, and still I couldn't enjoy her company.

We were so different. Everything she said, every belief and viewpoint, made me want to argue with her.

"We've decided to have dinner at Corrine's Place; there aren't many other places to choose from this evening, to be honest. You'll be joining us, won't you?" Helen asked of Janine.

"Oh, yes, that would be great, if you don't mind." She glanced up at me through a swept fringe.

"Of course not," I managed, quite civilly. Librans are known for their acting skills.

Tessa would be there, too, after which we'd arranged to go back to her place. I would be staying there for the night and driving back with her in time for court in the morning. Normally I would be looking forward to this, but a large part of me feared that it would leave Mark free to sit up late on the Napoleon balcony with Janine, or worse, perhaps.

Corrine's was run by a formidable lady, Paula, a matriarch and businesswoman with the cynical good humour of someone who had worked hard all her life and for little financial gain. Her sons were fishermen. Paula juggled grandchildren with fishcakes on a nightly basis without frying the grandchildren in batter. She fed us regularly during our stay on the island.

It wasn't the kind of place you needed to dress up for, but I had been dressing with far more care than I ever used to before Janine came on the scene. Mark had said, "Ooh, I like your shoes," when I'd donned a pair that evening. He'd had the small, patronising smile of a husband who wasn't used to seeing his wife in high heels.

Lately, I had become interested in the variations of female court clothes. Always black and white, of course; always a little suit jacket. But skirts of differing lengths and styles.

In short, the earring had made me grow shallow in my interests, but aware of what I looked like as I had not been since my thirties.

At Corrine's, we ordered our food and sat down to wait for Mark and some of the others who had stayed late at the courthouse. Tessa was working with Mark and would come with him.

"What sort of a day have people had?" I asked.

"Not bad." Helen grimaced. "Mark made one of the social workers cry."

"He does that to me sometimes." I grinned, before I checked myself.

Janine laughed. I shouldn't have said it for several reasons; that I didn't want Janine to make assumptions about my relationship with Mark, being one of them.

"Why?" I asked.

"He accused her of not doing enough for Cara and of making decisions that were not hers to make," Helen said.

"I don't think that is entirely unfair, having looked at the documents they managed to trace," Janine added.

"So, where are these documents?"

Janine shrugged. "It's a mystery, apparently. Filing systems on the island aren't good. Some doctors don't appear to keep records at all, not even for children. Documents in many cases have gone missing or have been shredded. I think Mark has a hard task ahead of him, and there are some people here, not islanders, but within the authorities, who are less than happy that he's here. He's opened a rather nasty can of worms and has been busy attacking government officials."

Don't lose it; hold hard, I told myself. She was starting to irritate me with her lectures and loyalty to my husband.

"Yes, well, I certainly get the impression that some of the officials who've come from the UK are rather complacent about their cosy lives on the island," Helen agreed, "not all, by any means, but some," she added.

It was just as our food arrived that a small group of people mounted the steps to the café, led by Sanele.

There were four young men following him. I recognised two of them from the Napoleon's courtyard. These two were wearing Manchester United football shirts. Sanele had swopped his Che Guevara tee shirt for one bearing the swarthy, bearded face of Fidel Castro, and was wearing the expensive-looking shades, which slightly dwarfed his small face. He looked confident and in control, a very different man to the one who had thrown up on the boat.

Paula, who had been serving us our food, now looked towards them with irritation. She rolled up her shirt sleeves in the manner of a woman who was preparing for a fight, revealing the forearms of a wrestler.

"Here come trouble," she said in a low growl.

"What?" Helen grinned.

"Nothin' funny 'bout it," Paula said. "Him, the boy from Johannesburg, 'bout time he went home to his mamma; he stirrin' up trouble with Saints kids." She stared long and hard at us before disappearing into the kitchen, muttering under her breath as she lifted a plump and healthy looking little boy from the top of the freezer to set him on his feet.

"She means Sanele, the interpreter, yes?" Helen asked, lifting her fork and wincing slightly as she took a sip of her unusual wine.

"He seemed nice enough," I said, perhaps a tad naively.

"He didn't do the guys from Zimbabwe any favours today," Janine said.

I stared blankly at her.

"He is an interpreter for a man who has been accused of molesting a young girl; one of the airport workers, not an islander. Sanele become a little too chummy with several of them; he shouldn't mix with them really, but according to Rachel he has. He was followed to court this morning by several of the man's friends. Sanele wore a suit, but the men came in their uniforms, which isn't a good advertisement for the company building the airport, especially as Jack is the man's lawyer, and it looks as though the man will be found guilty. What is worse is that his supporters sat on the cannons outside of court until they were told to move. They were quite noisy. Jack told me that he thinks Sanele is a bit of a rabble-rouser."

And this evening, Sanele seemed to confirm Paula's worst fears and suspicions by talking in a hushed voice to his young companions, who hung onto his every word. It was as though they were enacting Guy Fawkes' meeting with the Gunpowder Plotters.

Paula scowled at them from the kitchen hatch whilst savagely slicing the vegetables.

At last the legal eagles arrived, and there was a definite air of weariness about them.

Mark kissed me lightly on the cheek and collapsed into a chair, seating himself next to me.

"That was one of the most fucking horrible days of my life," Jack said, with feeling.

Edward winced at the term 'fucking', his gentle face shrinking into his shirt collar, tortoise-like.

Sanele half turned at Jack's voice, but he didn't acknowledge us, seemingly oblivious to our presence.

Jack now lowered his voice to a hissed whisper. "First the bloody awful rape case and then, of all things, I had to prosecute one of Declan's fishing friends for beating up a young man."

He tore a large finger into his neck collar as though releasing a noose.

"Make no mistake. I am going to be so unpopular for that."

"Sorry, old love... Shall I get us a bottle of wine?" Helen asked.

"Good idea."

"Where's Tessa?" I asked Mark.

"In the robing room, talking to a witness. She's going to join us later for a drink before she whisks you away."

I nodded, wanting him to sound a little more disappointed about it.

"They work very hard, don't they? Tessa and the other lay advocates. Do they get paid anything?"

"Nope." Mark took a swig of the cold beer Phil had brought to the table. "They work voluntarily, and yes, it's long, hard work, which is probably why they are finding it impossible to recruit new advocates. They get a small allowance to cover any expenses incurred."

Paula's feet slapped resentfully across the restaurant with plates of food for Sanele and his friends, her face puckered with suspicion and distaste as she slammed the plates before them.

I felt something brush against my leg and wondered whether Mark and Janine were playing footsie under the table, but it was just Paula's large ginger cat, in search of affection.

Our two tall South African friends entered the restaurant then, without the willowy blonde companion. Paula's hostile expression smoothed itself as she met them with a smile, knowing them to be big spenders. They greeted us with a nod and sat at the table nearest the pretty town gardens, beneath the colourful flags. For a moment, I wondered whether they were following us around the place, but then there were few places to eat in Jamestown.

Chapter 24

Cara

She was a small girl. At seventeen, although she might have been mistaken for a fourteen-year-old, the hand-me-down summer dresses her mother had left her almost drowned her, except where Cara had stitched the seams.

She was pretty, as her mother had once been, but prouder and tougher than her mother by far, although she had a waif-like vulnerability. Perhaps her strengths stemmed from a complicated childhood; perhaps, in her own way, Nina had protected her from the worst.

Nina, her mother, had once had a little pride too, but it had been bruised and punched out of her. Firstly lessened by Nina's own motherless childhood; then, when her drunken father had more-or-less sold her off to the man on Ascension when she was sixteen for the price of a few bottles of whisky, pride was hammered out by a succession of men, one of whom had introduced Nina to drugs.

Cara's father had been a Scotsman. That's what Nina had told her. Whether this man was dead or alive, Cara didn't know. Nina said she loved him for a while when she was young.

Nina was a Saint, which was funny because of course she wasn't anything like a saint except that she loved

Cara, which Cara understood. Sometimes Cara felt so angry with her mother, it was like a hard knot in her chest, but somehow she had defended Cara against all the shitty things that had happened to them on their travels. Almost always, in the end, they'd run away to another place, and sometimes this was after Nina had robbed the man first.

So, Cara found it hard to make friends. It didn't matter, she liked being alone.

Now she sat on the low wall between the cottages and looked up at the stars.

They said that when the airport came, you wouldn't be able to see the stars, not like this anyway, not a velvet black pincushion studded with small diamonds.

The stars had names, but Cara had never learned them. She could read and write, in fact she was good at English as one teacher had told her, but she'd never spent long enough in a school to find out about things like the stars.

Now, she had three cigarettes left; she'd have to go down the ladder into the town tomorrow to get more.

The ladder was steep, but it wasn't the ladder that bothered her. She didn't like talking to people, the nosy old women, the sneering men with nothing much to sneer about, the people who looked down at her, thought themselves better.

Once, after they'd been thrown out of America because of Nina's drugs charge, Nina had gone to Jamestown to get the shopping and a woman who remembered her had spat at her and called her a whore.

"I know her husband," Nina said. And Cara was old and wise enough by then to know what she meant. But having Nina as a mother made people think that Cara was going to be the same, she thought – not with bitterness but with a cynicism beyond her years.

Some people couldn't find it inside themselves to be generous, even when you were only thirteen and new back from the USA. Cara chuckled at the stars.

When Nina died, her voice muffled by the oxygen mask, she'd heaved and rasped the words, "Look up at the stars and you'll find me there."

It sounded like something from a Disney film, Cara had thought at the time. But she did look up at the stars, almost every night, hearing Nina's voice when there was still air in her lungs. Cara sang too; she knew she had a good voice; she got that much from Nina, and singing her mother's songs kept her from feeling lonesome. Nina had said they could earn money from her voice, but it never happened.

There was a song – everyone was humming and singing it right now; the loud car radios played it all the time. Cara sang it to the stars, knowing that her voice was clear and sweet.

"It's been a long day without you, my friend, and I'll tell you all about it when I see you again…"

Her voice carried through the cool air, to the rooftops and all the way to Arizona, Cara thought. In the end, it was lung cancer. The milder drug, cigarettes she smoked, sometimes thirty a day, killed her mother.

Right to the end, Nina was a beautiful woman. She had men sniffing after her right up to the point she went to the hospital, even when she leaned on a walking frame and could hardly breathe.

She was in her mid-fifties when she died, her small face shrunk in the long black hair, her large breasts flopping on either side of her thin ribcage.

Then, Cara had explored her mother's scars for the last time.

The cigarette burns, scars on her belly, made by a man when Nina was too high on drugs to feel pain; they looked like tiny white clouds, bluish white and puckered. Where had Cara been when that happened? Playing in a yard, or at one of the temporary schools? She only recalled bathing them in iced water later in the day, to soothe Nina's cries of pain.

Cara wasn't scared of being alone, not there, not amongst the handful of cottages at the old fort above Jamestown. There, she was comforted by the soothing breeze lifting from the sea and the smell of honeysuckle.

Not many people lived there. Aside from Stevie, who played his music too loud and had sometimes got into shouting at Nina if she complained, everyone there got along well.

Nina had been scared sometimes, not too long ago. Scared of wandering too far from the cottages along the road by the fort and at night. She said she could hear ghostly boots, like soldiers marching. She was convinced of it. But Cara never heard them.

There were three people on the island who Cara could call friends.

There was Miss Rachel and Miss Tessa, who found Nina the cottage when they first came back there to live, and then there was old Ebony, who lived in the cottage next door.

Ebony had brought Nina and Cara things, from time to time. Food, flowers, and things she didn't need anymore. Ebony was very old and very kind. She had known Nina's loud-mouthed, drunken brute of a father, or so she told Cara. Ebony was butt ugly but kind.

Cara plucked the purple flower head of a nearby weed, turning her thoughts to the two little girls she'd given birth to. She couldn't think it was love that made her miss their weight upon her arms; after all, they had been forced upon her by the man's rape. Sometimes she felt close to them, sometimes detached. Neither child belonged to her and she knew she couldn't give them the love that her own mother had given to her.

It wasn't there it had happened, but on a path going down to the sea, late one evening.

Cara was going down, and the man was coming up. She didn't know where he was going, but he was a little drunk. From the corner of her eye, Cara noticed him lurching as he walked. His footfall was soft, so she didn't notice him till he was a few yards ahead of her, then she waited, something inside of her warning her to take care. Only she couldn't move at the time; fear had turned her to stone. The man's face was kind of hot and heavy, which made her heart beat fast just as he came towards her.

He was not local, not anyone Cara knew of, but she'd noticed him ascending the hill once before and then he'd seen her and done nothing; maybe that's why she carried on being polite. But this time her grabbed her arm, crushing her down against the stones, tearing at her skirt and pants so she couldn't breathe, holding her so she couldn't escape.

She had seen him since; he still had the long scratch she made on his face, a deep scar that would never go away, that would mark his dark skin for eternity.

No good going to the police. They just say it was her fault, she asking for it. She was Nina's daughter. So she just climbed to her feet after it, her panties sticky and uncomfortable and cold, oozing with his disgusting cum, and she walked back to the cottage to wash it away. Only it didn't wash the two babies away.

It was a year after Nina died that it happened. It was old Ebony who understood that she was expecting a baby, two babies as things turned out.

Ebony simply asked her who the father was, after she noticed the swell in her belly. So Cara told her, said what he'd done. But when Ebony fetched Miss Tessa, Cara wouldn't say who the man was. He told her, when he got up and dragged his pants up, that he'd cut her if she reported him, so she didn't.

She didn't want his babies, two of them, two black-skinned little girls. She never asked for them, they were forced on her. It wasn't her fault and she didn't want no one's babies.

She told Miss Rachel she wanted them to go to good families, better than she had. She wanted that they stay together, if someone would take them that way.

She kept them till they had fattened, little chubby arms and bellies, fattened on her milk, till she was afraid she could feel herself loving them. Then she told Miss Rachel to take them away.

Now people stared at her like she was cold-hearted. Didn't matter, Cara didn't care, she was used to being stared at. Cara didn't give a monkey's about other people's opinions.

The new lawyer, the tall man, like that lawyer in the film; he would find good homes for them.

Tomorrow she had to go to court. Miss Tessa had brought her a black skirt and a white shirt during the day, drove up to see her and say she would fetch her tomorrow.

Cara lit her last cigarette and stared up at the velvet night sky again, wondering if the baby girls would look for her there, one day, just as she looked for Nina.

Chapter 25

Diary Nineteen

Tessa and I talked into the wee small hours. In the end, slightly tipsy by eleven thirty but relaxed and comfortable with her, for she was very funny, I was so glad that I hadn't let my neurosis about Mark and Janine stop me from coming.

She was a good talker, a good listener too.

The stars peeked through the blinds as we wandered from her living room and out onto the veranda to sit on the swing chair as the night air cooled. We took our glasses and a half bottle of wine.

So much quiet, with only the sound of the crickets and the wide view of the valley before us, with the few house lights remaining like fireflies in the velvet dark. No street lights, no light pollution yet to mute the starlight, and the distant bay hidden by the night, except for the lights of a large yacht which was moored there.

And every now and then, music would blare from a car radio, as a vehicle drove along the road and passed the house to intrude upon the quiet.

"It's so lovely up here, so peaceful."

I pushed my feet against the patio, rhythmically in step with hers, rocking us on the swing chair.

"It is, isn't it? I wouldn't want to live in Jamestown, too noisy."

I giggled. "Noisy? Compared with towns in the UK, it's a village."

"Sometimes," she whispered conspiratorially, as though someone might be listening in her garden, "I wander around the house in a bathing costume, you know? When the nights are so warm."

I spluttered a little over the wine, spilling it on my top.

"Tessa, do you think that's safe? You're a very attractive person."

"Old habit, hard to break, and such a lovely feeling." She grinned. "Sometimes I sleep out here on the porch swing... fully clothed of course."

We sat in silence for a while until she asked, "So, how are things with you? Still got the earring?"

I nodded. "I don't think Janine has missed it. Mark won't talk about any of it. I tried once; he just gets all cagey and defensive."

"He's a handsome man," she mused, "but that doesn't mean he's doing anything."

"I know his flirting gets me down," I sighed. "All flirting is cheating really, isn't it, if you're married?" I was aware that it sounded very puritanical. I wondered whether this had been my point of view in my twenties, but I felt too old to remember.

"How are you getting on with Janine?"

I twisted my lips in a grimace of frustration, avoiding her face.

"Well, I'm not keen," I said. Then I turned to her in a desperate appeal.

"It is her earring, isn't it? What was it doing in the collar of his shirt?"

"I can't answer all your questions, honey; maybe they were just dancing cheek to cheek."

"Just dancing? How dare he do that! Why didn't he take me to a dance?"

"At least that's not sex." She grinned, and I felt offended; it wasn't funny to me. Perhaps she saw this. She put an arm around my shoulder.

"So you don't like Janine at all."

"Well, not in the circumstances," I huffed, "but we're getting on okay, I suppose, a bit cool towards each other. I just get the feeling that they are quite close, you know, talking with their eyes, that kind of thing. I think he'd follow her like a puppy if I wasn't here."

"Mm... funny things happen in Saint Helena," Tessa confided, "with the local people for sure, but it's such a small island that others get the signals quickly, if you know what I mean. Then there are those who come to work here without their partners. Often, they get lonely, or they just think they are safe here to get away with it. You wouldn't believe how many affairs can happen on one tiny little island, often good people with reputations to keep."

"This started before Saint Helena," I pointed out.

She gazed into the distance. "I had this one friend, a senior nurse at the hospital; she was lovely. She fell in love with a married man, waited and waited for him to leave his wife but he never did. She died before he did... She waited all her life."

"That's sad," I said, without a jot of genuine sympathy for the woman. It was sad, but I felt sure that I wouldn't wait all my life. The thought surprised me; did that mean I didn't love Mark enough?

"So, have you asked Mark if there's anything going on between them?"

The question took me by surprise.

"I think I know instinctively that he wouldn't tell the truth," I explained.

"Pity, but I can see that. He's a good lawyer, isn't he? That's why Rachel wanted him to come here."

"You mean that would make him a good liar?" I smiled. "Mark is a very strong person in lots of ways, but he's also quite vulnerable sometimes, especially to female adulation," I murmured. "I guess I meant that he would never admit it to me."

Tessa regarded me, then patted my knee with a firm hand. "Hang in there, honey," she said.

I nodded. I had this sudden, overwhelming, impulsive feeling that I loved everyone in Saint Helena, even the imperfect people; that the place had crept inside me like a piece of magic, unseen. I wanted to cry, but didn't, staring out at the tranquil landscape instead.

Tessa wrapped her arms across her chest; perhaps sensing my sadness, she swiftly changed the subject. "There used to be a whorehouse on the island," she said suddenly.

"Did there?" I wondered what was coming next. There was a mischievous twinkle in her eye. I suppose it wasn't too much of a surprise; there had probably been whorehouses in the world wherever the navy went. My thoughts drifted to two great uncles who had both fought in the British Navy during the Second World War; had they used whorehouses? One of them was a good boy, the other more exciting but not such a good boy.

"Oh yes. That's how I first made some money, as a teenager, when I was at school."

My eyes widened like saucers as I gaped at her, and she rocked in the chair, laughing for a few seconds at the expression on my face.

"No, not doing that!" She grinned. "When I was younger, a few of us used to wait at the waterfront for the sailors as they came off the ships and take them to the whorehouse. Some of them were old, some young, but they all wanted to enjoy the same thing."

Her practical viewpoint of it put Mark in his place for a moment; just men, after all.

"I used to get angry alright, jealous, just like you, but my husband would never have dared to play me up like that. Once, there was a time when he used to go up to the ambassador's house, years ago. The man's wife was always calling him up there on one piece of business or another, and she was attractive, you know? So, one time, he didn't come back, and didn't come back, and his dinner got cold. When he did come back eventually, he brought a tray of cakes for our girls. Know what I did?"

I shook my head.

"I took the tray from him and threw it all over the garden for the goats and the chickens. I was so mad."

"I think I'll come back as a lesbian," I said.

"Good idea."

"Where do you suppose some of those men from the *Darkdale* were, on the night before she was torpedoed? In the whorehouse probably, their wives at home, protected from that knowledge."

I nodded and looked out towards the sea, shrouded by darkness, towards the place where the ship had gone down during World War Two.

"My grandma told me a story about a sailor on shore from the *Darkdale* on the evening before she sank. My grandma was a battleaxe." She shook her head in despair.

"Granny was a Scottish battleaxe, a true Celt, and my granddad a Saint, in all respects. The governor was terrified of my granny. She used to boss him about. Used to go up there in her finest clothes and lay down the law to him. She came to this island with her parents. My grandfather's family came over with other people from Britain after the Great Fire of London, after they lost their homes and all their possessions in that fire. That's where some of the Saint names come from, from the time of the Great Fire of London. My granny had to have the best of everything, the best. She was a proud woman, with high standards.

One day, before my mother met my father, when she was younger, she was hanging out the sheets on the line for my granny. A young sailor from the *Darkdale* was on shore. He was passing their house and saw this pretty young girl, hanging out the sheets, so he jumped out on her, making her shriek and giggle. Then they started having a game of hide and seek in the sheets until he caught her and kissed her. It was her first kiss. He said he'd come back the next day, but the next day they were all killed by that big explosion and sank to the bottom of the sea…"

I listened, entranced. I was about to ask her more about her grandmother when out of the stillness a firework cracked through the night, numbing our ears. I waited, watching the window for the splatter of firework lights, but they never came.

"What the heck was that?"

Tessa rose from the chair and looked down at the road. "It's coming from Jack's house," she murmured.

Jack had told me that he rented a house up in the hills close to Tessa, but I'd not been there. As she gazed into the distance, there was a second loud thwack, like some giant nail splitting a rock.

"Fireworks?" I suggested.

She shook her head, still waiting, and after seconds it came, ricocheting through the valley beyond.

"Gunshots," she said. "Someone is firing a gun close to Jack's house and the lights are on, so he's there…" She pointed towards the lights of a solitary house along the road, but there were no figures to be seen against the dark.

"Should we call the police?!" I shrieked in alarm.

"No point," she said dryly. "It is the police; it's retribution."

"The police are shooting at Jack?" It was a dreadful thought. "What do you mean?"

I was very frightened for him, and yet Tessa hardly appeared to take it seriously at all. I stared anxiously at his house, my arms held across my stomach, my mouth hanging open.

"Not all the police, just a handful; friends of the man he prosecuted today. They won't be shooting at Jack, only at the night. It's a warning, a telling-off. Most of them are decent enough, but the Saint Helena police see themselves as a tight-knit family. They like Jack, what's not to like? He goes drinking and fishing with them whenever he's here."

"Oh my God, it's like the Wild West – country music and shootings," I exclaimed, giving in to confused, disbelieving laughter.

"They're just trying to scare him a little after what he did."

She sat down in the chair once more, relaxed and resigned to it. "He's probably curled up in a chair with a book and a glass of Scotch, busily ignoring them," she said, stretching out, flexing her back, a small sigh of regret at such childish carryings-on.

"Well, I've got work tomorrow; perhaps we should be going to bed."

I nodded and picked up the glasses, still pondering on Jack. Tessa loved her work, hard as it was.

As we wandered back into the house, she asked me, "Talking of prosecutions, did Danny say much to you when you were on the *Puffin*?"

I shrugged. "My friend, 'you-don't-know-my-mamma' Danny?" I asked. "No, not really, but he did manage a smile."

"Good. I bin worried about him."

"Why?"

"Oh, he keep telling people he see a little girl in a white nightdress, close to his house, wandering about in the night, a little ghost girl; just wondered if he losing it at long last. But it odd."

"A ghost girl. Whereabouts does Danny live?"

Tessa nodded her head in the direction of the fort. "Up that way, in his daddy's old house. I think he must be drinking again."

She took me to her spare room and clicked on the light. A neat, pleasant bedroom in lemon and white.

"There again, lots of people believe in ghosts around here. It's a very spiritual island. My grandfather believed in ghosts. Grandma used to laugh at him, but he convinced. Every day he talked about this little girl who follow him down to the sea, and she had a white nightdress, so he say. My grandad never touch drink except at Christmas."

I shrugged. I had limited experience of ghosts, but I wouldn't discount them.

"Grandad used to walk down the hill to the harbour every day; he was the harbourmaster, see. He didn' tell it like it was a story, but like he was fond of the child.

"He'd get up early and take his lunch and walk the same way when the streets were almost empty. He told us most days a little girl came to join him; she appear from nowhere, a very sweet-faced little girl, and she walk with him as though she knew him, as though he were her grandfather, a skinny-limbed little girl. Grandma would tease him, but he told us that story again and again, like it was something true."

She smiled at the memory, laying out a dressing gown on the bed for me, giving me a hug.

When she had said goodnight, I lay in her spare room, staring through the curtains at the sky and the bright stars, thinking about Jack and retribution and the things Tessa had told me. It had taken my mind off Mark and Janine, but as I fell asleep it was still Mark that I thought of.

Half asleep, half awake, dreaming of a time, years ago, when we had played on a Dorset beach with the children.

Chapter 26

Diary Twenty

The weather changed overnight.

It has been stiflingly hot since our arrival; now the heat is still here, but the skies have clouded over.

Tessa drops me off outside the court. I don't return to the hotel straight away, but wander down to the harbour, following the steps of the 'ghost girl'.

The sea is very angry beneath the cloud-filled skies. It writhes and crashes across the shining black rocks, spitting spume at the harbour wall and at me. It grabs at the jagged stones, making them roar against each other with the sound of a menacing Grendel from the deep. At times the waves are high enough to throw an imaginary surfer against the sea wall, breaking every bone in his body. Foam showers the harbour wall with tiny flecks of spit.

It isn't promising for the passengers of the RMS, now waiting in the harbour to depart with the friends and relatives who must travel back to the UK and to other far-flung corners of the earth.

In a huddle, like frightened animals at the cattle market, is a very different group of well-wishers to those we met on our arrival. They kiss and hug their friends and relatives for the last time, and for a long time to come. Grandparents know that they may never see their children and grandchildren again. It takes half a lifetime to save for that golden ticket, and the air fare will not be much cheaper.

There is a heavy resignation upon their faces, beneath the forced, unselfish brightness.

The air is stifling, and everyone but the very young sweat profusely.

At last the passengers bound for the RMS depart, and the sad little groups of family and friends disperse to return to their lives on the island; to their jobs, the shopping and cooking and cleaning and the children.

I wander back from my early morning stroll. Mark will be at court and I wonder what case he is involved in this morning.

Past the courthouse, I walk up the slight hilly incline to the hotel. It is still early, the streets are quite empty, but as I get closer to the hotel I can see a lonely figure in the near distance.

Tall, angular, an older man leaning on a walking stick, his tread is heavy and his progress slow. His broad shoulders droop.

"Herman!" I call out to him.

It is Sarah's father, my coffee friend who sits outside the hotel each morning with her father and his friends. She has just left for the UK. Herman has been in the crowd of family and well-wishers; he will not see his daughter for several years, perhaps.

Herman turns to smile at me. I walk towards him, without knowing what I am going to say.

"Did Sarah get off okay?" I manage at last.

"Yes," he says, smiling, "I won't see her for a long time now."

"No." I reach up and kiss him on the cheek without invitation and think of my father. Just this brief parting in Saint Helena is enough to imagine how it must feel to be distanced from someone you love so much.

"Do you want one cup of coffee at the Napoleon?" I slip into Saint easily.

"Not today, dear, maybe tomorrow," he says.

"Can you get hold of her by email?" I ask anxiously.

"Oh yes." Then he asks me, "Would you like my email address?"

So, in the street we swop addresses, but I know what Mark will say to me.

He will say, *"You can't. You will be impeding my job. Please don't contact people. If you are seen to be doing that it might be taken that you are trying to influence them in some way. I can do far more than you can here; if you get too friendly with people, how can I represent them if they need me?"*

I feel my own loneliness of a sudden, with the knowledge that my friendships on the island can't be sustained.

I want to talk to my family.

I say goodbye to Herman and cross the road to the rather grand, square-faced Victorian Post Office opposite the hotel, in search of stamps.

There's a small queue. When I reach the front of it, peering through the old-fashioned grill, I come face to face with the kind of suspicious female who is used to tourists. She attempts a smile, the kind of smile that implies I have done something wrong.

"Do you want these new ones? You can have a picture of the airport or a picture of Margaret Thatcher."

"Why?" I want to ask her but don't. *"Why would you want to sell stamps with Maggie Thatcher on them,*

when she took away your citizenship, until Tony Blair restored it, after you loyally sent all of those men to the Falklands?"

But, "I'll have the airport stamps, please," is all I say.

When I emerge from the Post Office, it has begun to rain. I let my shoulders fall and then relax a little with the feel of it, happy to be drenched after the cloying heat.

Seeing Herman has reminded me of my father; it will cost a lot of money, but I am going to have a long telephone call with Lucy, who has time off work to care for Mum.

I run across the street, jumping puddles, racing up the hotel staircase to my room.

The telephone is by the bed. You can't use a mobile phone in Saint Helena, but you can make calls. The white telephone is an old-fashioned one. If you don't position it in a certain way the cord pops out. I wonder briefly if the people from the Foreign Office have bugged the phone. There is something about this island which makes you paranoid.

Tessa told me that, once upon a time on the island, you had to go through the operator for every conversation, and that the operator would often listen in; nobody's business was safe from prying ears.

I sit on the edge of the bed and dial the number for the UK and to Mum's home. I only wait a short while.

"Hello?" It's Lucy's voice.

"Luce? It's me!" I shout excitedly, as though fearing that my voice won't carry across the Atlantic Ocean.

She sounds happy to hear from me, but there's an unmistakable tiredness behind the act.

"How are you? How's Mum?" I ask tentatively.

"I'm fine, but things aren't too good with her."

"What's happened?" I ask.

Lucy breaks into a long sigh. "They've gotten rid of the tumour, but there are a lot of tiny cancer cells they can't get rid of. The doctors think there are more that didn't even show up on the scan, and the chemotherapy is making her very ill."

"Yes, I supposed it would..." I feel guilty, useless; sorry for not being there.

"She's being violently sick, bowls full of the stuff. Toxic, brown and disgusting. I can't get her to eat anything, either."

"Oh God, Lucy, I'm so sorry for her; sorry for you too. What about Dad?"

"Dad? I hadn't realised," she answered. "I hadn't realised quite how bad his memory is now. I think Mum must have had a hard time dealing with him. No wonder she kept getting irritable." She gives a dry chuckle.

"Why?" I bite my lip, waiting.

"He just keeps asking the same questions, over and over again. It's a good job I'm staying here, otherwise I mightn't have realised quite how bad he is. I've tried to tell him a million times what the matter is and why she's bed-bound, but he just doesn't seem to take any of it in."

"Maybe some of it is denial?" I suggest. "His mother died at a very young age from cancer, didn't she?"

"Yes, possibly, but when you get back I think we should get another appointment at the memory clinic. I ask him if he's had any breakfast and he replies, 'Yes,' then I discover he hasn't had anything at all, he's just forgetting to make it. Mum must have made it for him all the time."

Dementia, not denial, I think.

"What about your girls? How are they coping if you're not there?"

"I'm popping back all the time, at least when I can. Alex is still being difficult with John. She's a good girl, but she still hopes her dad and I will get back together. Still, after all this time." Lucy sighs. "She can be a bit, you know, meddlesome and manipulative sometimes. But she's helping me by sitting on Sophie to pass her GCSEs whilst I'm not there, so that's good." There is a slight pause. "Something odd happened."

"What do you mean?"

"Doug turned up."

Alex's father, handsome but hopeless. He and Lucy have been divorced for more than six years now. He lives in Newcastle and Alex goes to stay with him during her holidays, or at least she used to, before her teenage years.

"His father died," Lucy states. "He says there's nothing for him there, so he's moving back here."

"What does John think of it?"

She grunts. "They're getting on like a house on fire; they've even been to the pub…"

"Well, that's good, isn't it?"

"No. I smell a rat. I can't trust Doug; he's up to something. I don't like the way they keep calling one another 'mate', either."

I laugh. I'm not sure what she means; I wish she were here so very much. Talking to her has lifted me right out of Saint Helena for a while, which is perhaps what I needed.

"Can you take the phone up to Mum?" I ask.

Gladys comes to the open bedroom door and peers around it, bestowing her crooked smile upon me, sees that I am on the telephone and hisses, "No bother, sweetie. I come back."

"She's upstairs," Lucy says. "She's just stopped throwing up vile, brown, toxic stuff for a few minutes. Cancer is a shit. I feel so badly for her, so helpless…"

"But you are there, comforting her. I'm not, am I?"

When Mum speaks into the telephone, it is her voice, but as I've never heard it before. Our mother has a strong voice, an authoritative voice, but it's now weakened and so muffled that it is difficult to hear what she says. The feeling of wanting to put my arms about her is so strong that I find myself kneading the pillow beside me in frustration.

"Mum? Mum, I'm so sorry to hear what you've been through. It will make you better in the long run, the chemotherapy, although I know that's little comfort just now. I'll be home in time to decorate your Christmas tree…"

"I don't think I can be doing with Christmas this year."

The strangled, husky sound of attempted laughter.

"No, I don't suppose you can. Just get as much sleep as you can."

She asks me about the things we have been doing then, and I tell her as much as I can, whilst feeling spoilt and selfish in the face of all the things she and Lucy are going through, trying to avoid any mention of Mark's cases in case the Foreign Office has indeed bugged the phone, but attempting to entertain her, too.

When at last we say goodbye to one another I have tears in my eyes. I lean my head against the window pane for a while, staring down into the street. The gospel choir is singing rather mournfully once again.

I feel very emotional. I have tried to ring Henry, but so far he has avoided me. I resolve to try again tomorrow, after the ambassador's dinner. I don't really feel in much of a garden party mood.

"So, so you think you can tell... heaven from hell? Grey skies from blue?" Wyclef competes with the gospel choir, from within my head.

Chapter 27

Diary Twenty-One

I had never attended anything as sumptuous or as formal as the dinner at Plantation House. Mark probably had, Janine and Helen, too; certainly Edward, I remember thinking.

When Mark and I were younger, I used to accompany him to legal dinners and less formal functions, small banquets in a variety of strange settings. Mark was proud of me then, loved showing me off.

Our transport to the ambassadorial residence was not particularly posh, however. We were chauffer driven to the place in a white van, wearing our finery, the women careful not to catch flowing gowns in the heavy, sliding vehicle doors.

I had brought with me a long evening dress, bought at Debenhams, not particularly expensive, simple in its style. It was grey, with a Grecian shoulder to show off my tan. Jack, none the worse for being shot at, complimented me on it and was kind enough to say that I looked beautiful.

I was certainly not as young or as beautiful as the skinny Janine; there wasn't much point in pretending that I was. I wondered how old she was. She, too, wore a long evening dress, simple, black, with silver embroidery at the shoulder straps – eye-catching; certainly it caught Mark's eye, anyway. It complemented her figure perfectly. But in the van, he sat dutifully, I suppose, next to me.

The chauffer parked the van at the side of the large house, having driven through dense woodland first.

A squarish, white, colonial wedding cake of a house with many shuttered windows, Georgian and simplistic in its grandeur, it overlooked flat, green lawns. We entered beneath a porch which led to the entrance hall.

We were welcomed by the ambassador's smiling staff, proffering silver trays laden with drinks.

"When was it built?" I asked Jack, who appeared to know most things about Saint Helena.

"In the 1790s, I believe. Built as a country residence for the governor of the East India Company."

I accepted a glass of wine, following Mark and Jack.

"It's open to visitors on certain days of the week," Jack added.

I very much wanted to explore the drawing room, where we were surrounded by some interesting paintings and textiles. But Mark took my arm, leading me to the place where Helen and Janine were talking, so exploration would have to wait a while. I had been a little disappointed that Tessa and Rachel hadn't been invited, but they told me that they had been invited on several previous occasions and didn't particularly feel left out of the affair.

Mark's unspoken plan was to make sure that I was comfortable with Helen and Janine so that he could introduce himself to the ambassador. So I kept a fixed smile upon my face for Janine but couldn't resist a gasp of horror and a couple of giggles at Helen's entertaining story about a gangster who had shut his mother-in-law in the boot of his car, intending to kill her – only the brave woman leapt out when he opened the boot and clawed his face, escaping the plot. As the lawyers I have met are sympathetic, on the whole, with an understanding of the human race, I think they tell these stories as a way of coping with real life; although sometimes it gets out of hand, as one lawyer tries to out-do another in the ancient art of storytelling.

Every now and then, as I listened, I would peek at my surroundings and the invited guests. I knew very few of them. Jack joined us with a middle-aged, balding man with a rather anxious face and his less anxious wife at his side. This was the island's governor. The wife was called Caroline and I warmed to her immediately. She was very open and friendly, very much like Helen, in fact. She explained that they had four children under the age of twelve, whom they had left this evening with their nanny.

The time came for us to be invited through to dinner at the long table set for about twenty or so people. I was seated about five places down from the ambassador's wife at the head of the table, opposite Mark and between Edward and the kindly judge.

She, the ambassador's wife, was very elegant and erect, which I suppose is a good thing to be if you are married to an ambassador. When she first spoke, I thought she was American, but during conversation she explained to those sitting closest to her that she was Canadian.

She was attractive, certainly, with a rather pale, angular face and straight, honey coloured hair which reached her shoulders. Until she stood, I didn't realise that she had a slight disability and relied upon a walking stick, which leaned against the wall behind her, which a young staff member handed to her when she rose from the chair.

Mrs Dalby, Lauren, was someone whom I would like to know more about, I decided. She was friendly to everyone and a good conversationalist.

Her husband was seated at the other end of the table, quite good-looking, affable, with a ready laugh.

I had thought that any speeches would be given at the start of the meal, but along with a toast to the Queen they were kept until the end.

I was a little nervous about sitting next to the kindly judge, a knowledgeable and intelligent man with a keen sense of humour, but he put me at my ease early on in the proceedings by asking me about my family. He may not have been genuinely interested, but the point is that I felt very much more relaxed after a while in this splendid setting.

Intent upon the judge's questions and upon not spilling my fish starter, I hardly noticed Mark until the dessert arrived. Then, intent upon the conversation around me, which was less structured now that the diners had relaxed with their wine, I heard his voice directed at Mrs Dalby.

"For how long did you live in Kenya?"

She smiled at him. "I was at boarding school in England when I was a child; my father worked at the embassy in Nairobi. I became a teacher and taught at one of the top private primary schools in Nairobi for a few years, until I married. Then we lived in Panama, where our two daughters were born. We have been in Saint Helena for eight years now."

The Canadian accent was very slight. Too eagerly, Mark said, "Stephanie is a teacher, too..."

Now I would have to speak before the entire company, whilst all eyes stared at me. I found it a little daunting. "I used to teach," I said, "but not now." More was expected of me, whether they were interested or not. "In primary and secondary schools, although I prefer primary; younger children are interested in everything, aren't they?" I paused, looking around me. People seemed to require a little more of me. "In fact, Mark and I met whilst he was a lawyer and I a teacher in a prison. It was a temporary job, quite daunting, but I had some supportive colleagues."

I wanted the conversation to return to Mrs Dalby; after all, she was the hostess. "What age group did you teach, Mrs Dalby?" I asked.

The corner of her mouth dimpled as she smiled at me. "Please, call me Lauren," she said.

After that, she took up the conversation once more and I felt it was not because she had to be the centre of attention but because she wanted to help me out, so I liked her even more.

It broadened to a discussion involving the people around me. The subject of education grew to incorporate the unwieldy topic matter of Africa.

"So, how would you improve education in Africa? Where would you start?" The judge asked Mrs Dalby.

She shook her head. "Perhaps many Africans don't have the confidence to change things; they look to foreigners to solve their problems for them."

The subject matter boosted my lack of confidence. "Couldn't it begin with South Africa? If they got it right, ideas might flow into neighbouring countries..." My voice petered away after this. I was a primary school teacher, not a politician, not a diplomat; I expected the people around me to look at me with polite contempt, but they did not.

"That's the ideal that many politicians have," Mrs Dalby agreed, "but education, even in South Africa, has proved a complicated subject. So far, the government has not been able to supply enough classroom spaces for school-aged children or to train enough teachers. Then there are the corruption issues. The South African government has received over three hundred reports of school principals who appear to have stolen cash from school accounts, as I understand."

Several people were listening to her now, the conversations further along the table almost ceasing.

"That's dreadful!" Helen voiced, Janine nodding.

"The tragic thing is that even the poorest of parents sacrifice a substantial portion of their earnings to send their children to lower-cost private schools," Mrs Dalby explained.

I looked across at Mark for the first time all evening. He wasn't looking at Mrs Dalby, or in my direction. No, he was definitely, positively, staring entranced at Janine. His eyes shone with some magical intensity that hurt me beyond words.

After that I became a person with hearing loss, listening to nothing, stooped again by my own insecurity... until I saw that there was someone else gazing at Janine, equally entranced. From the little smile she returned him, Janine was aware of the attention. Janine and the ambassador, Mr Dalby, had locked eyes together in flirtatious interest.

A new feeling swept over me – indignance – but now in defence of Mrs Dalby, whom I glanced at. She smiled back at me. Her smile was like a Masonic handshake. Two women past their prime, who had grown used to being second best to other mistresses, acknowledging one another.

Chapter 28
Diary Twenty-Two

Over the next two days, the heat became so oppressive that the skies seemed to hang above us like swathes of thick blue material. On the second day, the heavenly washing line collapsed and the rain poured as though it would never stop, running like a river down the Jamestown gutters. It stopped eventually, and just in time for the annual, pre-Christmas Garden Party at Plantation House.

The rain had stopped at last, but the overhanging leaves of the many trees and plants flanking the drive to the house were dripping wet and showered us as we left the car.

So many cars were parked everywhere: on grass verges, on the sides of the road and in the long, curving driveway, leading to the grand house. It was as though everyone on the island would attend the event.

We arrived a little late, the lovely lawyer Mairead's fault. When we arrived at her flat to collect her, she was leaning out of the window, her blonde tresses caught up beneath a black fascinator as she waved frantically down at us.

"I've got a rogue mouse and I hate them; could somebody come and capture it for me?" A soft Irish accent gave way to a sudden girlish squeal.

There was a sad struggle, then, between Mark, Jack and Phil, about who should be the knight in shining armour to go to her aid. It rendered me speechless, my mouth falling open in, I'm sure, a suitably unattractive way. I am a primary teacher by training, small rodents are my speciality, but Mark? He still calls me to the bathroom when a spider lurks in the shower and would stand on a chair at the sight of a mouse.

I gazed out of the car window after them in wide-eyed cynicism, tapping my fingernails on the door handle until the men emerged at last, red-faced from their endeavours.

"Did you catch it?" Janine asked with a smile.

"No, too quick for us. Mairead has called the island's rat catcher," Jack replied, wiping his forehead with a large white handkerchief.

Mark held the door open for Mairead, who was younger and prettier than any of us in her tight-fitting, floral summer frock, and she squeezed her long legs and ample bottom between me and the car door for the drive to Plantation House.

Mark skilfully parked the car between two others after Jack had jumped out to remove a 'Please don't park here' sign, and we women teetered down the hill towards the grand house nestling in a leafy valley.

In front of it, a grand marquee had been erected against the rain; but other than the few smokers standing outside, it looked as though the entire population of the island was seeking shelter beneath it.

Drinks were being served on silver trays by the island's enthusiastic Brownies. Helen commented upon this, as under sixteen-year-olds are not permitted to serve alcohol in British shops, but 'there you go,' as they say in Saint Helena.

I had expected that we would meet with the ambassador and Mrs Dalby once more. But Mark told me they'd been called away at the last moment on a matter of urgency and the party would be hosted by the governor and his wife.

Within moments, we were standing before the smiling governor in his white uniform, a fixed, white smile to match the outfit. Beside him, his dark-haired wife, who rather reminded me of Anjelica Huston's portrayal of the grand high witch in the Roald Dahl story.

"Halloo, verry pleased that you could come..." She towered over me and I suddenly found myself inspecting the dark hair to see whether I could detect the joins between a wig and her scalp. I listened to her as she spoke to Mark about various inconsequential things, but the queue behind him was long and I assumed that she had little time to speak to individual guests and so their conversation wasn't long.

I followed Mark, who followed Janine into the marquee. Mrs Quelch, the Anjelica Huston look-alike, had very little to say to me beyond the fact that she liked my clutch bag, recognising that it had been handmade on the island.

Janine's dress was white, expensive, very flattering to her tiny figure, and she wore cork-bottomed sandals with a silver strap, on which I would have teetered uncomfortably, but which suited her. There were short, dangly earrings in her earlobes. In the car, she had smelled deliciously of expensive perfume. She made me feel very fat, although, honestly, I am not.

She immediately went over to talk with the judge's wife, once a lawyer in her own right so I had gathered. Mark followed her and I him. They all knew one another, and immediately began talking shop, about opposing barristers in the family division.

Not for the first time I wished that I had become a lawyer so that I could join in with more interesting things to say. So I smiled and listened carefully to what they were saying as an alternative.

As I stood there, like an extra in a film, I mulled this over, that he now had more in common with Janine than with me. It hurt horribly. It laid me low all of a sudden. We used to share so much, not just the children, but likes and dislikes and friends; now I hardly knew the people he met with. I gave myself a little shake, tried to fix all of my thoughts on the people around us.

Beyond the marquee a small, wooden stage had been erected. Tessa was one of the more important members of the brass band, all smartly attired in black trousers and white shirts. She was seated upon a stool with a trombone resting beneath her knees which seemed to dwarf her tiny frame.

I waved at her and she grinned back at me. The conductor drew the band to their feet and they started a rousing rendition of 'On Ilkley Moor Bar T'at'.

"Hello, you're Mark's wife, aren't you?"

A uniformed man, broad-shouldered, a confident half smile and blue-grey eyes, looked down at me.

"Yes, that's right, and you are?" I held out my hand.

"Ian Shaw, customs officer. I was just admiring your flower."

It was a mildly flirty introduction and I think I blushed, at least my cheeks felt warm as I tried to think what 'I like your flower' might mean.

Was it a medieval reference to some part of my anatomy? Then I realised that it was a literal referral to the bright orange flower now pinned to the cleavage of my fuchsia pink dress to hide some bad stitching.

His eyes twinkled in a way which gave me confidence too, and made me like him, I suppose. I tried to sum him up. He had sisters, daughters, a wife... I felt sure of it.

Grow up, I told myself, *this is exactly the kind of thing that upsets you about Mark.*

"So, you're a teacher, yes?" The question cut into my thoughts.

"Yes," I agreed, frowning a little because the next thing he said was, "Tessa told me."

"Ah..."

"What have you been doing with yourself whilst Mark has been beavering away and causing mayhem on the island?"

I accepted a glass of wine from a small, proud Brownie.

"Precious little that's of any use to the world," I replied. "Meeting people, swimming." I grinned at him. "Drinking in The Standard."

"And dancing, I hear..."

I winced and bit my lip. News travels fast; it was my own doing.

"Well, yes, on occasion..."

He grinned. "Just the kinds of things that I enjoy here; have to admit life has been quite peaceful for me in Saint Helena until now."

"Until now?" I frowned, uncomprehending.

"Now the airport is almost completed, things are hotting up. I have to begin a whole training programme here for the immigration staff."

I glanced towards Mark, kind of hoping he might notice me, but he was kneeling beside a very old lady in a wheelchair, with a flowery straw hat on her head and several medals pinned to her chest, trying to listen to her, whilst Janine laughed beside him at some anecdote she was relaying to him. They made a handsome couple, I supposed. Once upon a time he would have linked arms with me and insisted I was his companion.

"What does Mrs Shaw do on the island?" I asked the customs officer, turning away from Mark.

He blew out his cheeks in a soft sigh. "Mrs Shaw quickly got fed up with the restrictions here and missed our grown-up girls and her family, so she went back to the UK after a year. I've been here for three, with visits home, of course."

"Where's home?"

"Bristol, actually…"

That was the mild West Country accent I had been trying to place, and just as I was about to ask him what 'the restrictions' meant, he asked me, "So, will you come back with him, on the next trip?"

"The next trip?" I felt very stupid once more. Would there be a next trip? Of course, I would be the last person to know. He smiled in a kindly way at the confusion stamped across my face.

"They all want your husband to come back, according to Tessa and Rachel. Him and the other barristers, too. They've got the kind of expertise that's missing on the island, haven't they? I think the judge is talking about next spring."

"Oh…" That soon. I would feel torn. Perhaps it would be every year for the rest of his life. Our life would change, but it might change anyway, depending upon Janine's progress, I thought darkly.

The band finished playing to take a well-earned break, and we clapped them.

"You must be very proud of him," Ian said. "I've never known the ambassador to invite the residents of the old people's home before. Tessa told me it was Mark's suggestion."

"I am," I agreed, "proud..."

"I'm meant to be mingling," Ian said. "Care to mingle with me?"

I was tempted, for a moment, to attach myself to his arm in the absence of Mark and Mrs Shaw.

"I probably ought to catch up with Mark." I smiled.

He inclined his head in a half bow and nodded. "Then I hope we will talk a bit more, later."

But Mark had left the old lady when I turned around; he had disappeared, presumably with Janine in tow.

A small, weedy man was standing outside the marquee, strumming a guitar and singing a Joan Baez song badly, whether anyone wanted him to or no. I think the ambassador would have cheerfully cracked it over his head, from the look on his face, his expression suggesting his diplomatic skills were being sorely put to the test.

Jack was speaking to the lovely blondes, with an unlit pipe clenched between his teeth.

A woman was saying loudly, "But it's wonderful, isn't it? That no one has been killed or injured on such a complicated project as the Saint Helena airport..."

I raised my eyebrows at her, in honour of the Zimbabwean father who had been killed and who Josh had told me about.

I gazed across the sea of decorated straw hats and flowery dresses, searching for Mark, accepting a second glass of wine from a Brownie in an immaculately ironed uniform.

As I caught Rachel's eye, and waved, I passed Janine and Helen. Mark wasn't with them.

There was a small, circular wooden table behind Janine and on it she had placed her handbag. Jutting out of the unzipped top of the handbag was a small black diary.

No one was looking. I glanced around the room to see that Janine's thin-boned back was facing me. My heart thumped with adrenalin. What was I doing? This was becoming a habit.

I smiled openly at anyone close by, my chin lifted in innocence, before taking the diary swiftly and furtively, shoving it into my little cream bag from the craft shop and hiding it in the bottom where it wouldn't be seen, then made my escape to the loos. What else could I do? I couldn't murder Janine, after all.

Chapter 29

Diary Twenty-Three

I had little to say to Mark that evening, and he picked up on my silence and challenged me about it before dinner, but I didn't want another row, so I said that I had a sore throat instead of telling the truth, which was that he had ignored me for the duration of the afternoon.

It would be obvious to any idiot why I was upset, but Mark was the kind of person who could not have his behaviour challenged, and he wouldn't change it out of obstinacy.

I'd only been married once, so I couldn't say whether many men were like this; all I knew was that my sister's partner had fallen below the mark. Perhaps we had been spoilt as children by a father who was devoted to our mother, or a mother who wouldn't pretend to be less than she was. Or perhaps we had set the hurdle too high.

So, I didn't say, *"You didn't talk to me at all at that garden party,"* or *"Are you in love with Janine?"* And I waited for him to say something like, *"Let's go and have a meal on our own for a change,"* which would have made everything better, but he didn't.

At least I have the diary, I thought, vengefully, as though it were a weapon to hit him with.

Having clutched the bag to my side for the duration of the garden party, I longed to examine it, but I needed a quiet time, in a quiet place, alone.

Wellington House was a sparse but elegant building in the centre of Jamestown.

There were two large rooms, originally drawing rooms, with wooden trestle tables decorated with flowers.

The waiters and waitresses were young trainees from the school, and the food, although carefully prepared, resembled the pages of a 1970s cookbook.

The 'Tuna Surprise' was presented in upturned bowl shape with an olive on the top, so that Jack remarked that it looked like a woman's breast, whilst the lamb chops had little chef's hats on.

We had entertainment too, in the shape of an old, bearded sea dog called William, who bored us all into a mindless stupor after the fifth seafaring tale told in a sonorous monotone.

Heaven knew who he was or where he came from, but eventually the lady who ran the restaurant caught on and beckoned him from the door, saying, "Can I borrow you, Bill?" And as Bill shuffled away, she apologised for him.

"Sorry about that, he's lovely really, but he gets a little carried away sometimes," she said.

"Does he live here?" Helen asked.

"Oh no, he sometimes drops in for a drink and a chat and we tolerate him." She smiled.

I think Mark would have held my hand on the short walk back to the hotel; but I had noticed that although he did this in front of the others, he desisted when Janine was there.

I wondered whether she had missed the diary. She hadn't remarked upon it, or the earring, but then she probably wouldn't.

As we stood in the street outside the hotel, Mark asked, "Fancy a nightcap before we go to bed?"

My lips moved in a tight little smile.

"No thanks, it's been a long day. I thought…" – I was about to suggest 'we' but changed it to – "I might go to bed a bit earlier."

It wasn't the right tactic. I probably ought to fight for him; but there again, why should I? It was demeaning. I should have some rights after all these years.

Janine ran her fingers through her dark fringe and hooked one high-heeled foot behind the other. "I'd like one," she said, throwing me a happy smile.

How did she manage to keep her red lipstick intact? Mine always disappeared after a meal, I mused unhappily.

I said goodnight and turned my back on them, annoyed. I had wanted him to follow me, to make mad passionate love to me. Now I wished I had agreed to the late-night drink.

I don't know what time he came to bed.

Having fought with the bedclothes and wrestled with my thoughts for quite a while, I fell into a restless sleep.

I suffered some bizarre and unpleasant dreams and woke, eventually, drenched in sweat with my heart racing and Mark snoring heavily, lying on his back beside me.

Through the open window the church clock struck the hour whilst I glimpsed the lights of Jacob's Ladder, stretching to the dark sky like a diamond bracelet.

I watched Mark sleeping for a moment, with a mixture of tenderness and irritation reserved for a child.

Then I took a few sips from a tumbler of water. I crossed the room and leaned towards the window, expelling a small, lonely sigh.

In one moment, all of my pent-up fears and anxieties were vanquished. I stared, frowning through the darkness towards the shop lights illuminating the pavement opposite the hotel.

I could see her so clearly, alone and vulnerable. A little girl, a Saint, a long, dark plait running down her back, swinging from side to side as she ran. As I watched, she looked back over her shoulder; no ghost... a real child, bare-footed, eight perhaps, or nine?

Whether she was crying or talking to herself, I couldn't tell. She wore a light cotton nightdress, and the fingers of her left hand were wound in the hem as she pattered along the pavement.

That hand was desperate to be held by someone who loved her; the little voice was pleading for reassurance. What on earth was a child doing in the dark at this time of night?

I couldn't stand there as a voyeur any longer; I wanted to reach her, to put my arms about her. I grabbed the wrap from our bed and fled to the door, unlocking it.

I left the door open wide, with Mark still sleeping, to descend the staircase as fast as I could.

It was not the kind of hotel where the reception was open all night. The hallways were dark and silent, and at the foot of the staircase I snatched the bolt back and stepped out into the street, staring up and down at the houses and alleyways for the girl.

My own feet were bare, but I went down the stone steps, searching for her.

"Hello?" I called, not once but several times, and loudly.

She had gone. She could not have gone very far, into a nearby house perhaps, or along one of the street's little alleyways?

I recalled what Tessa had told me. In his cups, poor drunken Danny believed she was a ghost, but the little girl was flesh and blood and very vulnerable. He had seen her and now I had witnessed it too. I stayed in the street for some long while, hoping to find her crouching somewhere, or hiding in one of the alleyways. In my nightdress, I wandered up and down the road for about half an hour, but there was no sign of her or of anyone else.

It took me a long time to sleep after that, a long, long time; it washed away all of the other silly, trivial thoughts, leaving me yearning for the morning so that I could tell Mark or Helen.

When the pink light and birdsong penetrated the darkness, I got up and washed at the bathroom sink, then dressed and leaned across the bed to Mark, who was lying on his back, emitting male odours of sweat and wine and no doubt dreaming of Janine. He mumbled in his sleep but didn't stir.

Impatiently I picked up my bag with the diary inside it, along with Tessa's car keys to the borrowed car.

Only Gladys was in the dining room and she was talking to herself about yoghurt.

"Hello, sweetie, wanna cooked breakfast?" She beamed, in her cross-eyed fashion, as I approached.

"No thanks, Gladys. I'll just grab some of these to take with me, if I may," I said, reaching for a fistful of sweet rolls and a couple of cartons of juice.

At the hotel door, I hesitated. I thought about finding Helen. I must do something about the little girl, but Helen wouldn't be awake yet. I suspected that she thought me a little crazy at the moment, considering my hostility towards Janine. Perhaps she would think my mind had turned to ghost spotting; maybe she would believe that I was delusional. I went back up the staircase anyway, standing outside her bedroom door, chewing my nail. I didn't want to wake her, so I determined to seek her out later, before she started the business of the day.

I had always maintained that I wouldn't drive Tessa's car, and it was rather foolish of me to do so now as I didn't have my driver's licence with me, and I wasn't insured to drive her car as Mark was. There again, I felt pretty sure that several cars on the island were uninsured, and I had spotted families driving about with small children dangling from the windows; this was Britain, after all, albeit several decades ago.

I just had to make sure I did no damage to it, drive carefully; and I was a cautious driver; my father had taught me. So cautious that our daughter would berate me for being so slow when I followed her anywhere.

I had no satnav, but had looked at the map and felt pretty sure of the route I should take.

I wanted to get out of Jamestown, wanted to read the diary dates alone, somewhere undisturbed.

Tessa had told me where to find that kind of peace.

Diana's Peak was a place where she, her husband and children used to camp at weekends. Tessa had said it was very beautiful, and she was right.

The geography of the island never ceased to amaze me. I travelled the bumpy, winding roads, my hands gripping the wheel lightly. At this time of day there were few drivers about. I slowed down occasionally, to appreciate the low ridges and flat plains; the sudden, volcanic shapes in soft browns and mossy, vibrant greens.

There were many such peaks, but Diana's was perhaps the most beautiful of all.

A moss-covered, fluted, ridged shape rose from the yellow-green plains, where cattle slowly roamed, surrounded by pines and pretty woodlands. The colours were similar to those in the Mediterranean, but the landscape was Devonshire one moment and Brazilian rainforest the next.

The roads leading to the peak were gritty and narrow and in a bad state of repair; they were tracks rather than roads.

On my journey, a stranger or two waved to me from the roadside. I realised they probably thought I was Tessa and recognised her car, but then strangers did wave to you in Saint Helena; it was friendly like that.

Just beyond the peak I was searching for, I found a wider track and followed it to a cattle grid.

I stopped the car and got out to open a heavy spring gate with both hands, whilst the dopy brown cows stared moony-eyed at me.

As I let the gate go, too quickly, it sprung back at my head with unexpected vengeance. Clout, bang; blood burst, rising instantly to the surface and quickly dripping to the dry ground, and my head was in such incredible pain.

I clutched at my forehead and staggered backwards, swearing profusely.

"Idiot, bloody fool!" I yelled at the cows as though it was their fault.

I staggered back to the car for a tissue and to examine the cut in the driver's mirror. I didn't think it was deep, but the blow to my head had left me reeling with pain and feeling sick; my front teeth tasted of metal but were unbroken, thank God.

I got out of the car again, lying down on my back on the dry, warm earth, shading my eyes until I got my breath back – whilst the cows continued munching the grass, unaware, stupid and unsympathetic.

At last I climbed to my feet and determinedly lifted myself back into the car. I drove a little dizzily through the gate, afterwards lifting the latch with greater awareness and closing it behind me.

I drove slowly across the bumpy ground, parking the car close to the woods and getting out, still holding the tissue to my head. A warm wind tugged at my hair. The air smelled sweet, of sunshine after the rain, and mercifully the bleeding had stopped.

I began to walk, across fields where Napoleon and his entourage had once galloped their horses in a race, desperate for entertainment. No horses now, no interest in them perhaps, too difficult to bring them to the island on the RMS. Only the shaggy brown donkeys remained.

In the distance were the fields where the Boers had camped. They were treated a little better, or so I had read, than the Boer soldiers incarcerated by the British in the first concentration camps in South Africa. I supposed there was nowhere to escape to when you were so far away from another country, so the guards could be more relaxed. But so many young boys, some of them only sixteen, who would die in Saint Helena, never to see their mothers again.

I thought of Henry, eighteen. Where the hell was Henry? His elder sister hadn't seen him, neither had his aunt. Why wasn't he answering his voicemail messages? I would try to call him again when I got back to the hotel.

Despite the stinging head, blood now caking my forehead, it felt good to be walking, good to be alone. With my bag swinging from my shoulder, I felt like a sixth former on a Geography field trip. I had almost forgotten that I carried Janine's diary with me, almost didn't want to read it now.

But I headed for the woodlands to find a comfy place to sit in the shade and read the diary. I followed a rocky path, flanked by tiny, pretty flowers and with only the crickets for company, following the path upward to the summit of a steep hill. My head had stopped bleeding at last. I dabbed away the tiny rivulets of sweat from my cleavage with the bloody tissue as I walked, until I reached the hilltop and found a rocky outcrop, high above the shimmering blue sea, with a canopy of whitewood trees to protect me against the sun.

Then I sat for a while, staring down at the sunbeams on the bright, blue water far below me, taking out the little rolls and hungrily devouring two of them, none too delicately either, happy to eat my picnic without company.

Afterwards, I reached tentatively into my bag for the diary, fearing the peace I now felt would soon be gone. I wanted to read it. I did not want to read it. I had to read it.

I opened the cover, and on the very first page, in sloping, elegant writing, five numbers had been written.

The first entry was 'Royal Courts of Justice', 'Greg' written beside it.

The second was Mark's mobile number.

That, in itself, meant nothing, I reasoned. They knew each other well; they had worked closely together.

I turned the pages, scanning them quickly but efficiently.

'January 16th, Law Society dinner, meet Mark at six.'

I tried to think back, to where I had been, to what I had been doing. It seemed so long ago.

I pursed my lips. That one date meant nothing either. I wasn't a lawyer; why shouldn't he go with another lawyer?

But then I imagined her being collected by him, tried to imagine the dress she would have worn, the fun they would have had together. His escort, and it hurt.

I turned the other pages: trials, dates, advocates meetings, until February 14th, Valentine's Day. I remembered the sadness I had felt. How I had pleaded with him to let me stay with him in London, and how cross he had been then, on the telephone. Saying that he couldn't make it. He had too much work to do. He promised we would have our special evening on the following day.

It was the first time in our marriage we had been away from one another on St Valentine's Day.

There it was, clearly: 'Marlborough Hotel – Mark, dinner, 7pm.'

My shoulder's fell. I went on, reading through the diary.

There were about eight appointments with Mark in all, not all of them social. A judge's retirement dinner, an event at Waddesdon Manor in Oxford. Some of these dates had the name of a restaurant, others a hotel in the evening. What was I to make of that?

I stared down at the bright blue lagoon below me, encircled by rocks. I bit my lip as I tried to think what I should do now and how I should do it, but my legs were numb, heavy with fatigue and a kind of misery.

At last I got up, brushing bits of wood and an insect from my arm. As I did so a small, folded piece of notepaper fluttered from the pages. I stooped to pick it up, shaking off a brown-bodied cricket, unfolding it.

Mark's writing; I knew it well, elegant, sloping. 'There will be too many people; meet at my room, say nine o'clock?' As if that wasn't enough, a kiss. Mark, who had not punctuated texts or notes with kisses since we were younger. A kiss for Janine.

I pushed the diary down into the bag and wandered back to the car. The graze to my head was nothing compared to my bruised emotions.

Chapter 30
Diary Twenty-Four

It must have turned eleven o'clock by the time I parked the car opposite the courts.

The town was busy with shoppers and old people resting on street benches beneath the shade of the trees. Nothing seemed real; I felt as though I was on a film set.

I glanced across the street, waving to the judge's friendly chauffeur who sat outside the court. I wandered thoughtfully up the street and past the church, but paused, hearing the sweetest music from within.

The vaulted church door stood ajar. I went inside. The church was empty but for one person, an older woman. She sat on one of the front pews, her short fair head bent over the strings of a harp.

I couldn't tell what music she played, it was in part folk tune, but in my present wistful mood it had the quality of an angel's song.

The music lifted to the high ceiling of the church. It was beautiful and I found myself rooted to the spot, standing very still throughout, not wanting to disturb the musician.

When she finished there was complete silence for several seconds, until I said, "That was so lovely."

She was clearly startled at my voice.

She looked towards me and smiled – such a kind smile.

"Thank you," she said.

Stupidly, ridiculously, my cheek and chin started to wobble. I stuck my tongue inside it. I didn't wish to cry in front of a stranger.

"Is this your first visit to the island? Are you on holiday?" she asked me, leaving the harp and walking towards me. A few paces in front of me she asked, in a kindly way, "Would you like to sit down? I could make you a cup of tea. It looks as though you have injured your head."

She smiled again, her head on one side, waiting.

Sympathy is lethal when you are trying not to cry.

I took a deep breath. "I'm fine, really, but thank you. It's just a small cut. I think it's healing up now."

She nodded, held out her hand. "I'm Greta," she said, "the vicar's wife."

I told her a little about who I was, said I would come back and look at the church properly on another day. Then I thanked her again for the lovely music and, aware of the tears that had appeared in my eyes, laughed self-consciously. "But you're not supposed to make people cry," I said.

Outside, once again in the sunshine, I saw a figure crossing the road.

Janine was wearing a tight-fitting but elegant black skirt and, despite the heat, a black jacket. Her hair was tied up in a ponytail and in her arms she held a bundle of files.

She didn't see me, even as I watched her walk to the little door on the right of the courthouse and she turned and pushed the door open with a high-heeled foot.

I watched her go inside, biting my lip thoughtfully. She looked so much younger than me. I felt so tired and had no excuse for feeling so; I wasn't working hard, as they were.

I returned to the hotel and slept for a while, not having slept well on the previous night. I realised that for the past few days, despite my mother's cancer, despite being concerned about Henry, all of my thoughts had been centred upon Janine and Mark.

When I woke up, I hid the diary in a washbag in my case and wandered downstairs to the coffee shop.

Helen was there, talking to Edward.

I waited until their conversation had finished and Edward had gone and Helen was tidying the bundle of notes that they had been looking at together.

"Hello, stranger, where were you at breakfast?" she asked me. Then, "Ouch, what happened to your head? You have a small golf ball there."

"It's nothing, really, I'll tell you about it later," I said. Then, "Helen, do you have a few minutes to spare?"

"A few. Got to get back to the court, but go on…"

I told her, all about the last night, and the little ghost girl, hoping she wouldn't think I was delusional. Then I waited, half expecting her to suggest a psychiatric assessment, but she didn't.

She frowned. "That's too suspicious, especially at the moment…"

"What do you mean by especially at the moment?" I asked.

She grimaced. "I can't really tell you. But there's something going on, and it doesn't sound as though the child was sleepwalking. She shouldn't be wandering about at that time of night." She regarded me for a minute. "I'll have to go, lovey, I'll be late for my meeting. But I'll do something about it. I promise to have it investigated. I will do something about it today, so try not to worry."

I knew she would. I trusted her. I felt happier than I had done all day in passing it onto her. I was not in a position to do anything, but Helen was. I could have told Mark, of course. Peculiar that, in an instant, my trust in telling her was stronger.

I bought a cup of takeaway coffee in the shop and took it back upstairs to retrieve my watercolours from the bedroom. A child's set, but they could be used to good effect.

I had been thinking about painting the harbour for some while, as a gift for Helen. Perhaps I could paint for Tessa and Rachel too.

Painting is as soothing as playing the harp. Perhaps it might still the panic inside me since reading Janine's diary and the note, I hoped.

I found a shady, solitary spot beneath overhanging brown rocks and overlooking the broken harbour wall. Not so far away, I could see that one or two small vessels were moored there, which I could paint into the scene.

The tiny black crabs scuttled from beneath my shadow as I sat down, arranging the paints and a cup of water, and started to sketch the sea and the horizon.

I had made quite a lot of progress and was in a soothing world of my own by then, so absorbed that I didn't hear the footfall approaching me, or see the shadow until the very last minute.

I looked up, startled out of the scene by another human being.

"Hello, Danny." I turned my startled expression into a smile, looking up at the craggy features, the mottled cheeks and heavy eyes.

He wore grey fisherman's overalls and his usual stern expression, which resembled a bear, mid growl. He held a can of beer loosely in his hand. He was clearly very interested in the painting, staring down at it with his head on one side.

"That good; not many paint like that," he said.

"Thanks, Danny." I felt so pleased at the compliment from the man who had said, *"You don't know my mamma,"* that I followed it up with, "Want me to do one for you?"

"Yeah, sure, if you got time…"

"Oh, I've got time, I'm on holiday. I'm doing this one for Helen…"

"Helen, she the lawyer who jus' come, pretty one?"

He grinned. He seemed to be questioning something. His large, brown, red-rimmed eyes lifted a little.

"Helen is pretty," I said, "but I think you must be talking about Janine."

I looked towards the sea to mask my feelings.

"Janine…" He said her name slowly. "Yeah. She spend a lot o' time with your husband, don't she?"

He was becoming offensive now. The more familiar, sullen thoughts were replaced by mischief.

"They work together, on the same cases," I said, aware of the edge in my voice.

"It make you mad?"

I sighed. There was hardly any point in denying it. "It make me mad that he work with a lot of pretty lawyers," I said.

"But that one special?"

I shrugged, and twisted my lips primly.

"I like you," he said. This was definitely a change of tune.

"I like you too," I replied, smiling up at him. I'm not sure if it was true, but I liked him more since I'd met him on the boat, and certainly I liked him more than Janine.

"Miss Tessa say you all goin' to the light show, at High Knoll, on Saturday."

It was the first I'd heard about it. "Do she... I mean, does she?"

"Yeah. Your husband bought tickets today. I helping with the electrics." He took a swig from the can.

"You make yourself useful on the island, Danny, a man of many talents."

He nodded.

"See you up there, then, at the Knoll. Think you done my paintin' by then?"

I nodded. "I'll do it by then, sure."

I watched him walk back towards the port. He turned back once and grinned happily, if not a little beerily.

Chapter 31

Diary Twenty-Five

When Mark came into the bedroom later, he looked tall, handsome and very preoccupied with the court cases.

He pulled off the white shirt and threw it onto the bed. I wondered briefly whether Janine had seen the muscular brown back and dismissed the idea before it could poison me.

"Barclays have been trying to get hold of me," he grunted. "Someone has taken three thousand pounds out of an account. They must have had my pin number."

He turned to glare at me. I shrugged and stared back, genuinely mystified.

"Well, it wasn't me. I wouldn't do that," I said defensively, then remembered Henry. I swallowed. I had let Henry, only the once, use it to purchase music on the internet.

Henry wouldn't take three thousand pounds, surely to God? But I had to confess it to Mark now, even though he would denounce me for the simpleton I undoubtedly was.

I told him, and his face turned puce with anger.

"How stupid..."

"Yes, you've a right to be cross, he promised me he would never use it again. But three thousand pounds? It's rather a lot for Henry's needs."

He gave a snort of derision.

"You'd better talk to the bank, then," I said. I would have to call Henry now; what the hell was going on?

But he went into the bathroom first, for a hasty shower, and I waited until he had emerged. I needed a long time to make the call, and I needed to do it away from Mark. I trusted Henry for the most part, he was a good lad. I felt sure that he wouldn't do such a thing, but I knew that both Mark and I had our suspicions, and when the cat is away, mice will play.

"I'm going down to the bar to get a drink," Mark said when he had dressed. "Then I'll call the bank from the reception phone."

"Okay," I smiled, with cleverly faked enthusiasm, because I didn't feel very sociable, or that I wanted to be party to his little games with Janine. "I'll be there shortly."

At the door, he glanced at me, openly mistrustful, which I resented, one eyebrow raised. "You will tell me what Henry has to say?" he demanded.

I smiled. "Of course I will," I assured him.

Incredibly, this time Henry answered. It was so good to hear his voice that I shrieked down the mouthpiece. "Henry, oh Henry, it's so good to hear you. Where have you been? I've been trying and trying to get hold of you!"

"Stay calm, Mum. I took some money out of Dad's bank and I'm in Harari."

"You are where?" I spluttered. "What do you mean, in Harari?" I wondered whether I had heard him correctly.

"Harari..."

"What? Harari? Harari in Zimbabwe?" I asked stupidly.

Of course. JJ, his dearest rapper friend... No way. Henry wouldn't go all that way; he had to be joking.

"I figured that if you and Dad could spend all that money on going to Saint Helena, you wouldn't mind if I did something just as important. I know it was a bit spontaneous, and I'll pay you back, promise."

"Are you on your own?" I asked in squeaky panic. I knew little about the place, except that I didn't believe it was the safest place for a naive British white boy to be, or a naive would-be British black boy like JJ, if it came to that.

"Cyril came with me. In fact, we're staying with Cyril's family. They've got a great house, Mum, and servants. We're not roughing it in the slums; they even have a pool. You mustn't worry, I swear we're okay."

There was a long pause, some voices in the background. Had the thousands paid for Cyril's ticket too, I wondered? It seemed not to matter just then. Just that Henry was safe.

"I'll pay Dad back, I promise. I'll get a job. But I want to find JJ and help him to get back to England."

I covered my face with my right hand, staring at the wall through my fingers in despair.

"When are you coming home?" I asked, feeling a panic inside of me that was far greater than any insecurity about Mark and Janine.

"Soon, I hope."

"What do you mean, soon? When is your return ticket for?" My voice rose to a shriek.

"I don't have one yet."

"What?" I groaned. "How are you intending to get JJ here, Henry? It's lunacy! It's one thing to visit him, but you will never get him out of Zimbabwe, for crying out loud! What exactly are you intending to do, smuggle him onto an airplane without a passport?"

There was a pause, as though he hadn't considered that and was mulling it over. But then he said, "No, of course not. I brought an application form for university with me. I'm going to get him to fill it in, like the immigration lawyer said. Then he can come back properly."

It was sensible. Who was going to pay for it, Mark and I?

"But why did you have to go there? You could have sent it to his dad's address. You didn't need to go there and spend all that money. From what I know, Zimbabwe can be a pretty dodgy place, Henry. Anyway, love, his parents don't have the money for him to go to university and he's not a British national, even if he should be!"

"I came here with Cyril because we can't find him. He's gone from Facebook; he's not answering his phone anymore..."

The last text JJ had sent me had said that he wanted to come home to England and could we help him. But then the texts had stopped.

"He was living with his dad and working on a farm, but he left and didn't come back, so now we're trying to find out if he's okay."

I groaned, filled as I was with a mixture of exasperation and pride.

"What if he's not okay? What then? This is too much, Henry; what do you think you can do then?"

"Please stop worrying, Mum. Enjoy your time there. I had to do something, he was so depressed, I know it. Cyril's family are great, they're looking after us well. You'd really like them. Cyril's uncle has a lead on it; he thinks he might know where JJ is, so we're going there today."

I didn't want to lose contact with Henry. I grabbed a pen and the hotel notepad.

"An address, Henry, give me an address. Where are you staying?"

He gave me Cyril's uncle's address, which sounded like something from the English suburbs. I read it over again to him to make sure. "Do you have enough phone credit?" I asked.

"Of course, I have enough money, and I'll pay you back, promise."

"That doesn't matter right now. Just stay safe, Henry, and please answer when I call you!" I shouted. "I love you. Please, please take care! Find out the address of the British Embassy, just in case…"

"I will. Love you too…"

"Henry, don't forget!"

But he had gone.

Chapter 32

Diary Twenty-Six

The many cases were drawing to their final judgements, which was just as well as we had only three days to go before our return to Cape Town on the RMS *Saint Helena*.

The cases that had not been concluded would continue in England, and Mark and Helen would return to the island in the spring, as well as Janine of course, which was a problem for me, not much point in denying that.

I think the judge, so calm throughout, became a real human being to me as I caught sight of him outside the robing room, pacing up and down, so deep in thought and with a cigarette held between his fingers. Solomon about to give judgement.

As for Mark, he was too preoccupied to be angry about Henry for long. A little surprised at his decision, but proud too, perhaps.

Sometimes Mark returned to the hotel with an infuriated expression on his face, and on others a look of triumph. This way, I got an impression of how the cases were progressing.

Twice he was absolutely, bloody well hopping mad. But I was used to these end-of-the-day reactions.

Although I wanted to know what was happening, I could only surmise the reasons from his moods and the snippets of conversation from various lawyers. I knew nothing very much. I didn't mind his moods, so long as he loved me and had not been carrying on romantically with Janine. But I suspected he had.

I felt listless, lacking in enthusiasm for the 'murder mystery', giving it up for the time being. I had never been good at making up my mind in a hurry, and consequently I was a little fractious and frustrated those last few days on the island.

But I managed five watercolour sketches for various people, including Danny, and I visited the little photocopying shop, where they sold clip frames, to mount the paintings.

I spent some of my time thinking things through in the island's fabulous swimming pool, pursuing rigid, military lengths whilst chewing life over like a dog with a bone. I visited people to say goodbye and to thank them. I really felt as though I couldn't bear to be parted from these new friends.

The light show took place two evenings before we left the island.

Before then, I had not realised how many cars there were in Saint Helena.

Most people parked at the foot of High Knoll and walked up to the fort with their picnic baskets, carrying small children upon their shoulders.

We arrived shortly before sunset and went first to the ramparts of the fort.

I thought about the description that some of the islanders used for their home. They often found it small, had even described it as a slightly claustrophobic place to live; but at the very top of High Knoll, a fort built by the East India Company and a prison where the more rebellious Boers were incarcerated, it feels as though you are at the centre of a vast earth, a vast, panoramic, mountainous earth suffused in a heat haze.

The sun had swathed everything in pink and gold, colours stretching to the pastel blue sea which you could turn three hundred and sixty degrees and never miss. The cooling wind tugged at you from every angle.

I turned to smile at Mark, forgetting what I felt about him inside, somewhere back in the past now, when we were young, and he took my photograph.

I let him (I usually protest), shading my eyes with one hand and holding my hair back from my face with the other, trying not to be self-conscious whilst wishing that my face looked less lined.

Afterwards, he clasped my fingers and kissed me, briefly, on my mouth.

In an instant it felt as though he had kissed it all away, all the anxiety. Then he turned to Helen and Janine, standing together further along the wall, and took their photograph.

I was forgotten once more, a pet that the master is too used to and must replace with a younger bitch.

We descended the battlements to the shelter of the old fort, where the light show would take place, to meet the others and set out blankets borrowed from Tessa. We added our offerings to the picnic, bought at the supermarket. Some meats, cheeses, bread and, of course, wine.

Rachel and Tessa were there. Rachel cleared the blanket beside her for me to sit down.

"Have you heard what happened to Sanele?" she asked.

"The interpreter?"

She nodded. "He's been arrested."

"What?" My eyes widened as I stared at her in amazement. "For what?"

"He came here to stir things up. He's been teaching some of the less responsible local youths to make homemade bombs from charcoal. They, the South African police, have been following him. They believe he is responsible for burning down the Boer museum."

I thought about Paula's criticism of him at the restaurant. My mouth opened to speak just as she said, "It's quite annoying really, he was a very good interpreter; we needed him."

"So, what happened?" I asked.

"The two South African men, they came over on the boat with you?"

"Yes, Helen's gunrunners, you mean?"

Rachel leaned closer to me. "They aren't gunrunners, they're SAPS."

"What's 'SAPS'?" I asked blankly.

"The South African Police Service," she explained. "They've been following him for some while; he's considered to be quite high risk, apparently. Pity, he was such a nice young man in many ways."

I nodded, biting my lip to resist the smile at her description of him, whilst feeling shocked and a little shaky. There was really nothing funny about it; I too had thought him a 'nice young man', albeit a little vain. But I liked him.

I thought about his parents, first and foremost. They would have been so proud of him. What would they feel now? I wondered how I would handle it if someone told me that Henry was a terrorist, a freedom fighter, a revolutionary, or in whatever way you chose to describe it. That he intended to blow people up and had been arrested for it. Nelson Mandela was surely a 'nice young man', Guy Fawkes, too. So many nice young men intent upon injuring others. Although, in this case, I didn't understand his cause.

I stared from Rachel to Janine, who was lightly touching Mark's shirt sleeve. He had his legs stretched out before him, swinging one foot across the other in tune with the first chords of the 1812 Overture, which was being piped through a distant speaker.

Janine was on the other side of him, her slim legs tucked lightly beneath her summer dress. She raised her skirt to scratch gently at a mosquito bite, and Mark's eyes dropped to her legs. I found myself turning away completely, to mask my annoyance and disquiet.

I turned towards Helen instead. I wanted to ask her about the little ghost girl. Perhaps suspecting it, she said in a whisper, "She's been taken to a safe house. I'll tell you more about it later. She will be looked after whilst the children's services talk with her."

I was glad, but dreaded to think what might have been going on.

A rather plump young man sat beside her on the rug, his fair hair already receding, although he could only have been in his early thirties. He wore a lovely, gentle smile.

"Sam is the human rights officer for Saint Helena," Helen said.

I asked him about his job, about the people who came to him. I thought, all of the while, that he looked as if he wouldn't say boo to a goose and that some government officials on the island must be very glad that he was their human rights officer.

But perhaps he had gained something since Mark and Helen had arrived, for he said, "Seven people came to see me yesterday; nine the day before!" in a way that suggested a boost to his confidence and that few people had visited him for help before.

As the music began and night set in, so did the light show. People stopped talking, except for the young children there, who continued to play between the colourful picnic rugs, chasing one another.

I got to my feet again after a while, careful not to disturb the others, in search of Danny. I'd brought his painting with me, rolled up in a cardboard tube. But I couldn't find him and expected he'd be 'backstage' somewhere, working on the electrical side of things.

Suddenly there was a burst of neon colour on the fortress wall; the light show opened with a projected map of St Helena, vivid blue dolphins leaping across it. The sound of cannon fire, not real but simulated, impressive nonetheless, made us cover our ears. The pageant had begun, so I found my way back and sat down again.

Opposite me, Jack was eating his third lamb roll and swigging his Namibian beer.

The committee who had organised this, a combination, I think, of the new tourist board and the Heritage Society, had gone to great lengths to put the show together. It was impressive indeed.

"Isn't that your friend Danny?" Jack hissed at me after about an hour, nodding into the distance.

It was. He was leaning against a wall away from the lights, but close enough to be reflected in them, so his face was a ghastly green one moment and a devilish red the next.

He held something in his hand, a torch, and he was staring towards our group, but I had the feeling he wasn't looking for me.

I decided it wasn't the time to scramble over the picnickers with my painting.

Hungry, I bit delicately into a lamb roll. I hadn't seen Janine eat anything and my waist was at least two sizes larger than hers.

"Does anyone know where the loos are?" Janine whispered then.

"There are toilet cubicles set up next to the old stable block," Helen said.

She leaned on Mark's shoulder as she got up. He smiled up at her. I flared my nostrils in annoyance. I watched Mark in profile until Janine was some way from him. He must have been aware of it and turned to me with obvious guilt written across his face.

When he had turned away, I looked towards Janine's figure once more, clad in jeans and an expensive cashmere sweater. She was wandering alone now, in the shadow of the fortress wall, towards the place that Helen had indicated.

Just as I turned away, I saw something no one else appeared to notice, and my heart squeezed itself of all oxygen in a split second. The large figure of Danny was following her, with the torch in his hand. But the torch wasn't turned on, and his movements were furtive, hesitant, like a child in a game of hide and seek. His shadow seemed enormous, grotesque in the stage lighting, a monster in a black and white movie.

Was he...? No, it couldn't be, and yet this was Danny in pursuit of Janine.

"Will nobody rid me of this damned woman?" The words came into my head and I held my breath for an instant, remembering his comments to me about her.

I must have said, "Oh no..." aloud, or something like that, because Mark asked me, "What is the matter?"

I ignored him, scrambling to my feet with less grace than Janine, then dodging and leaping over the picnickers as I hadn't done since my youth when I could sprint, racing towards the two distant figures.

I took the fastest route, my mind madly calculating the maze of family groups so I would avoid jumping on an innocent picnicker. For a moment my figure was haloed in light. I heard a few grumbles of annoyance as I spoiled the light show.

My heart was a small, pounding cannon itself, as I kept my eyes upon the two figures, running faster than I'd done since the parents' race on sports day, terrified that the worst would happen and I wouldn't reach them in time. All of the while, the bars of the 1812 Overture pounded all around us in tune with my heart.

Then at last I caught up with him, skidded behind Danny, panting as I came to a halt, and there were just the three of us, hidden by the fortress wall.

He was lifting the torch high above his head, above her head, but I don't think he meant to turn it on. He had a very different plan.

He turned towards me in surprise, the heavy torch raised in his hand then, and stared at me in a very Neanderthal way. His eyes were wide in the large forehead, his mouth slightly slack at the corners as if in a trance, before he brought the torch slowly down to his side.

And Janine turned too, giving a small yelp of surprise at the two people standing close beside her. Her eyes went from Danny, to the torch, to me, with a question in them. I will never know to this day if she understood anything, but I don't think I've ever seen anyone look so scared.

"I decided to go as well..." I began, thinking on my feet. "Danny brought a torch for us, as it's rather dark out here, isn't it? Not very good lighting for the loos."

Neither Janine nor Danny said anything. They were staring at each other.

"Didn't you, Danny?" I nodded eagerly at him, waiting for a response, jabbering wildly. Do you want to turn it on?"

He nodded slowly then, staring at me as though he had been sleepwalking.

"Do you want to turn it on, then?" I encouraged him, smiling as you might smile at a small child.

His finger moved to the button, and we had light.

Chapter 33

Thadie

After Thadie had stayed at The Jolly Sailor for a week and a half, she and Alan settled into a non-communicative but peaceful co-habitation which Molly had encouraged. Molly understood the importance of keeping the customers satisfied. She could not, however, encourage Alan to warm towards Sanele, who scuttled away from Alan with the speed of a small lizard each time the man approached him. It was Molly who greeted Sanele with a smile, served him breakfast and chatted with him.

It was only after a rather crudely named game of cards, played out in near silence between Alan and Thadie, which Thadie won – accumulating the ten Saint Helena pound bet they had placed – that Alan, warming to her, suggested, "Wanna come and see that wreck I told you about, the one in the photo you ask me?"

Thadie twisted her face so that her eyes met his across the bar. "You mean a dive?" she asked quietly whilst playing with the pack of cards in her hand.

"Sure. I understand if you afraid," he said, smiling. "Like I say, it's unstable in places."

Thadie stared at him for a moment, noting the challenge in his expression. There was no one in the bar, none to hear their conversation, but she dipped her voice anyway.

"Sure," she said at last. "Only problem is, I'm not supposed to dive unless it's part of my work; I could lose my job and I take that seriously. There's important work to be done here."

He grinned, shrugging at her. "Turtles? You mad about the frickin' turtles. They won't stick around when the planes start coming in." He shook his head slowly. "No need to say nothing to no one, honey, not even Molly. She be sound asleep and dreamin' at that time in the morning."

The following day, Alan crept down the staircase of The Jolly Sailor to retrieve his diving gear from the chest in the outside lock-up. He closed the door softly behind him and crossed the silent car park in front of the church to the place where Thadie had parked the borrowed Land Rover.

"Hope you're a good driver," he mumbled. "I don't trust women drivers as a rule."

"Oh, I am," she assured him, patting his knee whilst staring straight ahead.

"You know something? I have a daughter 'bout your age."

"You do? Where is she now?" Thadie's voice was distant.

Alan grunted. "As a matter of fact, I don't have a clue. In the UK, I expect, where her mamma took her when we split up. They left when she was tiny, not seen her since. Got all the equipment you need, missy?"

Thadie smiled, nodding as they ascended the hill through Jamestown.

"Good. Well, you're in safe hands," he assured her.

"You too." Thadie smiled, thinking of Maya.

As she drove, Thadie thought about the humpbacked whales, the pilot whales she had helped to save after they had become stranded on various beaches. It was the terrible scene of carnage on the vast, endless Australian beach that had moved her the most, the memory of which came to her at night and sometimes in flashbacks in the daytime. Almost a hundred of them, their bodies smooth and too warm, like grey-blue boulders, their grunts as they breathed like old men with emphysema, dying in the hot sun. None could be saved.

Stranded, forced to leave the sea because of pollution which was killing them, mentally impairing their babies, poisoning them and forcing them into shallow waters. Pollution and environmental factors forcing them to relocate.

Intelligent, sociable creatures, relatives of the dolphin, without the despicable traits of humans.

Thadie's smile was fixed upon her face as she drove towards the cove. She had never believed in God, anyway.

Chapter 34
Diary Twenty-Seven

So, thanks to Helen, the little ghost girl is safe.

I don't know her name to this day; it isn't something any of us need to know.

There is nothing else, except that she is safe now, and her long-term future will be in the hands of the family lawyers, the guardians, a more permanent future carer, and a happier life. She will want to return to her parents, because children love and are trusting in that way; no matter what they face, they still love their parents. She has a grandmother, I think.

The baby twins will have a happy life, too.

Mark and Helen have to return to the island, I understand that.

As for me, I am anxious about Mum; I desperately want to see her. I am very anxious about Henry, too, and I want to be with him.

I am not sentimental, not really, although I used to be when I was younger. Now that I'm closer to fifty, I tend to be cynical about so many things. But despite anxiety over Mum and Henry, the love and regard for the people I met in Saint Helena is overwhelming, and when the time comes for us to leave I feel such admiration and affection for them that I am almost as torn as Herman; one foot on the island, one in the UK.

Even the lovely blondes have a place in my heart, now.

Gladys and the hotel ladies, Helen and I have hugs after breakfast. Helen and I take more photographs of them in the little courtyard of the hotel. I fight the temptation to stuff cuttings from the trees and bushes into my bra to smuggle them through customs.

Our cases are taken down to the port. I think everyone is there. They are there for the lawyers, for Mark and Helen, for Phil and Edward and Janine; but some of them are there for me, too.

Janine has said little to me since the incident at High Knoll. I've caught her looking a little oddly at me sometimes. Danny thanked me for his painting – seconds after his attempt at murder, if that's what it would have been – just as though nothing was amiss. Perhaps in his own mind, nothing was.

The kisses and hugs of the townspeople are the ones I value the most. Once my wish might have been, 'Bury my heart in Cornwall'; now it would be, 'Bury my heart in Saint Helena'.

My cousin's mother and father come to see me off, and I will see them back in England very soon. Herman is there, and Rachel, with her children, amongst many others.

We leave Jack behind, for the time being, telling him to keep safe from men with shotguns, then say farewell to the judge and his wife, and of course Tessa, who whispers in my ear as she raises an eyebrow in Janine's direction, "Watch that one, she's as bold as a brass monkey."

I giggle, kissing her cheek, although I wish Janine were staying behind on the island, too.

Then, as I promise my cousin's mother that I will visit her back in England, a figure pushes his way through the throng of people at the Customs House – Ned. He stares about him as though searching for someone and my heart does a little dance as I imagine that he is looking for me. Silly, I tell myself.

But he sees me, and this wide, glad smile appears within the beard. He walks briskly towards the group around us, stopping before me. "You didn't say goodbye..." He frowns, without inhibition, before Mark and Janine and all of them, and I am so stupidly flattered that I don't know what to say to him. Before Mark's startled gaze he puts his arms around me, lifting me off my feet, holding me tightly to his chest so that I feel the bristles on his cheek and smell his aftershave. I think for one moment that he might kiss me on the mouth, which would be going a tad too far, but he kisses my cheek instead before setting me back upon my feet, holding me tightly in a hug.

"I'm sad that you're going. You will come back?" he asks.

"Hope so," is all I say. He nods. Everyone has stopped talking. Mark is frowning at me as though I must have done something terrible, unimaginable, but all I can think is that I want this from somebody, from Ned. It is a weakness, having to be loved by a man, but in this instant it is what I want. Mark doesn't love me. The thought is terrible to me but made better by this realisation.

Then Ned turns to Mark and shakes his hand. Mark's return is half-hearted to say the least, but he can hardly decline it. Ned turns back to me with a warm smile.

"I've always wanted to say this to an attractive woman… Here's looking at you, kid."

I laugh, though nobody else does.

A few days before, the sea had been angry beneath a cloud-filled sky, writhing and crashing across the shining, black rocks, but now it is blue and calm and the RMS *Saint Helena* floats at its mercy but is as steady as a rock.

We all say our final goodbyes and cross the little white bridge to the immigration building, and after a short wait we are ferried over to the ship.

A short while later, I stand upon the bridge with Mark in silence, watching the sea change colour as the ship blasts its goodbye to the island.

I look up at him, thinking how much I will always love him. The light shines upon the grey in his hair in rainbow colours, like oil spilled on sunlit water, glinting with every shining colour of the spectrum.

He rests a brown hand upon my arm. Forgiveness for Ned, forgiveness for whatever.

Thadie crosses the deck towards me, she is leaving too, but she tells me that she has been asked to return next year; she still has work to complete. I'm so glad she is travelling with us. I like her very much and would like to remain as friends. Such a calm and genial young woman, a happy person.

After a while, as the island recedes, I go down to our cabin, resounding with 1970s music piped through speakers.

I sit upon the bed and write the note to Mark. I will slip it into his pocket when we get to the airport in Cape Town.

I tell him how much I love him. I tell him what I believe has happened with Janine. I ask him to help Lucy to care for Mum, to get her any treatment, anything that she needs until I come home. I tell him that I am going to purchase a ticket to Harari, to join Henry.

I will slip it into his pocket when we reach Cape Town airport, then pretend that I need the loo and escape.

The '70s music stops and the heartfelt Saint Helena jingle begins.

Lightning Source UK Ltd.
Milton Keynes UK
UKHW011603050521
383165UK00001B/81

9 781839 750892